Murder at
Wittenham Park

Murder at
Wittenham Park

R. W. HEBER

ST. MARTIN'S PRESS

NEW YORK

A THOMAS DUNNE BOOK.
An imprint of St. Martin's Press.

MURDER AT WITTENHAM PARK. Copyright © 1986 by Thornton Cox Ltd. All rights
reserved. Printed in the United States of America. No part of this book may be
used or reproduced in any manner whatsoever without written permission except
in the case of brief quotations embodied in critical articles or reviews. For
information, address St. Martin's Press, 175 Fifth Avenue, New York, N.Y. 10010.

Production Editor: David Stanford Burr
Design: Ellen R. Sasahara

Library of Congress Cataloging-in-Publication Data

Heber, R. W.
        Murder at Wittenham Park / R. W. Heber.
                p.   cm.
        "A Thomas Dunne book."
        ISBN 0-312-16938-8
        I.   Title.
PR6058.E26M83   1997
813'.54—dc21
                                                                97-16906
                                                                CIP

First Edition: October 1997

10 9 8 7 6 5 4 3 2 1

To my daughter, Lorna

Murder at
Wittenham Park

1

 "DARLING," Lady Gilroy was asking, her normally relaxed East Coast voice strained, "is this 'murder weekend' really going to make money?"

"Should do." Lord Gilroy glanced at his wife across the tea-table, set with Spode china cups and an elegant George II silver teapot. He didn't like her tone. Outwardly Deirdre Gilroy was straight out of the pages of a society magazine. Her fine blond hair was held back by a black velvet band. Her pretty, though somewhat sharp features, were only lightly made-up. Because this was a chilly early-summer day, she was wearing a cashmere twin set and pearls over neatly tailored fawn slacks. As she poured a cup of Earl Grey tea for him, she looked poised and self-assured. But Gilroy knew that his American-born wife sometimes lacked confidence. Not in herself. In him. And her voice told him this was one of those days.

"Dee Dee darling, the murder weekend's a bloody clever idea," he insisted, feeling able to say so because it had not been his own. "That promoter fellow knows his onions. We've got a full house for tomorrow, haven't we? How can we lose? He said anything to do with Agatha Christie would pull in the punters, and he was damned right. They'll spend a fortune on booze alone."

"You mean we will," Dee Dee cut in acidly. "You should never have made it all-inclusive."

"But they're paying the earth!" Gilroy protested. "The weekend must show a profit."

"I darned well hope so." Dee Dee was sadly aware that most of her husband's waking hours were spent devising schemes to make money out of his ancestral home; and very few of them worked. "For your sake I darned well hope it does."

Owning a neo-Gothic mansion on fifteen hundred acres of the finest English countryside, and having a title to go with it, might sound like a dream-world; the ultimate distinction in a society of wannabees. The only other thing you would need is cash. But of this Lord Gilroy was perennially short. His grandfather had been given a peerage for "political services" in the 1920s. As the owner of a coal-mine he had been a particularly tough boss during the 1926 General Strike. So he was duly rewarded and soon after bought a massive Victorian "castle" called Wittenham Park to dignify his new title. But in 1946 the mines were nationalized and death duties became crippling. By the time that Algernon, Third Baron Gilroy, inherited Wittenham, there was precious little left except for the title, the land and the impossible house.

Traditionally British noblemen solved such problems by marrying American heiresses. This was what the outside world assumed Gilroy had done. Unfortunately for him, the outside world was wrong. Dee Dee Gilroy was the daughter of a prominent New York financier who had been a high-roller when she married, but had tripped up in the futures market and lost twenty million dollars almost overnight, leaving her an heiress no longer.

Worse, Gilroy had a more personal problem than money; one that his bride from Long Island had assumed she could change, but which had proved as ineradicable as a criminal conviction. He looked like a used-car salesman.

However well Lord Gilroy dressed, he still looked like a man whose dearest wish was to ease you into the driving seat of an insurance-write-off Ford, with a stolen engine and the odometer turned back. He looked like one in a City suit and in grouse-moor tweeds; above all he looked like one in a blue blazer and flannels, his favourite gear. At school his classmates had nicknamed him Fast Buck, after he had tried running a book on the Grand National. In the Coldstream Guards it became simply Buck, which he welcomed, not realizing that his fellow officers were shrewder than he thought, because "Buck Gilroy" made him sound like a womanizer as well as disreputable. And even in the dark blue "boating jacket" of his regiment, tailored at huge expense by Welch and Jefferies of Savile Row, and adorned with gleaming gilt regimental buttons, he still looked as though he belonged in a midtown showroom.

The explanation may have been that his chin was too round and dimpled, it may have been the way his thick dark hair slicked unevenly across his forehead, as though he were an overgrown teenager, it may have been his all-too-effusive smile, or the way he naturally adopted a self-confidently lounging attitude, as if trying to shake off the discipline of his brief military career. Whatever it was, Buck Gilroy exuded the impression that if he hadn't just sold you something, he was assuredly about to try. This was why he had never been offered the City directorships that other peers seemed to pick up like flowers from the wayside. Now, yet again, he was chasing a brilliant new idea for improving the family cash flow and, yet again, his wife was getting cold feet about it.

"Is this promoter on the level?"

"Why shouldn't he be?"

"He says he's sold all the rooms, but where's the guest list? Who is actually coming?"

Her tone made it very clear that if they did not clean up on the forthcoming weekend, there was going to be hell to pay. As a débutante she had imagined that a title and a grand house automatically spelt money; a misconception in which her financier father had encouraged her. Now, at thirty-five, with two children being expensively educated on top of maintaining this vast mansion, she knew better.

"He promised he'd fax us today. I'll go and check the machine."

In the Agatha Christie thriller on which their weekend was to be based, last-minute news would have arrived by the afternoon post, brought on a silver salver to the drawing-room by the butler. The Gilroys were more reliant on technology, and anyway the butler was having this Thursday off in compensation for working on the weekend. Gilroy had already decided, with what was for him striking originality, that the butler's role could be that of the butler. Dee Dee bettered that by observing that the simplest way for her to avoid having to be with their guests all the time was for her to play the first "victim." She could then refuse to appear again, except at meals, which would be hard to avoid, since "dining with Lord and Lady Gilroy in the aristocratic setting of their Wittenham Park dining-salon" was part of the deal. And she could make sure that the family silver did not become part of the "all-inclusive" deal. Dee Dee Gilroy was quite possessive about her husband's heirlooms.

When Lord Gilroy returned, holding several flimsy sheets of paper, he had a look of puzzlement on his face, as if he had just inadvertently purchased a rebuilt wreck himself.

"The bloody man's gone and hired an actress."

"What on earth for?"

He read aloud. " 'As your lordship appreciates, nothing is worse than guests' being hesitant about throwing their heart and souls into getting the action going. We have accordingly hired the talented actress Priscilla Worthington to take the part of the villainous companion and co-murderess.' "

"So talented she's out of work, I'll bet," Dee remarked acidly. " 'Resting,' don't they call it. And just how much are we paying her?"

"Doesn't say," Gilroy admitted, realizing he had allowed the promoter far too much leeway, then defended himself. "Actually, it makes sense. The only people we can rely on to make an effort are that retired insurance fellow and his wife."

Only one of the few replies to Gilroy's original advertisement in the personal columns of *The Times* had converted into a paid-up booking, and that was from a father and daughter called Jim and Jemma Savage, the father revealing that he had been a professional insurance assessor and that he was mad about Agatha Christie. He had also mentioned that Jemma worked for a magazine called *Crime and Punishment* and was certain to write up the weekend. Dee Dee recognized at once that they ought to offer a discount to a crime reporter. Accordingly Buck wrote back offering them ten percent off for being the first to book.

In fact, they had been very nearly the last to book as well, because no one else replied, save for an events promoter who specialized in country-house events. Without him, the weekend would never have materialized and the enthusiastic Mr. Savage would have had his deposit returned; albeit reluctantly, if Buck had anything to do with it.

"And who else is on the list?"

Gilroy began reading through the other names, but stopped abruptly half-way through. "George Welch?" he asked his wife. "Why do we know that name?"

"Welch?" For a second or two she was bemused. "My God, that's the lousy property developer we refused to deal with! Don't tell me we have that creep as a guest?" Dee Dee's normal self-control faltered as she confronted the prospect of entertaining one of the most unpleasant men they had ever met for an entire weekend. "I don't believe it!"

If his wife was outraged, Gilroy himself was astonished. He had recently been exploring every possible way of turning some of his fifteen hundred acres into cash without destroying the character of the estate, or losing control of it.

The estate mattered, both emotionally and practically. Buck Gilroy might look like a crook, but his heart was in the right place when it came to inheritances and his children's futures. Six years as a Guards officer had taught him that if his son Edward was ever going to marry serious money, he would need the estate. The marriage market, like any other trading business, was getting tougher every year. Too many titled gentry no longer inhabited, let alone owned, an ancestral home. If your parents had donated it to the national Trust and you retained a wing, well, that was acceptable, though it meant you had sightseers swarming all over the place at weekends. But then, most stately-home owners suffered that and spent happy hours counting the gate money on Sunday evenings.

But a title without any "stately" attached was worth little more than being one of those two-a-penny Italian counts, living in some tumbledown Venetian palazzo that any decently rich American would only go into to get out of the rain; and would regret having done so the moment he started scratching himself. No, in these highly competitive days only the genuine article would bring in the marital punters. Take Dee Dee's own father . . . Gilroy sighed to himself, as thoughts and memories ambled through his brain. He actually preferred not to think about Dee Dee's near-bankrupt father, but what had happened did prove the point.

Gregory D. Gregorian, a man of whom even Wall Street Masters of the Universe lived in terror at the time, would never have approved of his only daughter's marrying Gilroy before he spent a weekend at Wittenham. Previously Buck had been the sort of dubious young débutante's delight on whom ten cents spent was ten cents wasted. In those days he was only Lieutenant The Honorable Algernon Gilroy, and although Dee Dee adored him, Gregorian was sceptical. But then Buck's father had invited him and his wife, Estelle, up for what the old boy still called "a Friday to Monday"; and Gregory Dwight Gregorian was hooked. The mock battlements might be crumbling, the William Morris tapestries that had come with the house might have long been consigned to Sotheby's auction rooms, the butler might look like an aging waxwork whose facial structure had begun to droop, but none of this mattered. Wittenham was the real McCoy, with portraits and deer in the park and signed black-and-white photos of royalty in silver frames. Gregorian had been hooked. So had his wife. The butler even overheard Estelle, wandering in one of the stone-flagged "cloister" passages, mouthing the words "Lady Gilroy"; "Deirdre, the Lady Gilroy"; "Lady Gilroy of Wittenham," as if practising some witches' chant.

And then Greg discovered that the father had served on the Allied staff of General Eisenhower. Gregorian himself had been named Dwight on account of the liberation of Europe. That finalized the deal. Dee and Dee and Buck were married that summer at the Guard's Chapel, in the Wellington Barracks, right by Saint James's Park, and the names of the wedding guests took up four inches in *The Times*.

Even so, Dee Dee's marriage settlement had not been breathtaking. "Don't worry, boy," Gregorian had assured Buck repeatedly, "every cent that is mine will be hers one day. Whoever gets Dee Dee is some lucky guy."

If Buck really had been a used-car salesman, he would have wondered about the "whoever gets" bit and recognized the patter. But he was now a newly promoted captain and feeling too good about life to worry. Besides, Greg was unfailingly generous in everyday matters and Dee Dee had a substantial allowance. Then, in what seemed the twinkling of an eye, but was actually a series of events spread over two years, old Gilroy died, Buck was obliged to quit the Coldstream Guards to run the estate, and a new trans-Atlantic phrase impinged itself on his limited financial vocabulary. The phrase was "Filing for Protection under Chapter Eleven." Gregory D. Gregorian's company was going bust.

In practice, going into Chapter Eleven was not the disaster Gregorian pretended. He had to sell his yacht, but only the 120-foot *Estelle*. Another remained snugly moored up in Long Island, where the five-bedroom clapboard house on Beach Road in Southampton remained in the hands of a trust. The Sutton Place duplex went, but it was replaced with a comfortable apartment on Sixty-seventh Street, near the Frick. And Dee Dee's allowance went too. As she remarked to her husband, in a moment of disloyalty to Daddy, "Your motto may be 'Always Faithful,' ours is 'Me First!' "

Gilroy's accountants soon pointed out that, given the tax bill which he would have to settle, thanks to his father's early death, Wittenham Park would either have to be made profitable or be sold. Dee Dee set her teeth against selling; and Buck further enlarged his financial vocabulary with phrases like "bottom line," "deficit carried forward," and "profit centres." It was locating the last of these three that kept him permanently scheming.

Three years ago they had opened a Lion Park. Last year Dee Dee had converted the stables into a Period Gallery, displaying everything from Victorian dresses to an old fire engine. A shop sold Wittenham Park honey and curios, all labelled with Gilroy's crest of a stag rearing up, apparently trying to escape from a coronet in which its hooves were caught. No one could deny the energy with which Dee Dee threw herself into these enterprises. Why worry that the Marquess of Bath had long been famous for his lions and that the Duchess of Devonshire sold coronet-labelled honey? The moment the Gilroys read about someone else's smart idea, they copied it. Inevitably, they had the idea of a golf course.

Gilroy was thrilled. He could visualize a hundred spin-offs, such as selling golf balls adorned with a coronet and a limited-edition membership. Then he discovered that, although they had a suitable five hundred acres of land, the capital outlay would still be vast. This was how they had met the developer, George Welch.

Precisely how Welch came to hear that there was land on offer at Wittenham Park the Gilroys did not know, though it had coincided with their originating the murder-weekend project. At all events Welch had telephoned back in January and insisted on coming to see them. The moment his Rolls-Royce scrunched on the gravel and halted in the drive, they knew what he would be like. The Rolls was painted in an iridescent apple-green, with white sidewall tyres. In the old days Rolls would have refused to paint a car that colour, and if they'd found one that had been so painted, they would have done their damnedest to buy it back.

Sure enough, Welch had been a burly fifty-year-old, dressed in a Mafia-style blue suit, with wide lapels, and a multi-coloured kipper tie that appeared to have been attacked by a graffiti artist. He referred to his car as a "Roller."

"Oh God," Dee Dee had whispered as the butler announced him, "what have we let ourselves in for?"

Welch didn't waste any time letting them know.

"Hear you've got a bit of land up for grabs," he said, as soon they had sat down in the drawing-room, "now that could be interesting to a man like me."

"We're thinking of a golf-course development." Gilroy had said, only to be shot down at once.

"Golf course?" Welch had said dismissively, "what d'you want one of those for? Leave that to the Japs. The whole bloody country's going to be golf courses soon." His tone became more aggressive. "Nice little estate you could 'ave 'ere. Very nice little development. Five hundred acres, you said. Do a lot with five hundred."

"You mean houses?"

"Houses?" Utter scorn had entered Welch's roughly accented voice. "No way do I mean 'houses.' Homes is what people want, old cock. Homes, not bloody houses. Right then, five hundred acres. Say four to an acre. Knock off ten percent for roads and such. Eighteen hundred homes, you could 'ave. And you've the perfect place for 'em." Welch had got up and gone to the high windows that looked down towards the lake. "Took a gander at your little property on the way, I did. Got the perfect site down there, you 'ave. Right by the water, good access so long as you widen that drive of yours. How much d'you want, eh?"

Both the Gilroys had gazed at him in total horror. The man was proposing a vast residential estate in full view of the house.

"I don't think you've quite understood." Gilroy had said, almost stuttering with indignation, "the five hundred acres is at the other end of the park, by the old farm buildings. Would you like to see the site?"

"Don't waste my time, old cock. Down there's what I want. Have to get rid of those lions, though. Nasty, dangerous animals. Frighten the kids." He had returned and seated himself at a table, pulling a cheque-book and a flashy gold pen out of his inside pocket. "What's your price? A million? All right, then, if you're a bit short, say two." He had flourished the cheque-book. "What's a million between friends."

"Listen," Gilroy managed to say, "that is not the land involved; and anyway, we don't want houses."

"Homes!" Welch corrected him with an incisiveness that reminded Gilroy painfully of the Regimental Sergeant Major on parade, "not bloody houses. Two and half, then. And that's my final offer."

"Mr. Welch," Dee Dee had interrupted in her most glacial voice, "I don't think you have quite understood. None of our land is for sale, least of all by the lake. We are looking for a co-developer for a golf course."

"All right, then," Welch had replied in a resigned voice, "three million it is." He laid the cheque-book on the table and unscrewed the top of the gold pen.

"It absolutely is not all right," Dee Dee had said. "Our land is not for sale."

"Thought he needed the lolly," Welch had said, almost conversationally, then jerked his head towards Gilroy. "What does he do for a living then? Can't spend his whole time grinding the faces of the poor, not these days."

"We have our own business," Gilroy interjected.

"Ah. Thought you might. Wouldn't like to buy my Roller,

would yer? Only thirty-one thousand miles, and not been clocked either. Only a fool clocks a Roller. I've seen a new model I rather fancy."

"He is not a car dealer," Dee Dee had cut in.

"No offence meant, lady." Welch swung round. "Okay then. You've twisted my arm. Three and a half million." He had squared up to Gilroy with all the amiability of a retired prize-fighter who had just decided to return to the ring. "Three and a half; and that's my last word."

"No!" Dee Dee had burst out, exasperated at last. "No, no, no. If you can't understand, you'd better go."

Welch had eventually left, with a very bad grace and a final re-mark that they had not forgiven him for.

"Homes are what the people of this country want! And the sooner sods like you start getting them what they want, the better." He had marched off down the wide stone steps, slammed into his apple-green Roller and accelerated away, scattering gravel onto the surrounding lawns.

And now he was on the guest list for the weekend!

"You must speak to that promoter man at once," Dee Dee or-dered. "What was his name?"

"Wilkinson."

"Well, ask him what the hell is going on."

Gilroy departed to his office, holding the faxed guest list as if it were in flames and burning his hand. He returned fifteen minutes later and dropped heavily into the sofa.

"Nothing we can do about it," he announced. "Bloody man's paid in full and threatens to sue if we cancel. Wilkinson got him on the blower. What's worse, one of the others works for him."

"You're joking!" Dee began to feel seriously alarmed.

" 'Fraid so." Gilroy consulted the now crumpled fax. "There's a couple called McMountdown. Welch must be bloody keen to do this deal. The McMountdown wife is his lawyer."

"All ready to draw up a contract, I suppose. Who are the others?"

"McMountdown himself's in Lloyds, and there's another couple called Chancemain, friends of theirs from the same village."

"How very cosy!" Dee Dee said caustically. "It'll be just like 'Neighbours.' And who else?"

"Only Welch's wife. Her name's Adrienne."

"Buck, darling," Dee Dee only called him Buck when she was furious, yet controlling herself, "we have been set up." She felt like screaming and tearing her hair. Instead she was icy. "How the hell did you let it happen?"

Mercifully for Gilroy, they were interrupted at this moment by the maid, Tracy, a girl of monstrous girth, but great good nature. In keeping with the times, she did not wear a uniform, only an apron over a bulging print dress. She held out a letter.

"Registered, my lord." She was aggrieved and sounded it, since this was the butler's job. "He made me sign for it."

If their minds had not been distracted by the awfulness of the guest list, the Gilroys would have recognized this moment as being portentous. In uncannily correct Agatha Christie fashion, the afternoon post had arrived.

"Could be a cheque for four million," Gilroy suggested cheerfully, oblivious of the portents, "that would be Welch's style. Trying to force our hands."

"I wouldn't sell for twenty million!" Dee Dee snapped.

"Twenty? You think . . . ?" There was a sudden diminution in his son Edward's landowning prospects.

"Forget it. Get a grip." Dee Dee had not devoted herself to saving Wittenham in order to be deprived of the social rewards just as they began to matter. A housing estate in full view of the house would mean selling up completely, as Welch had astutely realized. "Where would we hold Sophie's coming-out dance? How could you dream of cheating her!"

Easily, was the true answer, at least for twenty million, but Gilroy kept quiet and attacked the envelope, trying to slide his forefinger under the flap, then impatiently ripping it apart. The letter inside was on thick, pale-yellow paper from a London literary agency at an oddly residential address off the Fulham Road. He was instantly suspicious. It was the sort of address at which married Members of Parliament kept their girl-friends. As he read it he winced.

"Oh Christ!" he said. "Now we are in the shit!"

"Don't be so mysterious. What does it say?" Dee Dee could hardly imagine a problem worse than having Welch as a house guest.

Gilroy handed her the letter, adding vengefully, "It was your bright idea to use Agatha Christie. All I wanted was a perfectly straightforward murder weekend."

Dee Dee sat upright on the long sofa, every inch the "grande dame," and gasped in turn. The letter began, "Dear Sir," and she understood why her husband had winced. Even creditors used his title. Especially creditors. But this was a cross between a creditor and the bailiffs. This was the representatives of one ancient British institution getting tough with the representative of another. As she read it, Dee Dee realized that Mike Tyson's manager would have insisted on "no contest" in the threatened fight, or, in football terms the result could only be "Agatha Christie (deceased) ten goals, Lord Gilroy of Wittenham nil." What the letter stated, unequivocally, was that Agatha Christie's literary executors could not agree to any use of material from her books, or of her characters or plots. They would appreciate Lord Gilroy's confirmation that he would not make any such use.

"Brilliant," Dee Dee said savagely. "Blame me, that's the easy way out. You're supposed to be the brains of the outfit. What do we do?" She knew the answer, of course, but let Buck sweat it out for a few minutes. "We have eight paid-up guests. We have Welch's lady lawyer ready to sue us if the toast is burnt. We have two Agatha Christie buffs. They all arrive tomorrow afternoon; and now we have no characters and no plot. What are you going to do?"

All Gilroy could bring to mind was the classic military message: "The situation is desperate, but not serious." That pretty well summed up their predicament.

"We'll have to work out another plot," he suggested.

"Great." She gave him one of those looks which implied that with his intellect he ought to be a road sweeper. "I suppose I'll have to do that. And I tell you what, Welch can be the first victim."

"Leaving him with nothing to do except harass me?" Gilroy did not often become indignant with his wife. She might be relatively penniless, but he loved her. However, this idea was carrying conjugal fidelity too far. "To hell with the actress," he insisted, "I have to keep Welch out of my hair. He can be the murderer."

"When we have a story-line," Dee Dee said, getting in the last word. "Damn Agatha Christie!"

2

THE NEXT day, while Buck and Dee Dee Gilroy were still struggling to eliminate Agatha Christie from their murder plot, some of their guests were involved in arguments that would have worried the noble lord even more than the prospect of being sued by the Queen of Crime's executors.

Imagination was not a gift with which the Creator had over-endowed Lord Gilroy. He had shuddered with horror when he first saw Welch's apple-green Rolls-Royce defacing his driveway, because it was so obviously ghastly. But he would never have guessed at the cold-blooded conversation going on inside it on this sunny afternoon, as its owner drove down the motorway towards the leafy lanes of rural Oxfordshire and the unexploited acres of Wittenham Park.

George Welch's robust physical appearance owed a great deal to the breweries. Drinking as a young construction worker had given him a beer belly, which later dietary intrusions by his wife Adrienne had not greatly reduced. At forty-nine, his complexion had a ruddiness unconnected with a healthy open-air life, even though in the tweed jacket which he reckoned appropriate to an upper-class weekend he could have passed for a choleric farmer. But the impression other drivers gained, as the outrageous Roller swept past them, was of a fleshy-faced photofit of road rage, who would cheerfully carve anyone up if they dared overtake him. If Welch had been an actor he would have been in constant demand to play self-made bastards like himself.

Seated beside him was a pretty blonde in her thirties who might have been assumed to be his wife, but was in fact his lawyer, Dulcie McMountdown. His wife, Adrienne, was behind in the deep white leather cushions of the back seat, together with Hamish McMountdown, making the most of the walnut-veneered cocktail cabinet and listening to stereo music, while the two in the front talked business.

Dulcie was petite, with thick, short-cut blonde hair, a tip-tilted nose, a determined little chin, and a wide, generous mouth that had prompted Hamish to nickname her "frogface" when they were first married. Now that he was heavily into an affair with the wife of a neighbour she refused to be called "frogface" any more, just as she refused to let their terrier be mated with the neighbour's bitch. A woman had to draw the line somewhere!

In fact, if her philandering husband didn't stop, she was going to draw that line in the divorce court, though she could hardly believe he could be serious over such a feather-brain as Loredana. Not that Hamish knew that she knew. He and Loredana both thought they were being blissfully clever and discreet and that neither of their spouses suspected a thing. Quite possibly Loredana's husband, Trevor, didn't. But for the moment Dulcie had other things on her mind. She was George Welch's legal adviser and George was being difficult.

Dulcie was a hundred and four pounds of bounce and energy, while the sleekly brushed thatch of blonde hair concealed an acute brain. Anybody who treated her as a bimbo would live to regret it, a point which had not yet occurred to Loredana. Now Welch was suddenly treating her as one. Why?

"Is the bloody contract watertight?" Welch was asking. "If Gilroy signs, can he back out?"

"There's no cooling-off period, if that's what you mean, George. It's not like one of those time-share contracts the law forces us to offer." Dulcie bridled. Was she likely to draw up a document that wasn't enforceable the moment it was signed and witnessed?

"And how's the land marked out? Thought of that, have you?"

"We have large-scale maps of the whole area. Plus photocopies." What had got into George today? Normally he would trust her grasp of detail. "The real question," she added grittily, "is how you're going to talk Gilroy into agreeing."

"He needs the money, doesn't he?"

"He's lost a lot on Lloyds." Dulcie kept her comment brief. This was dangerous ground.

"As who hasn't." Welch glanced sideways at her. "As who hasn't, eh, my girl?"

In the silence that followed, Dulcie was tempted to reply that since he had been fool enough to let her husband Hamish manage his Lloyds insurance commitments, he deserved to lose his shirt. But she held her tongue. And anyway, Hamish had only done the same as most Lloyds professionals, even if collectively they had created a catastrophe which had shattered thousands of people's lives and was threatening now to bankrupt Welch himself.

When the Lloyds insurance market had turned into an international can of worms, Hamish unquestionably ranked among the canners. He didn't rank high, but he had been in there exploiting the weaknesses of an eighteenth-century organization that existed on mutual trust and which had become a British institution. Its top men always had become extremely rich. Even Hamish had made a modest pile out of Lloyds. But any City institution that depended on mutual trust was wide open these days. Unsurprisingly, the fraudsters had moved in.

And yet, she thought, gaining time by swinging down the sun visor in front of her to inspect her make-up in its little mirror, and catching Hamish's unhappy eye in it as she did so, she did not want him ruined. She was not vindictive. She wanted to kick him in the teeth, of course, but that wasn't the same thing. And if George Welch sued him for fraud, which she was afraid he might, Hamish would be ruined. She was always pretty sure that he had never actually broken the law, not because he was clever, but because he'd never needed to.

The Lloyds system was what her Australian cousins would have called a "beaut." The managing agents like Hamish could hardly fail to get rich. Through them, wealthy individuals, known as "names," pledged their assets to make money as insurers by joining underwriting syndicates. The agents collected a percentage on their "names" profits, but suffered no deduction on losses. It was an absolute beaut of a situation. Whether their advice was good or bad, they could not lose.

It was highly attractive for the "names" too. All the professional work was done for them and they made their assets work twice, once as stocks or property or whatever they were, a second time through Lloyds. When Hamish was wooing potential "names," he became quite ecstatic about it. With Welch he had needed to be. Anyone who persuaded George to part with money had to be convincing; and he had underwritten huge amounts.

Poor old sod, Dulcie thought as she wielded her lipstick and tried to anticipate Welch's next remark. "So proud of being one of the Perthshire McMountdowns, and what happened? He joined a gentleman's club and discovered he actually had to work."

Two hundred years ago, fifty years ago, even thirty years ago, Lloyds was effectively a gentlemen's financial club. And it was prudently run, even when accepting such bizarre risks as insuring Marlene Dietrich's legs.

In the rare event that claims were not covered by premium income, then the "names" had to pay up. So they took out "stop loss" policies to protect themselves against being wiped out. This was where some of the fraud began in the 1980s.

"If what's been going on ain't fraud, I'd like to know what is," Welch said, mirroring Dulcie's thoughts.

By the late 1970s the gentlemen had been ousted by, or themselves turned into, ambitious and greedy salesmen, who took on open-ended risks that their forbears would never have touched. Lloyds itself relaxed one crucial rule, namely that a person's home could not be counted as an asset. With that barrier out of the way, the managing agents went down-market and courted people who could not really afford the risk. The lure of easy money was powerful. The downside featured very little in their expansive—and expensive—lunch-time briefings. The cut they made was never mentioned. It was not the sort of thing gentlemen discussed. Hamish was always skilful at implying this. Lloyds was still presented as an exclusive and profitable club.

Tennis stars, authors, actors, army officers and widows were among those suckered into signing up. So were Buck Gilroy and George Welch. Gilroy could not afford it because Wittenham Park was his only major asset, George Welch because his capital was tied up in his business. A further call from Lloyds for a few hundred thousand could wreck the lives of either of them.

While Dulcie was wondering just how deep in the mire George had got himself, the man who had sweet-talked him into it was sneaking an early Scotch and soda in the back of the Roller, earnestly wishing that he were somewhere else. The wish was re-doubled when he overheard Welch's next comment.

"Something bloody well has to be done by Monday, my girl." Welch spoke roughly, but with intensity. Inviting Hamish along to this weekend was far from from being a gracious gesture. Whatever role he might have in the forthcoming "murder," he had a far more important one in Welch's plan. But Welch did not intend to spring it on him until escape was impossible.

"Such as?"

"Telling Lord Toffee-Nose as how the call what's been posted off today is for the worst losses ever. Even if they ain't. 'Sign with me now, be safe on Monday,' that's the message."

"And just why should Hamish do that?"

"Call it a favour to a client what's suffered."

"You can't blame Hamish for your losses," Dulcie said. "You wanted to be on high-profit syndicates."

"Risky maybe, fraudulent never."

Fraud was close to the heart of it. A few Lloyds professionals turned out to have been charging for stop-loss insurance but not providing it.

Court cases followed. American "names" refused to pay. Year after year brought more "calls." All over Britain, country houses, racehorses and heirloom antiques were sold. For George Welch the only way to meet his obligations was to find more building land and then borrow both against its purchase and its future development. Naturally he blamed Hamish.

"If you're accusing my husband of fraud," Dulcie said coldly, "you can tell him so yourself, not hide behind me."

"Maybe I will and maybe I won't." Welch backed off a little. At heart he was frightened of lawyers, even his own. "Who else have yer brought with her to make this flipping party swing? Hope I'm getting value for me money."

"Our next-door neighbours are coming," Dulcie said, remembering Welch's pursuit of waitresses in restaurants, and adding mischievously, "Between you and me, Loredana Chancemain quite likes a little bit on the side. She might be delighted to find a new man in her room."

"What about her husband, then?" Welch lowered his voice conspiratorially.

"Oh, Trevor probably won't turn up. He's in Africa on business."

"Is he now!" Welch was interested and his attitude changed. "Likes a bit of nooky, does she?"

"Loredana may look cold but she's not underneath," Dulcie said, getting an unexpected kick out of this situation. When Hamish had suggested, a little too casually, that the Chancemains might make up the numbers, she had known exactly why. Bedrooms in these huge country houses frequently had two doors. Imagine Welch entering by one and Hamish by the other! That would wipe the smirk off Loredana's face for once. "She's quite sexy, in fact," she added, "Not to mention attractive." She might have added, attractive if you like them dumb. But he could find that out for himself.

Welch was prevented from asking more by his wife, who leaned forward and tapped him on the shoulder.

"And what are two getting up to, may I ask?"

Dulcie twisted around in her seat, in so far as the seat-belt allowed. "It's the contract details. We can't afford to make any mistakes this weekend"—she included her husband in the glance—"can we, darling?"

"Personally," Hamish said, sensing double meanings and changing the subject, "I'm hoping they make me Hercule Poirot, the detective."

"You hardly look like a Belgian with a waxed moustache," Dulcie commented. In fact, Christie's detective hero had been quite a small man, and so was Hamish, but in every other way they were opposites. Hamish had undistinguished features and a bland, faintly superior expression, which seldom displayed emotion. His personality was a level playing field—at a very good school, of course. What had attracted Dulcie had been their their shared love of opera. It had not proved enough.

"They must expect us to dress the part," Hamish insisted, earning a look of amazement from Dulcie. What was he up to?

"You really think so?" Adrienne brightened. "Then we might all get a bit of a giggle after all."

WHILE DULCIE was considering how to handle this delicate subplot to the murder weekend, two of Gilroy's other guests, approaching from the London direction in a Ford, were debating quite different concerns. Jemma and Jim Savage were father and daughter, and Jemma was airing a reasoned mistrust of what her father had arranged.

"Daddy," she was saying, as they approached the Oxford bypass, "are you sure you explained? I mean, sharing a room with you would not be my idea of a fun weekend."

"Nor mine, as a matter of fact."

"So what did you tell them?"

"What should I have? That I'm a redundant insurance adjuster of fifty-two, who would have opted out of the weekend if his daughter hadn't railroaded him?"

"What did that counsellor say?" Jemma was shepherding her father through the traumas of a redundancy that had come within months of his second wife's leaving him. "He said you must go on with whatever you've planned. Don't let anyone know you're upset. Come on, Daddy, you'll enjoy the weekend, and it's not as though we're completely broke."

"No thanks to Pauline."

"She's off the payroll. Forget her." Jemma never had liked her stepmother much. "At least you got the American Express card back."

"Eventually. Anyway, I did not tell Lord Gilroy that I was out of work. I told him I had a journalist daughter who was an Agatha Christie freak—"

"Daddy! I've never read any of her."

"—and who," Savage persisted, "is absolutely fascinated by the whole idea."

"So he expects me to write about it? You're a pig. Why should I?"

"All the best frauds originate in telling someone what he or she wants to hear. Lord Gilroy wants publicity."

"Really, Daddy!" Sometimes Jemma was astonished at her father's innocence. "If I'd known, I might have got it for free. Except that my mag isn't interested in hypothetical crimes."

"You want real blood all over the floor?"

"You know we do."

"Or blondes in black leather with whips?"

"Daddy, please! *Crime and Punishment* is a monthly review of interpretative analysis and holistic vision, devoted to improving understanding of the criminal mind. So there."

"Talking of which," Jim remarked, "Lord Gilroy has quite an unusual handwriting. If I was assessing a claim from him I'd go through every detail with a fine-tooth comb."

"I bet you would. With a very fine-tooth comb. Whatever that is." She smiled, teasing him about the cliché, yet remembering his reputation as an assessor whom it was hard to fool. Her father had the memory of an elephant, coupled with great persistence.

The relationship between the two of them had always been close, and his wife Pauline's precipitate departure had strengthened it. Not that they were physically alike—"Thank goodness," Jemma would say, "no way would I want his nose"—except in a few characteristics. And intellectually he was contemplative, she intuitive; although that distinction was blurred because his job had necessitated a degree of intuition.

What she most admired about her father was his even-handedness. He was slow to reach decisions, but when he reached them they were reasoned and dispassionate. This made him seem a rather dry character, yet underneath he was giving and warm, with occasional sparks of unexpected humour.

This air of detachment was reinforced by his appearance. To look at, Jim Savage was an unobtrusive middle-aged man, with a good head of a hair and a waistline kept trim by golf and tennis.

Today he was wearing dark slacks and an open-neck shirt under a blue sweater. He could have passed for a civil servant on holiday, except that he had deep-set pale-blue eyes which disconcerted people when he asked questions. Many years of assessing insurance claims had made him very good at asking questions.

By contrast Jemma dressed with easy style, adorned her basically mousy hair with blonde streaks, had only a very diminutive version of the Savage nose, and kept her figure without noticeably taking any exercise. "Lucky me, I have the right metabolism" she would say cheerfully as she bubbled her way through parties. But she had the same pale eyes as her father, and journalism was rapidly teaching her to see through other people's façades too.

"So why don't you trust Lord Gilroy? she asked.

"There was something smarmy about the letter he wrote. You know, after I sent the deposit." Savage remembered the personal letter from Gilroy. The notepaper was headed with a stag rearing up out of a coronet, apparently trapped by its hooves. This crest was embossed on the paper, not merely printed, which displayed class. But the text was studded with gushing phrases like "delighted to know" and "assure you this will be a weekend to remember."

"What I fail to see," Jim went on, "is how he's going to get away with it."

"What do you mean?"

"Well, they can hardly steal the plot of one of Christie's books. Someone will know the ending."

"He must have thought of that. He's probably changing it."

"Lucky the old girl's dead. She'd have a fit. Not the kind of person you could take liberties with."

Years ago, when he had been investigating an arson claim in Devon, Savage's senior had taken him to Agatha Christie's house for tea. He had been left with three abiding impressions: of the house's glorious views over a river estuary; of the lady's collection of ornamental teapots from canal barges, all of a kind, yet each one different; and of her strong sense of propriety, coupled with humour. He was pretty certain the sense of humour would not extend to her stories' being altered.

"I suppose there's nothing much anyone can do about it, now she's gone," he observed.

"D'you think they allocate the parts before they've even met us?" Jemma asked. "And who else will be there?"

"He didn't say."

They had reached a turn off the A-40 road signed "Wittenham." "Well, we'll know soon enough," Savage said "Let's hope they don't make me the murderer."

"Why should it be a him?" Jemma demanded. "There you go. Sexism again."

"FINISHED!" Dee Gilroy exclaimed triumphantly, rising from a desk in the library and crossing towards the high Gothic windows, scanning her notes. "In the nick of time. You're lucky to have such an inventive wife, not to mention devoted." She looked aggravatedly at her spouse. "You might say something, for God's sake, when I've just saved our reputation. What would be the point of all this"— she gestured around the Gothic splendour of the library, its solid furniture rearranged for the benefit of their guests, with teacups, plates and cakes set out on a vast side-table—"what earthly point would be there if I hadn't concocted a simply brilliant murder."

"You're a genius, sweetheart," Gilroy managed to say. "Only you could have done it." He hesitated, uncertain whether he was supposed to have second sight. "That's to say, what have you done?"

Dee Dee gave a tiny moue, vexed at his wanting explanations on top of assurances, then over-handed the final sheet of paper on which she had listed the cast in her rounded American handwriting.

"Even Agatha . . ." She cut herself short. "No. This is nothing to do with the wretched woman, but it is a family set-up her fans would like. A perfectly beastly family called Sketchley. I shall be Mrs. Louise Sketchley, an extremely rich widow, who is a pain in the butt to everyone and won't hand over the boodle. Not a cent. She has two grasping sons; they can be played by these fellows McMountdown and Chancemain."

"And she gets murdered?" Gilroy suggested.

"How else am I going to get out of playing games all weekend with these odious people? Of course she gets murdered. First thing in the morning. Before breakfast. You can have breakfast with them, darling."

"And who murders her?"

For a moment Dee Dee's confidence faltered. "Well, we have options. If you want to keep Welch occupied all the time, and out of our hair, then he ought to do it."

"Any reason?"

"He's her brother and he's lost everything on Lloyds."

"Getting a bit close to home, aren't we, darling? Anyway, how do you know Welch hasn't?"

"Alternatively"—Dee Dee wasn't giving up at this stage—"it's done by his wife. The actress could play her. Wouldn't that be brilliant? She's determined to save her husband."

"Must be the only person in the world who is," Gilroy commented. "But don't we have to write clues? And character descriptions? I mean, we're supposed to hand those out after tea."

"All done." Dee waved a sheaf of further notes. All I have to do is get them on the word processor. While you entertain everyone."

Gilroy's none-too-agile mind fumbled with another problem. Remembering the plot that they had not been allowed to use, he recalled all sorts of minor characters, like the doctor, the local policeman and the detective.

"So who's the sleuth?" he demanded.

"Obviously this insurance-assessor man. And his daughter can be . . . " Dee Dee faltered. She had never realized how hard it was to construct a murder plot. "She can be a reporter."

"Which she is anyway. At least she won't forget her role."

"She's the only one who isn't after Louise Sketchley's loot."

At the risk of wrecking his marriage, Gilroy asked the crucial question. "How is Mrs. Sketchley killed?"

"Poisoned. A good old-fashioned British murder."

"So it's a murderess?"

"How do you know?"

"English wives always poison their husbands. Either that or they grab a kitchen knife in the middle of a row. Odd how there always seems to be knife handy at the time."

"Actually," Dee Dee said, "it'll be Mrs. Sketchley's brother, played by Welch, and her companion, who get in cahoots to kill her. So everything depends on noticing who drinks what in the evening and who is around the bedrooms at the time."

"Which is?"

"Sometime between midnight and seven-thirty A.M. There'll be lots of to-ing and fro-ing during the night."

"Well, darling, if you're going to get all that typed up you'd better get your skates on. What time are they due?"

"We said tea-time." Dee Dee consulted a tiny jewel-encrusted watch, a memento of the days before Gregorian D. Gregorian invoked the salvation of Chapter Eleven. "It's half past three now. Any moment, I should think."

Alerted to the imminence of this, Gilroy looked out of the windows, across the broad lawns and towards the lake. On the far side a bright green shape was progressing slowly through the park, driving across the grass, far from the road. It stopped and two people got out, spreading what might have been a map in front of them. They began pointing in various directions.

"My God," Gilroy cried out. "If that bastard's staking out my land, I'll murder him."

3

THE MOMENT the butler ushered Jemma and Jim into the Gothic library at Wittenham Park they knew the weekend was starting badly. A small group of people were standing in constrained attitudes at the far end of the gloomily cavernous room. Among them a ruddy-faced, coarse-looking man was confronting a younger, more slenderly built one, whom Jemma recognized as Lord Gilroy, having seen his photograph in a magazine. The coarse man was speaking so vehemently that the butler was obliged to pause and wait.

"First it was bloody Agatha Christie and now you say it ain't," the man was almost shouting at Lord Gilroy "You've sold us—"

"M'lord, m'lady." This denunciation of his employer was too much for the butler, who cleared his throat and intervened loudly. He was elderly, with a lugubriously pallid, haughty face, which fitted well with his black jacket and rigidly pressed pin-stripe trousers, and was known by his surname, Dodgson, as though his station in life disqualified him from the luxury of a first name. But he had a penetratingly nasal voice of a timbre which, given a chance, could bring down ceilings.

"M'lord!" he screeched again, then realized that in the stress of the moment he had forgotten the names of the guests he was about to announce. The procedure had only been adopted for this weekend as a piece of showbiz, to make the clients feel they were getting full value. There was a lingering silence. The coarse man stopped in mid-sentence. Everyone turned towards the butler, who was now gasping like a landed fish. Jemma whispered in his ear and he wound himself into top gear again. "M'lord, m'lady. Mr. James Savage and Miss Jemma Savage."

Jemma noticed a tall blonde woman wince at the butler's ineptitude and glance accusingly at Lord Gilroy, before advancing to meet them, stretching out her hand in welcome.

"I am Deirdre Gilroy," she said in a cordial yet cool New England voice. "How nice that you could come." There was a distinct implication that any new arrival must be preferable to the people already here. They all shook hands. "Let me introduce you to my husband."

Lord Gilroy seemed abashed. "You're the Agatha Christie buffs, aren't you?" he inquired. "Well, I'm afraid that for legal reasons we've had to alter the plot. Can't use Christie."

"False pretences," the coarse man began again aggressively. "That's what it is. Not what we paid for."

"This is Mr. Welch," Gilroy said, distaste articulate in every syllable, "who is a property developer, and his wife Adrienne."

"Pleased to meet you, I'm sure." Adrienne was anxious to smooth over the clash of personalities. She'd spent a lot of money on new clothes for this weekend and intended to enjoy it.

"Mr. George Welch?" Jim Savage asked politely, but with an abstracted look in his eyes, which Jemma knew well. Her father had a million-megabyte memory and something about the property developer was being downloaded from it.

"And why shouldn't I be George Welch? Heard about me, 'ave you?"

"Everyone in the property business has."

Jemma guessed that his memory must have brought up something fairly discreditable about Welch. But Welch himself took the two-sided remark as a compliment.

"Well," he said, grinning, "even if I says it meself, I am the tops." He nudged Gilroy in the ribs. "You 'eard that. Couldn't want a better name to do business with."

Gilroy recoiled as fast as if God were trying to extract a rib from him and start restructuring the human race along the lines of Welch. He hastened to introduce Dulcie and Hamish McMountdown, followed by a tall, elegant woman with high cheek-bones and carefully coiffured, though thin and mousy, hair, whose name he had difficulty pronouncing.

"Loredana," the woman corrected him, "Loredana Chancemain." She extended her hand to Jim Savage as if she expected him to bow and kiss her fingertips, then glanced at Jemma. "This is your . . . ?"

"Daughter," Jemma said quickly and firmly. "We're a father-and-daughter team."

"Oh." Loredana sounded disappointed, as if deprived of a useful scandal. She turned to Gilroy. "So we're all here now, except for my husband?"

"Should we start without him?"

"For all I know, he's still in Nairobi." She looked around, seeking approval from the others, and got a quick smile from Hamish McMountdown, while Dulcie said nothing, and what little of her forehead was visible under the blonde thatch was creased by a frown.

Watching them, Jemma decided that there was something going on there, too. Why was Loredana so unconcerned about her husband? And why did Dulcie frown? What kind of man was Hamish? She noted that he wore thin-soled, soft black shoes, what her father in his old-fashioned way called "very Italian," while his equally thin lips had cracked into a private, inward kind of smile. Not to be trusted, Jemma decided.

However, Gilroy was too relieved to notice any of this interplay between the three. "In fact, there is one more person to come," he said happily, "but we needn't wait for her."

"Then let's all have some tea," Lady Gilroy suggested "and my husband will explain what's going to happen." She nodded towards the butler, who had been haunting a long side-table laid with teacups and plates of cake. "We have China or Earl Grey. It will be easier if we all sit near each other." She led the way to where chairs and sofas had been arranged in a rough semi-circle around a massive Victorian stone fireplace with a coat of arms carved into the overmantel hood.

Gilroy waited until everyone had whatever they wanted, then

placed himself in front of the fireplace, slouching slightly with his left hand in his trouser pocket, and launched into his spiel.

"Ladies and gentlemen. It is a very great pleasure to welcome you all to our weekend of intrigue, mystery and, of course, murder. As some of you already know, the literary agents of the late Agatha Christie have objected to our using her excellent novels. Personally I would have expected them to welcome an event that might boost her sales." Here Gilroy gave a delicate shrug, as though there was nothing to be done about the incomprehensible except fail to comprehend it. He followed this with his most winning salesman's smile. "However, it's an ill wind that blows nobody any good. My wife has been writing a whodunit herself, so we've utilized that." Having unburdened himself of this total lie, he instantly embroidered on it. "Naturally enough, she has set her story in a country house like ours, which makes the perfect setting. So our only problem is in allocating the roles. We'll do that in a moment, when you've all had a chance to read the background briefing." He beckoned to the butler. "Dodgson will now hand out the first set of papers."

The outline was commendably brief. In fact, Dee Dee Gilroy was proud of it, and could not resist smiling as people read her text.

"It is Friday night," the paper said, "in a house like this. The owner, a rich widow named Louise Sketchley, has summoned her family for what will be a painful reunion. She is facing a massive blackmail demand. Before calling in the police, she has decided to consult the family. Privately she suspects that one of them may be involved. And there is not a single person here who does not have an interest in her fortune."

Gilroy scanned the faces of his guests. "With it so far?" he asked. "Excellent. The characters come on page two. My wife will be playing the widow, Louise." He gave them a sideways smile. "It may turn out to be quite a small part. Now let's look at the others. First, there is Louise's fifty-five-year-old brother Norman."

It needed only seconds to take in the unsavoury character of Norman Carr, a villainous, self-centred younger brother, always resentful of the wealth that marriage had brought his sister.

"Well," Gilroy said, savouring his moment of revenge for Welch's outburst, "I'd say our developer friend should have a go at that. He's in the right age bracket. How about it?

Welch glowered at him. "Its a bloody insult. What if I won't, eh?"

"Then you can be the butler. Means your wife has to play the maid. Have to sleep in the servants' wing too, of course."

"Really!" Adrienne protested, pronouncing it "reely." "The very idea! We didn't pay good money to pretend we're servants."

"Oh, have it you're own way, then," Welch conceded. "What do I have to do?"

"That comes later." Gilroy had scored on points and intended holding on to the advantage. "Mrs. Welch can play your wife. As you see from the notes, they've had a bit of a row and she sleeps in a separate room."

"Not beyond imagining," Adrienne remarked acidly. She had already noticed that George had his eye on Loredana. "I hope it's a good room."

"One of the best. The Blue Room in the west wing."

"And what about me then?" Welch demanded.

"You're next door to Louise Sketchley, on the main passage. Strictly speaking, it's a dressing-room, but quite large."

"I'll make up me mind when I've seen it," Welch said cantankerously and continued muttering.

Gilroy dealt with the Savages next. They were given the roles of the police inspector and a young crime reporter, respectively, and reassigned to small bedrooms at the end of the long main passage leading to the east wing.

This left the roles of Louise Sketchley's two sons. As soon as Loredana read the character of James's wife, Estelle, she became determined to play her. "A beautiful gazelle-like creature of passionate sensitivity" was what Dee Dee had called her, and there was no way Loredana was going to let that label be attached to Dulcie.

"Estelle sounds exactly right for me," Loredana insisted brazenly, "and since my own husband hasn't come, the only man left is Hamish."

"What a clever idea," Dulcie breathed to Hamish. "You'll enjoy that, won't you, darling. And the role's cut out for you. 'Handsome but indolent. A pseudo country squire who's at his wit's end for cash and hates his successful brother Tarquin.' "

"If you say so, darling," Hamish said, pretending to be bashful and smiling in that private way. He looked at Gilroy. "Which room are we in?"

Dee Dee gave him a sharp glance. She could just imagine the creaking of bedroom doors and floor-boards there would be tonight and she didn't welcome it. Not for moral reasons. These wretched people could screw each other's spouses rotten as far as she was concerned. She was worried because the "murder" demanded various goings-on in the evening as well.

"You and your real wife will be in the Pink Room on the other side of Louise from Mr. Welch," she told Hamish.

"And what about little me?" Loredana demanded.

"You and your husband are in the Chinese Room in the east wing, beyond the Savages."

Gilroy hastened to explain. "The main part of the house is between an east wing and a west wing. My wife and I use the west wing. There's a plan with the papers."

"That leaves me with a room but not a role," Dulcie remarked, faintly annoyed at being left out.

"How about the doctor?" Gilroy suggested smoothly.

Dulcie wrinkled her nose. "Why not Tarquin? He's described as a great contrast to his brother." She gave Hamish a sweetly ironic smile. "Intelligent. Successful in the City. I suppose he's gay?"

"Well . . ." Gilroy was embarrassed. "Actually yes. Ask my wife. She invented him."

"Yes, he is," Dee Dee confirmed. "But not outrageously. The important point is that he notices things some men might not."

"Done," Dulcie said. "I'll be Tarquin. And if Trevor does pitch up, he can be the doctor."

"Excellent." Gilroy rubbed his hands together as if he had just made a sale.

"Wait a minute," Dulcie said, consulting her cast list. "We're still one short. Who plays Louise's companion?"

"A Mrs. Worthington." He had no intention of revealing that she was a hired actress. Must remember she needs a background, he told himself. "She rang to say she'd be late. Now Dodgson will show you all to your rooms. Then you might like to visit our Lion Park before we have drinks and the first clues are handed out."

"Bloody waste of time," Welch muttered.

"Oh, but we must!" Loredana exclaimed. "I've been on safari and I know all about lions. Such exciting creatures. So virile and masculine."

"I'll come," said Hamish.

"So virile and masculine," Dulcie murmured, which Hamish affected not to hear.

"Then we meet at five-thirty," Gilroy ordered.

The guests all moved off except for Welch. "Now listen 'ere," he said to Gilroy and Dee Dee. "We ought to be gettin' a discount when it ain't the genuine article. Stands to reason."

"Mr. Welch." Dee Dee could freeze a furnace if she chose. "If you wish to leave, Dodgson will pack your bags."

This called Welch's bluff, even though he had not yet unpacked. Leaving would defeat the purpose of his being here, not to mention that Adrienne would kill him. And the way that little piece Loredana had smiled at him gave him hopes for the night, what with both of them being alone in their rooms.

"You're not getting rid of me as easy as that," he said hastily. "I'll stay. But I want a proper sit-down discussion with your lordship, right?"

"If you must," Gilroy agreed. "After dinner this evening. In my office, off the hall."

"Soon as we finish the nosh," Welch said, adding, in an effort to be conciliatory, "what does me wife wear for the Lion Park?"

"Claws," said Dee Dee and left the room.

Upstairs Jim and Jemma Savage were settling into their chintz-furnished rooms. Each had a tall Gothic window overlooking the park and the lake, with elaborated swagged curtains that matched the wallpaper. When Dee Dee had done the house up after their wedding, her father was still paying the bills. Hunting prints hung in Jim's rooms, prints of Guardsmen and officers in Jemma's. Vases of flowers stood on side-tables. The only snag was that they had to share a bathroom.

"Daddy," Jemma exclaimed, coming into her father's room, "this is the real thing. This is how the nobs live."

"Probably nothing on the Blue Room, the Pink Room, and the Chinese Room."

"I'm going to take a peek at all of them. And sneak a few pictures. There has to be a story in this. Will you enjoy being the cop?"

"Within limits." Jim Savage had reservations about the way the police worked.

A light knock on the door interrupted them. Jim called out, "Come in," and to their surprise Lady Gilroy entered. She had changed into jeans and a sweater, presumably for the Lion Park excursion. She apologized for disturbing them.

"Please don't get me wrong over this," she said to Jim, "but you are some kind of real-life detective? Is that right?"

"Not exactly. I was an insurance assessor."

"I suppose that would do." She was doubtful, then became more positive. "We certainly want to avoid insurance claims."

"You've taken special cover for this weekend?"

Dee Dee's face fell. "I bet that husband of mine hasn't. The point is, we have some nice things here, especially the silver. We don't want to lose them."

"You mean your guests might steal the spoons?"

"How can I stop them? Would you keep an eye on everyone for me? It would be a huge relief. After all, that is the policeman's role."

Jim felt obliged to agree and instinctively began asking questions. Whom did she have fears about?

"I wouldn't put it past that ghastly man Welch. Or his wife. Between you and me, he's after our land for a housing estate. We refused. You heard how rude he was."

"Could he turn nasty?"

"If it's possible to be nastier than he's been already. He's an absolute shoot. And he's got some trick up his sleeve. I feel it. That blonde is his lawyer."

"I'll keep a discreet watch on him, Lady Gilroy. If it's any help."

"That's really kind of you. Thank you. See you downstairs."
Lady Gilroy exited stage left, as they say, and left the field clear for
Jemma.

"Is Welch a crook, Daddy? You were giving him one of your
looks."

"Let's just say that one way of cashing in on an unsold building
is to burn it down. Nothing was ever proven, but we felt he was a
bad risk. He was on our blacklist."

"Does he know you know?"

"I doubt it."

"Doesn't take long for reality to intrude, does it?" Jemma observed reflectively.

"Never does. That's the problem with amateur dramatics. Someone always hates someone else's guts and the next thing you know
there's blood on the floor."

In other spacious rooms along the thickly carpeted main corridor of the house, the other guests were preparing for the Lion Park
outing and considering the conveniences and inconveniences of
their rooms. The corridor led off in both directions from the head
of a magnificent oak staircase, with newels carved in the shape of
unicorns. It was wide and well-lit.

Loredana, luxuriating in the pagoda-and-willow-tree wallpa-
pers and silk curtains of the Chinese Room, which had been lav-
ishly done up for Mr. and Mrs. Gregorian, appreciated that for
Hamish to get to her in the night would involve his passing the
doors of "Louise," Welch, and the Savages. Thank goodness the car-
pets were deep. She wished the rooms had telephones, like a hotel.
Then Hamish would be able to alert her when Dulcie was out of
the way or asleep. She went through into the bathroom and began
laying out the bottles of Clarins body lotions and astringents, of
scents and oils which she could not manage without. There were
sixteen of them, which she considered was traveling very light. At
home her thirty-five bottles left Trevor no space at all for his
shaving-kit. If only they had a bathroom as large and luxurious as
this one!

Then her thoughts reverted to the coming night. That loathsome man Welch had been looking her over in a very suggestive

way. Just let him try propositioning her! But how was she going to get together with Hamish? They had discussed slipping a pill into Dulcie's last drink, just to make sure she did sleep. Well, that was his job, not hers. Dulcie had been making some oddly knowing remarks, too. Was she getting suspicious?

Dulcie herself was being blandly polite to Hamish as he unpacked, noticing with disgust when he laid his pyjamas out on the bed that they were stained as usual, and thankful that the butler was not unpacking for them. However, she had more important things on her mind. Welch had just told her triumphantly that his meeting with Gilroy was scheduled for after dinner and she must be ready with the contract.

Hamish himself had not yet been told of his intended part in the business, yet he seemed on edge, Dulcie thought. Perhaps he guessed that this weekend was no free lunch. Or was he nervous over sneaking out to the wretched Loredana's room? When Trevor was away and he slipped out, after she was asleep, to go to Loredana, she would watch him return across the village street in the dawn, then go back to bed and pretend to be still asleep. Had that saved their marriage? It didn't seem to have. In fact, he was behaving with unbelievable gall. As she changed, Dulcie confirmed her decision to have it out with him this weekend.

She heard a car scrunch on the gravel outside and looked through the window to see a taxi disgorge what could only be the last guest. From above, her face was obscured by a large straw hat extravagantly decorated with flowers. It was odd that a woman should come on this kind of weekend by herself.

Priscilla Worthington arrived from the station complete with a huge suitcase and a model's make-up box. She was around fifty, slim, of average height, and with an exceptionally pretty face that had not quite withstood the attentions of time. She needed a good friend to tell her to use less make-up.

She had been talked into this job by her agent and, more convincingly, by the arrival of her quarterly telephone bill. Normally she would never have taken such a dubious form of acting. Not an actress of her talent. Not someone who used to appear on TV and was asked to open supermarkets. However, the gloomy splendour of

Wittenham Park and the suave appearance of Lord Gilroy in his
boating jacket when he greeted her persuaded her that it might be
quite amusing after all. She began to cheer up.

"What a perfect setting for a murder!" she gushed after Gilroy
had introduced Dee Dee. "This is going to be the greatest fun."

"I'm so glad you feel like that," Dee Dee said quickly, "because
you're the murderess."

"Why not! I was a great hit in *The Mousetrap.*"

"If you don't mind," Gilroy said, "we'll explain the plot straight-
away. We're running to rather a tight schedule this evening. Have to
get the show on the road and all that, and luckily the rest are upstairs changing."

Having thoughtfully provided Priscilla with a stiff gin and tonic,
which Dee Dee guessed she would prefer to tea, they launched
into the details.

As the characters of Louise and her family were outlined,
Priscilla began calculating the many opportunities that the staircase,
the stone-flagged Great Hall and the library offered for dramatic en-
trances and exits.

"Being the widow's companion," Dee Dee explained, "you have
more access to her private rooms than anyone else. You're also determined to get your legacy. When, over dinner, it sounds as though
she'll rethink her will, you decide to act. You don't know who the
blackmailer is, but you suspect it's her brother. He's sleeping in what
had been her husband's dressing-room, next to hers. So it should be
easy to throw suspicion on him."

"And how do I kill her?"

"Poison," Gilroy said. "You put it in the bedtime drink you
bring her every night. But tonight you talk her brother into taking
it for you."

"Are you sure he won't see through that, darlings?" Priscilla
slipped into her theatrical way of calling everyone "darling" without realizing it. "Or is he an utter fool?"

"Why should he suspect anything?" Gilroy reacted as if insulted,
but it was being called "darling" that had upset him more than the
implication of idiocy.

"Well, I would."

"Then you'd better sort out some stage business with the coffee-cups. Or the after-dinner brandy. Talk to Dodgson. You can work it out between you while we're at the Lion Park. Give you a chance to get to know the house too."

"Just what kind of poison is it?"

"What kind?" They hadn't bothered with this aspect. It was as bad as those army instructors who always wanted to know the calibre of weapon you were using. "The fatal kind, of course. What does it matter?"

"An awful lot, darlings. Cyanide is very quick. Arsenic's very slow. There's hemlock and aconite. You ought to read Agatha Christie."

"We have, God help us," Gilroy exploded "Until the cows come home."

"In fact," Dee Dee confessed, "we're probably the only people on this weekend who've read a word of hers."

"I thought they were all enthusiasts."

"So did we."

"But, darlings"—having acted in many murder plays, Priscilla was very positive about crime—"the kind of poison makes an awful lot of difference."

"Mrs. Worthington." Dee Dee decided to call a halt and did so with a barbed remark, given whom she was talking to. "This is only play-acting. The game is for everyone to identify the murderer."

Priscilla's eyelids quivered, as though she was about to cry. "I've brought several costumes. Are your guests dressing up?"

"Only to their own satisfaction. I have to warn you they're a tough bunch. Getting any enthusiasm out of them is going to be hard work. The man Savage and his daughter will enter into the spirit of things. The others won't."

"We rely on you," Gilroy said, "to get things going."

"And keep them going," added Dee Dee firmly. "It's going to be a long, hard night."

Priscilla gazed at her hosts, so affable at first, now so demanding. "It'll be a fun weekend, so you won't mind the fee being rather small, will you?" the agent had said. What *had* she let herself in for?

"A hard night for all of us," Dee Dee said, softening the blow a little. "Would you like to see your room?"

Priscilla was so overwhelmed that she did not dare ask for another drink. Luckily she had a half bottle of gin in her make-up case.

4

THE ASSEMBLED group almost caused Dee Dee Gilroy to burst out laughing. Each person had a different idea of the right clothes to wear for seeing the lions. Welch was in one of the loudest checked jackets ever seen outside a race-track, while his wife bulged in a green spotted silk dress more suitable for a garden party. Hamish had opted for soft blue canvas loafers and a blazer with buttons bearing the lion crest of a London store. Loredana was in a Chanel-style beige safari suit, with large pockets and a silk Hermès scarf tied around the crown of an Australian bush hat. Dee Dee thought. Only Dulcie had on common-sense jeans and a sweater, as had Dee Dee herself.

Two Land Rovers with viewing hatches cut in the roofs stood in the drive. Beside them waited Ted Matthews, the Lion Park keeper, wearing cords and an old sleeveless safari jacket. He was a youngster compared to most of them, with a fresh, freckled face and a boyish smile. He was in a more or less constant dispute with Lord Gilroy, who wanted him to sport a full-scale African hunting out-fit, as the rangers did at rival safari parks. Ted, who had a zoology Ph.D. and had spent five years in a South African game reserve, ar-gued that it would look absurd in rural England, even if this was more show business than animal management. Since Ted had both the experience and the instinct for handling big cats, Gilroy had so far given way.

Gilroy introduced this motley group to Ted and apportioned them seats, taking care to put Welch in the vehicle Ted drove. He knew exactly what kind of remarks Welch would make during the "safari" and had no intention of being subjected to them. Naturally the McMountdowns went with Welch, leaving Loredana to flutter her eyelashes vainly at being left to the mercies of Gilroy himself, together with the Savages. Loredana was making a big thing out of having been on safari in Kenya and was not pleased to discover that Gilroy and Dee Dee had been there frequently, while Jemma had been in the Masai Mara reporting on the murder there of an English girl. "I don't remember that," Loredana protested. "Who killed her?"

"They pretended it was a lion, but really she'd been hacked to pieces."

"How absolutely horrid. Men are beasts."

"What about women?" Jemma said, earning a disdainful frown from Loredana. "Don't lionesses usually do the killing?"

"Only because the males are too lazy."

"When did you start the Lion Park, Lord Gilroy?" Jim asked, elbowing his daughter in the ribs to shut her up, but noting that Loredana took offence easily and had little sense of humour.

"The only one in this part of the country," Gilroy said with pride, as they were let through a high gate in the electrified fence. "They have a hundred acres all to themselves. It's a big attraction."

There were still visitors from the afternoon driving round in their saloon cars, past signs warning them it was forbidden to feed the animals, sound their horns, or—most importantly—get out of their vehicles.

"People think they can go up to the lions and stroke them," Gilroy said. "Not that I'd be sorry if that fellow Welch tried."

The lions themselves seemed healthy enough, if incongruous lying in the shade of oak trees in English meadows.

"Caesar's our largest male," Gilroy said, stopping the vehicle to point at an impressive black-maned lion squatting over a lioness and very actively mating. "Don't see them at it all that often. Not that there's much else for them to do."

"Darling!" Dee protested.

"I'd like a few cubs born here. Tremendous publicity."

At this moment the other Land Rover drew up, also to watch

Caesar in action. Jim studied the occupants' faces through his binoculars and was amused. Mrs. Welch was affecting embarrassment, Hamish was expressionless, as though this sort of thing were beneath him, Dulcie was openly laughing and Welch had his own binoculars raised to get a close-up view. That pretty well summed them up, Jim thought. Hamish was a cold fish and Welch a sex-obsessed rogue.

As they watched, Caesar dismounted from the lioness, biting her neck gently, then ambled away to lie down by himself.

"He's limping," Loredana said. "Poor old thing. He must have a thorn in his paw."

"No thorn-bushes here," Gilroy countered, aggravated that he had not noticed the limp himself. "Whatever it is, Ted'll fix him up."

"How? I mean, I find it hard enough with my cat." It was clear that she felt deeply about cats, or at least about her own one.

"Dart him with a tranquillizer," Gilroy said, casually emphasizing his expertise, "deal with the paw, then inject him with the antidote and get the hell out of his way again."

"But wouldn't Caesar be grateful? My little Timmy would."

"How would little Timmy like having a hypodermic fired into his little behind?" Dee Dee asked, nauseated by all this tweeness.

"Oh, he'd hate it!" Loredana instantly reversed her attitude. "He's a lion at heart. And he hates the vet. He knows when we're going there. But he's so old now, he's going to have to be put down."

"It's a lot kinder," Jemma said. "I'm all for euthanasia."

"Regardless of age, I hope." Dee Dee reckoned they had several euthanasia candidates here this weekend.

"She was thinking of me, rather than her, I think," Jim suggested.

"Oh no, Daddy. Never." Jemma leaned across and squeezed his hand.

Far from laughing along with the others, Loredana was annoyed by this inconsequential small talk. Nobody understood her problems. "I only wish I could put darling Timmy to sleep myself," she moaned.

"Come on, darling," Dee Dee said to Gilroy, having had enough of this inane chatter. "We haven't seen the Conservation Centre yet."

But Loredana wanted the last word. "You have one? How marvellous!" she cooed. "And I must talk to your keeper. Lions are so fascinating."

"Compared to humans, unquestionably," said Dee Dee.

The Conservation Centre was a skilful adaptation of an old timbered Elizabethan barn, the only surviving building of the original estate. It housed an exhibition area, a cafeteria, a souvenir shop and the lion keeper's offices and laboratory.

The two Land Rovers arrived almost simultaneously and Gilroy gathered his group to show them round, not omitting the shop with its car stickers boasting "I've heard the Wittenham lions roar!" and mugs emblazoned with the family crest of the stag. In fact, he took them there first, pretending it would shortly be closing. He'd once heard a marketing man say, "The sale you lose today can never be made again." It had taken him time to understand the concept that tomorrow is inescapably another day, but once he had, this became a prized motto. Predictably Adrienne bought a crested mug and Dulcie a tea-towel because she felt obliged to, while the others firmly bought nothing.

The exhibition was more rewarding. There were photographs and wildlife montages, while looking down at them were the mounted trophies of the first Lord Gilroy's big-game hunting. This collection of slightly moth-eaten heads—buffalo, numerous antelope, tiger and, inevitably, lion—had formerly graced the Great Hall at the house. They had been Dee Dee's first target for eviction after her marriage.

"Bet the animal-rights girls like those!" Welch commented sardonically. "Get a lot of protests?"

"In fact, no." Gilroy knew what was coming and tried to steer past it.

"Have to close the lions down once our homes is built," Welch said. "Frighten the families."

"The Lion Park is not going to be closed," Gilroy said firmly, which was a way of saying that the houses would be built over his dead body. But there had been a sting in the tail of Welch's remark.

This week he'd received a letter from the local council questioning security and claiming that local residents were concerned about certain dangers. He had asked Ted to draft an answer.

Luckily Dulcie came up at this moment, saying, "I've something to show you, George." She grinned at Gilroy. "I've never seen lions screwing before. Quite a giggle." She then led Welch off to examine a map of the estate that she had found hanging in the cafeteria.

"Disgusting, I'd say," Adrienne chipped in. She was out of temper. It had been hot and bumpy in the Land Rover. She'd imagined they were going straight on to drinks, which was why she had put on the silk dress, and now it was stained with sweat.

"What they were doing was entirely normal," Gilroy said stiffly, then quoted from his own brochure. "We aim to show the King of Beasts in a completely natural environment."

Loredana now insisted on having her little talk with Ted. Gilroy directed her to the unobtrusive office door in the far wall of the exhibition area. Characteristically she did not knock, but went straight in.

The keeper's office-cum-laboratory was thoroughly modern. A wide chrome-legged desk and several filing cabinets stood at one end beneath a window. There was another door in the outer wall, and at the opposite end a long laboratory bench had a steel sink set into it. Two empty glass vials for samples were by the sink. Shelves held a range of bottles and there was a rack of veterinary instruments.

The only thing missing was the keeper himself.

Tempted by his absence, Loredana explored. A letter from the local council lay on the desk, suggesting that the electric fence put children "at risk" and mentioning local fears about lions escaping.

Beside was Ted's draft reply, stating that the fence had a five-thousand-volt pulse, but very low amperage, and could not kill. He had pencilled on his draft: "The talk in the village is that a developer has been paying people to write to the council complaining. They get £10 a letter. I'm trying to find someone who'll admit it and name the developer, or his agent. Then we can go to the police."

Not hard to guess who that is, Loredana thought. Hamish had told her what Welch was after. She wandered across to the laboratory bench. Lying on it was a thin metal cylinder, about four inches long, with a needle projecting from one end. A vial of colorless liquid was beside it. She realized this must be the tranquillizer dart, ready for filling. The needle was almost an eighth of an inch thick. Small wonder the lion objected to being hit by that! She picked it up, tried to see how it worked, failed, and put it down again. She was examining the liquid when she heard the handle turn in the outside door. She put the vial down again, telling herself that she was being extremely naughty.

"Hallo, there," Ted said cheerfully, though with a question in his tone.

Loredana explained about her interest in lions with unusual brevity.

"It was you spotted Caesar limping, then? Glad to meet you." He shook her hand warmly, finding her response firmer than he would have expected from her delicate appearance. "I'll have to take a look at his paw tomorrow, it's too late today. He's a magnificent animal, but easier to approach in the heat of the day when he's sleepy. So, how can I help?"

"How do you keep them fit?" She gestured towards his medicines. "I give my Timmy all sorts of tablets, but what do you give a lion?"

Few professionals do not enjoy talking about their profession. It was a full twenty minutes before Ted escorted Loredana back into the exhibition hall. He took with him his draft reply to the council to give Lord Gilroy.

"We were wondering where you'd got to." Hamish came up to her immediately. "We're off to the house for drinks."

"But I must change first! I simply must." Loredana reverted to her normal demanding self, though making a point of thanking Ted with the sweetest of smiles.

Gilroy was relieved to see her too. The moment he needed to assemble a group, its members started to wander off. It was one of those immutable laws of nature, the kind they had taught about at Eton, like gravity or the way peas fall off one's fork. A professional tour leader's life must be absolute hell!

Before anyone else could stray, he and Dee Dee ushered all the guests into the vehicles and so back to the house. The serious business of the weekend was about to begin. Ted waved before taking his Land Rover again and Loredana blew him a kiss. "Such a darling man," she said, causing Hamish to look at her askance. He expected her to be faithful in her infidelity. Dulcie noticed the blown kiss and her husband's expression, interpreted it correctly and quite suddenly decided that tonight would be the night. If Hamish took a trip down the corridor later on, it was going to be on a one-way ticket.

"Ladies and gentlemen," Gilroy announced when they were all in the hall, "drinks will be served in the library at six-thirty, that's in half an hour, and we'll be handing out the first clues. From then on it's murder time."

Mrs. Worthington clapped, to Gilroy's consternation, and the others followed suit faint-heartedly. She had spent an industrious hour with Dodgson, working out how the notional poison would be planted. After that she had taken on board a little fortification, in the shape of the gin from her suitcase. She was now all set for her role as animator-in-chief.

"Darlings," she announced, "I don't know about all of you, but I can't wait for the first clue."

"Speak for yerself," Welch was heard to mutter, before Dee Dee firmly chivvied them all upstairs to change, Mrs. Worthington included.

"Am I dreaming," she asked Gilroy, "or has that woman been at the bottle?"

"Sounded a bit like it," Gilroy agreed gloomily. "Have to tell Dodgson to keep the drinks locked up."

"Which you cannot do, honey. This is an all-inclusive weekend, remember? Right through from the beer to the brandy. When are you seeing Welch?"

"After dinner."

"Well, for God's sake, don't sign anything." Dee Dee was

tempted to insist on being present, but that would be too demeaning for her husband. "Now, I am about to transform myself into Mrs. Louise Sketchley. And don't you dare applaud when I come down."

Half an hour later, rather too punctually, Jim and Jemma Savage descended the great stairway. Jemma paused to fondle one of the carved unicorns at the bottom. "It is rather splendid, isn't it, Daddy. Think of the work this must have taken."

As they stood there, the muffled sounds of an altercation came from somewhere close by.

"Officially it's murder time," Jemma whispered. "We'd better listen."

The voices were easily traceable to an oak door off the hall, leading to the room that was Lord Gilroy's office, though neither of them knew this. It sounded as though two men were arguing, but not loudly enough for the words to be distinguishable. Then suddenly one bellowed sentence came through distinctly.

"You bloody well will! Or else!"

There was a brief silence. Then a third, less belligerent, voice added, "You haven't any option."

The reply was inaudible. It also sounded as though the threat might have ended the conversation. Jim and Jemma backed away from the door in case it was opened.

"That was Mr. George Welch shouting," Jim remarked. "No question about it. God, he's a thug."

"It did sound terribly real," Jemma commented. "I mean, not like acting at all. But who were the others?"

"No idea. Better make it the first of my detective's observations." Jokingly her father pulled out a small red spiral-bound notebook and recorded the time, 6:31 P.M., and the words. Then they went through into the library, where the butler was on duty with a drinks tray.

They were the first arrivals. Dee Dee greeted them, looking superb in a long flame-coloured dress, with a diamond choker and diamond earrings.

"Meet Mrs. Louise Sketchley," she said genially, "rich widow and blackmail victim. This might be the last occasion she'll be able to wear her best jewels, unless the blackmailer is defeated, so she's loaded on the lot."

"Which will remind her relations of just how much she's worth and what they stand to inherit," added Gilroy, who wore a well-cut dinner jacket, yet somehow still looked as if he had only hired it for a salesman's conference. "Since you're the first down, would you like to read the first clue?"

"Why not?" Jemma agreed.

"But first," he said, childishly pleased with all this "first" punning, "you can be the first to have the first drink. What's your poison, ha ha?"

"An orange juice and lemonade, please. And I hope it won't kill me!"

A look of panic came over Gilroy's dimpled features, as though he had suddenly realized that his rented trousers were unzipped. For a moment Jemma thought she might be the first intended victim. What had actually taken him aback was that he had failed to reckon on non-drinkers. They had orange juice on the drinks tray, but Dodgson needed to go to his pantry to fetch lemonade. It was a relief when Jim Savage asked for an ordinary "G and T," the standard drink of the Surrey stockbroker belt where he and Jemma lived. Gilroy winced at the expression, but at least gin and tonic was easy and he poured it himself, mixed another for Dee Dee, and gave himself a Scotch and soda.

"Here's to the weekend." He raised his glass and they all toasted its success. "And here"—he took two slips of paper from a small pile on a table—"is the first clue."

The text ran: "This evening two characters are overheard in fierce argument. Who are they and why are they in dispute?" Dee Dee was planning to stage an argument with Welch, which would not be hard to bring about, and give a red-herring clue as to why he might be the murderer.

"We seem to be ahead of the action," Jemma remarked to her father as she read this.

"Possibly," Jim conceded in his dry way, appreciating that during this weekend his own instinctive caution was going to be overruled by his daughter. Just as she had insisted that they didn't cancel, in spite of his losing his job, now she was going to find mysteries at every turn. She had all the curiosity and ghoulish imagination of a born crime reporter.

Gilroy overheard Jemma's comment and had an alarming presentiment that events were already spiralling out of control, in the way that his business ventures invariably did. He had begun to think of it as the curse of the Gilroys. If he really had been a car salesman, pieces would have fallen off his cars during the test drives and gearboxes disintegrated. It would be typical of his luck if there actually was a murder this weekend. What exactly had the girl meant? What row could she have already overheard? There was going to be one with Welch, all right. But that would be after dinner, and he thought he'd been pretty clever to weave it into the "murder" clues. "Dashed neat, darling, don't you think?" he had said to Dee Dee. So what the heck was all this?

"When will this argument be?" Jemma asked, sounding innocent.

"Could be any time." He tried to put a bold face on the reply, but his discomfort showed through. Luckily he had to break off to welcome Dulcie and Hamish, who were soon followed by Loredana and then by Welch and his wife. Dee Dee had already guessed that only Dulcie and the Savages would put any effort into making the weekend work, and she was right. Loredana's interest in the evening went precisely as far as tricking herself out in a skimpy, clinging silk dress, which revealed a great deal more than it concealed and kept both Welch's and Hamish's eyes on her most of the time.

However, Hamish had dressed decently, almost overdressed himself, in a dark-blue velvet smoking-jacket with enough loops of black braid on its sleeves to satisfy a four-star general.

As for Welch, he was in another of his Mafia-style blue suits, causing Adrienne embarrassment and anger. She had told him to pack a dinner suit and he'd refused. "What, tog meself up for that toffee-nose?" he'd snorted "You have to be joking!" Why did George have to be so obstinate and always put people's backs up? There were times when she had really had enough. "Reely," she'd told her mother last week, "now I've wormed that million of insurance out of him, I'd be better off if he did drop dead. No more having to beg him for money all the time and I'd be able have my friends round when I want."

It had taken little short of the rack and thumbscrews to get George to buy that insurance, but the threat of more Lloyds losses had done the trick. She'd pointed out that Lloyds could take every penny if he died unexpectedly, whereas an insurance payout would be inalienably hers. She suspected he'd given in because having done so gave him a kind of licence to womanize. She felt a lot more secure as a result, but was still furious at the way he kept sneaking glances at Loredana's well-defined nipples. That woman was no more than a high-class tart, she decided. Trust George to be spellbound!

Gilroy's fears regarding his guests' enthusiasm were justified when the rest were given their clues. Welch read his and scrumpled it into a pocket. Hamish made a sotto-voce comment and did the same. Loredana handed hers to Hamish, protesting she had nowhere to put it. Possibly not, Jemma thought wickedly, since she was neither carrying a handbag nor wearing a bra, though lacking a handbag was strange. She was probably worried she'd end up leaving it in the wrong room. The vibes about Loredana and Hamish had been easy to pick up.

Dulcie's reaction was the most intriguing. She smiled to herself as she read the clue, then carefully folded it and tucked it into her evening bag. What caused that smile? Jemma wondered.

The stilted conversation was mercifully cut short by Priscilla Worthington making her entrance, wearing a low-cut black evening gown with a gauzy see-through top up to her neck and down to her wrists. Priscilla knew how to pile on the glamour.

"Darlings," she announced, swaying slightly as she accepted her clue, "how too mysterious for words. We must all keep our ears to the ground!" She advanced on Dee Dee. "Dear Mrs. Sketchley," she accented the "dear" heavily for effect, "how good it is of you to ask all your family for the weekend. Such a privilege for me to meet them all again. A companion's life is not always a happy one." Then she added to the others in a hissing undertone, "Actually I hate the old bitch."

Total silence greeted this theatrical foray.

Hamish's face froze, as though she'd impugned the honour of the McMountdowns, or a cab driver had addressed him as "friend." Hamish was starchily snobbish about virtually everything.

Dee Dee decided Priscilla must be tanked up to the eyebrows, and was working out how to prevent her getting any more to drink, when Dodgson saved her by announcing that dinner was served. As soon as the guests had gone through, he whispered throatily to Dee Dee that Tracy, the maid, insisted on speaking to her.

"This moment?"

"Yes, milady."

Oh God, Dee Dee thought, she can't be going to give in her notice now! She agreed to see the girl very briefly and, when the guests had been taken to the dining-room, Tracy came in looking flustered.

"Well, Tracy," Dee Dee demanded brusquely, "what's the problem?"

"I'm not taking him his early-morning tea. No way." Tracy's language was an odd mixture of shop-girl English and TV Americanisms.

"Who?"

"That Welch. When I went to make up his room he pinched my—"

"Goosed you?"

Tracy's face reddened. "Yes, milady. I won't do it. No way when he's there, I won't. He can have a tray left outside his door."

Normally Dee Dee would never dream of her guests' not having tea taken in to them. The place might just as well be a hotel. Damn Welch! But it was a solution. Instead of castigating the maid, she beamed at her.

"What a clever idea! But you must do the same for everyone. And if he bothers you again, we'll call the police." Dee Dee rather hoped he would, though the idea of anyone goosing a girl as fat as Tracy was bizarre. Then it occurred to her that while she had the chance she ought to remind her about tomorrow morning's happenings. "And don't forget, you come to the State Bedroom at seven-thirty, pretend you've found me dead, run out into the passage and start screaming the house down."

Tracy brightened up. She'd enjoy doing that. "Yes, milady," she said enthusiastically. "I'll scream like a banshee."

"Perhaps not quite so loud. Just so that everyone hears."

With this agreed, Dee Dee made her way through to the dining-room and was pleased to find that Dodgson had followed her orders implicitly. There was silver everywhere. A pair of massive candelabra graced the long mahogany table. Between them stood a silver statuette of a Guardsman in a bearskin. Silver salt-cellars and pepper-pots, solid silver cutlery and slender-stemmed wine glasses all helped complete the atmosphere promised in the brochure.

Welch had been audibly impressed, while Jim Savage understood why his hostess was concerned about theft. He wouldn't put it past Adrienne or the tipsy Priscilla to slip a souvenir into their handbags; nor Welch to pocket a spoon. Even the seating plan was indicated by crested name cards held in little silver clips.

Where to put people had worried Dee Dee. The main thing was to keep Welch at one remove from both herself and Buck. So he was on one side of the centre facing Hamish, with Jemma and Dulcie separating Gilroy from them at the far end, while she had Savage on her right and the two remaining women on her left. Loredana sat smirkingly next to Hamish. Trevor Chancemain had still not arrived and it had occurred to her to invite Ted, the lion keeper, to improve the balance, but he had no small talk.

Overall it was not a bad plan. Jim Savage could tip her off if anyone did start stealing the spoons and she could keep an eye on Priscilla's drinking. But she had overestimated her ability to insulate Welch from Buck. Unexpectedly the man who broke the barrier was Hamish.

The prawn with thin slices of avocado had gone down well and Dodgson was about to go round with a dish of chicken Maryland when Hamish leaned towards Buck.

"Sorry to be the bearer of ill tidings," he said, "but just before I left the office I heard that Lloyds has posted another six-billion loss. Calls for up to half a million will be sent out tomorrow morning."

Gilroy's face paled and the impact on him was so obvious that even Priscilla stopped chattering, though she ostentatiously held up her wineglass for it to be refilled by Dodgson.

"That don't worry me," Welch said quickly, "I ain't on the worst syndicates." He caught Hamish's eye and Hamish nodded half-heartedly, or so it seemed to Jim.

"How d'you know about Lloyds?" Gilroy asked.

"For my sins," Hamish said unctuously, "I work there."

At this point Jim Savage began taking serious note of the conversation. There was something staged about the remarks Hamish was making, and about Welch's intervention. He glanced at Dee Dee and saw that her expression was tight and angry.

"Are you heavily involved?" Dulcie asked Gilroy with polite concern.

"Yes, damn the buggers."

"I'm so sorry." Her concern now sounded more deeply felt.

"It's the estate I'm worried about," Gilroy said, disregarding a warning look from Dee Dee.

Behind him Dodgson, still holding the decanter of white wine, stiffened and Jim saw an expression of extreme dismay cross his drooping face.

"How do I stop those bastards from taking my land?"

"Speaking as a lawyer," Dulcie said quietly, "probably the only way out is to raise money on it and deposit that in an offshore bank account ahead of getting the demand. If you say you've already spent the money, how can they prove you haven't?"

"That's an idea," Gilroy conceded, but before he could say any more he was firmly interrupted by his wife.

"If we must talk business, let's at least talk the murder plot." Dee Dee made a sign to Dodgson to start serving again, then fixed her gaze on Welch. "Now, let's get one thing utterly clear. I am not about to be blackmailed."

"Accusing me of blackmail, are yer?" he reacted quite violently.

"Since you have the nerve to ask, yes, I am."

There was another moment of absolute silence.

"There's witnesses to that," Welch said venomously. "I'll sue yer. And your perishing 'usband."

"That will be difficult," Dee Dee said calmly, having made the real-life point she intended, "since my husband, John Sketchley, has been dead for eleven years."

Priscilla tittered and gradually the laughter of nervous relief spread around the table, as everyone else realized that this was play-acting and could be the dispute referred to in the first clue; everyone, that was, except Welch. He glared at Dee Dee.

"Too bloody clever by 'alf, ain't you. Thought you 'ad me on the hop, eh? You make accusations like that again and we'll be meeting in court."

"You should have read the clue, Mr. Welch."

"People are as guilty as they think they are," chimed in Priscilla, gesticulating with her newly refilled glass and spilling some on the table. "As Carr, you must be the blackmailer, Mr. Welch."

"I think it's time for the next clue," Dee Dee said, as Welch lapsed into a sullen scowl, his face becoming more highly coloured than ever, "even though you mustn't throw away the first one."

Since Dodgson was busy serving the chicken, Gilroy got up and handed out the second set of clues.

"Watch out for who drinks what," the slip of paper advised. "And whoever is last to bed, please turn out the lights."

"The proverbial coffee-cups, I suppose," Jemma said to Gilroy.

"Have to wait and see." Gilroy was still trying to figure out what exactly his wife had been doing in challenging the property developer, even though he recognized an underlying purpose from her tone. It had been Dee Dee's "telling you off" voice. Was she trying to warn him of something? Certainly Welch had been blustering and unpleasant, but he had made no threats. So what was all this about? Gilroy hated being talked to in riddles.

The rest of the meal was uneventful, although Welch attempted to engage Loredana in conversation across the table, while Hamish surreptitiously stroked her thigh underneath it. They all returned to the library for coffee. Dee excused herself early and one by one the others drifted off, though not before Priscilla, now decidedly tipsy, asked Welch if he would take a bedtime mug of cocoa in to "Mrs. Sketchley."

Welch erupted as violently as one of those volcanoes that gives jets engine failure and halts all traffic for hundreds of miles.

"Take it yer bloody self. What d'yer think I am, a bloody skivvy? You can bloody well tell that doddering butler to send me up a whisky, too. And not a glass. A bottle."

He charged out of the room like a bull that couldn't wait to gore the next matador. However, Priscilla decided to do as he had asked, and get a small snifter of the right stuff for herself at the same time. Accordingly, she rang the bell, and after a wait Dodgson appeared. He was reluctant to send Welch an entire bottle, but graced the refusal by saying he would place a small decanter and a bottle of soda in his room. Prudently, noting Priscilla's condition, he fetched her only a cut-glass tumbler and served her there and then in the library.

Meanwhile, as Jemma and Jim were going upstairs, they again heard noises from the room off the hall. No one else seemed to be interested, or perhaps they all recognized the clue "row" as having been the one at dinner. Jemma tiptoed to the door and put her ear to it. She heard what might have been Dulcie's relatively deep voice say, "Go ahead, then!"

Gilroy came striding through the hall and she hastily backed away. He opened the door and went in. She noted the time. It was nine thirty-six.

"We seem to be having a very early night, Daddy," she commented. Early nights were not her big thing.

"Speak for yourself, my dear," Savage commented wryly.

Savage was one hundred percent right. Whereas he swiftly fell asleep in his room, she could not get to sleep, so she lay in bed reading. Shortly before midnight she heard surreptitious footsteps pass her door, going towards the east wing. Then she did fall asleep until she was woken by a knock on the door and the maid's voice.

"Your tea's outside, miss."

She checked her watch. It was 7:10 A.M. Early to rise was no more Jemma's motto than early to bed. She had to force herself to get up, sleepily open the door and bring in the tray. As she did so she realized that there was activity down the passage towards the west wing. That was to say, she heard noises. All she actually saw was the back of a tall woman in a lacy night-gown disappear into one of the doorways farther along, and she only glimpsed her from the waist down, because she was leaning forwards as she opened the door.

Jemma stood in the passage for another moment, holding her tray and wondering who would emerge next from where. However, nothing happened and she felt stupid standing there. The time was seven-fourteen. She went back to bed. Minutes later she thought she heard footsteps in the passage, but could not be bothered to move. It was bad enough that at any moment there would be a murder.

Fifteen minutes later, piercing screams from the maid shattered the quiet of the house.

Jemma shot out of her room, as did her father out of his. A door at the west end of the passage opened and Dulcie came out, a short coat on over her night-dress.

"She's dead!" Tracy screamed, as soon as she had an audience. "Milady's dead!" She stopped, realizing she had got it wrong, mumbled something and started again. "Mrs. Sketchley's dead!" It was not an easy name to scream, so she added an easier word: "Help!"

This brought Loredana along from the east wing, followed by Priscilla, whose room was even farther along there. Both were in their night-dresses, though Loredana had a cream silk dressing-gown over hers. Priscilla was clutching a gown, while the lace trim on her night-dress swirled as she ran to join in the drama.

"Oh my God," Priscilla yelled, making a rush for the State Bedroom door, only to have it firmly shut in her face from the inside. This did not deter her from her mission. "Mrs. Sketchley's been murdered!"

Next on the scene was a bleary-eyed Adrienne Welch, also wearing a night-gown trimmed with lace. She saw that her husband's tea-tray had not yet been used, since the cup was clean. "No point disturbing him yet," she said. "All I'll get is an earful. See you all later."

Finally Hamish came up the stairs. "What's the matter?" he asked, as if unaware of the plot.

"Where have you been?" Dulcie demanded.

"Went down to get some coffee. You know I never drink tea."

Dulcie gave him a filthy look. A moment later Lady Gilroy came out of the State Room dressed in a resplendent, all-enveloping, red satin housecoat. Jemma noticed a flare of white lace from the bottom of a night-gown, which the housecoat did not totally conceal. Lace must be this year's Harrods' fashion, she thought.

"Well," Dee Dee said, with a definitive edge to her words, "since Mr. Chancemain has not arrived to play the doctor, you can all take it that Mrs. Louise Sketchley has been murdered. A medical bulletin will be issued later. Breakfast is at nine." She swept off down the passage to the east wing.

"Speaking for myself," Dulcie said, "I am going back to bed."

One by one they all drifted off. Jemma was not surprised that Welch had not appeared. As his wife had implied, he was so surly, and so uninterested in the plot, that nothing could be expected of him. She went back to her room at seven forty-four and the landing was deserted once more.

5

BREAKFAST was an anticlimax after the 7:30 A.M. commotion. Dee Dee had misjudged the effect of having the "murder" discovered so early. Her guests' first instinct was to get back to their morning tea, then to dress. When they did come down for breakfast soon after nine, they were more interested in real food than fictional crime. Furthermore, it was a genuine country-house breakfast, not a hotelier's make-believe, with silver dishes bearing bacon, eggs, tomatoes, kidneys and mushrooms, lined up on a hotplate for everyone to serve themselves as they felt inclined.

Dee Dee and Gilroy breakfasted elsewhere and only Priscilla tried to steer the conversation onto the "murder," an attempt not helped by her being in the grip of a hangover.

"I don't know about all of you, darlings," she quavered, embracing Hamish, Dulcie and Loredana with what was intended to be an encouraging smile, but emerged as a conspiratorial giggle, "but I quite definitely heard footsteps in the corridor during the night. I'm sure something dastardly was going on."

"The question is what," Dulcie remarked, looking sideways at her husband, who flushed, while Loredana became intensely interested in a boiled egg which she had only been fiddling with before.

"I heard a midnight person," Jemma cut in. "And I saw a woman in a night-dress this morning who can't have been the maid."

"Must we take this nonsense seriously?" Hamish asked in a lofty way. "Personally I came here for a relaxed weekend."

"We came because we were invited," Dulcie said coldly.

Listening, Jim Savage realized whose voice they had overheard in the hall before dinner. Dulcie's last remark had the same low, scornful, and almost masculine intensity that had characterized the words "You haven't any option."

"None the less, Mrs. McMountdown, you have been joining in," he protested, wondering if he would catch her on the hop. "Jemma and me heard the 'row' before dinner. Mr. Welch took part, didn't he?"

"Before dinner?" Dulcie was caught unawares, but recovered quickly and laughed in a dismissive way. "You've fallen for a red herring. Lord Gilroy lent him the room for a business discussion. There was no row. George always expresses himself, well, vividly. The row during dinner was the one we're supposed to remember."

"Libellous that was, all that about blackmail," Adrienne said indignantly. "Just deliberately getting on George's wick. No wonder he went bananas. And fancy making him sleep in a different room to me." She stopped, then added with a trace of concern, almost of guilt, "I think I'll go and see what's keeping him. It's not like my George to be late for a meal. Likes his food too much." She put down her napkin and left the room.

"I need to talk to him, too," Dulcie said.

"So do I," Hamish echoed her words, making Jim wonder if he had been the third person involved in the row. It was clearer than ever that those three had an agenda of their own this weekend, just as it had been obvious that Lady Gilroy's antipathy to Welch was real and that Loredana was involved with Hamish.

"What I simply don't understand," Priscilla said plaintively, holding her hands to her head as if in need of steadying her brain, "is what we do when we've guessed the clues."

"Oh my God!" Jim exclaimed, reminded of his duties, "I'm meant to be the detective." He ought to have made notes about everything in "Mrs. Sketchley's" room—the position of the body, all that kind of thing. Although he could hardly have done so when the "body" had sailed imperiously off to the Gilroy's private quarters.

"You'll have to make up for lost time, Daddy," Jemma chided him. "Shall I come with you?"

"Good idea." He swallowed down the last of his coffee and the two of them left the room.

As they reached the top of the great staircase, Adrienne appeared from the dressing-room, where her husband was, looking frantically around, her handbag swinging. When she caught sight of Jim and Jemma she hurried down the passage to them.

"Please help me," she said, her voice only just under control. "It's George. I can't wake him up."

She led them into the dressing-room. It was simply and traditionally furnished with a mahogany chest of drawers, an Empire-style single bed, a mahogany wardrobe and a bookcase. Welch's underclothes were lying in disarray on an armchair. The curtains were drawn across a high window and there was another door, presumably leading either to a bathroom or to the State Room next door.

Jim began making these mental notes the moment he saw George Welch's corpulent body, lying propped up with pillows, on the elegant bed. He was wearing a dressing-gown over his pyjamas and might have been reading something when he collapsed, because a pair of reading glasses lay on the bedcover. Jim stood by the bed, took his wrist and felt for a pulse. There was none.

"We need a doctor," he said. "Jemma, go and rout out the Gilroys. Quick."

"He's not dead!" Adrienne half-screamed, beginning to lose control, as Jemma ran out into the passage. She took her husband's arm and tried to lift him up further on the bed. "George, George," she cried out. "What's happened?" There was no response and he was too heavy for her to shift.

"They'll have a doctor here in no time," Jim said. It was pointless to offer hope, but he felt Welch's chest as a gesture. There was no trace of a heartbeat.

Adrienne gave up her efforts, sat down heavily in the empty armchair and began to sob.

"Can I get you a cup of tea?" Jim offered.

She nodded.

Before leaving the room, he made a further quick survey of what was in it. A small decanter stood on top of the chest of drawers. It looked empty. It struck him that something was missing, something that should have been there, but he could not think what it was. He would have liked to look in the bathroom, but felt obliged to go out by the main door.

Downstairs he encountered Gilroy, calling the doctor from the phone in the hall, with Jemma beside him. He fetched a cup of sweetened tea from the dining-room and took it up. The only table was the bedside one. Balancing the teacup in his right hand, he used his left to lift the table across to Adrienne.

"I never knew he had a bad heart," she said. "It must have been his heart, mustn't it? I can't believe this is happening." She began to sob again. "I reely can't."

"The doctor'll be here soon," he assured her. There wasn't a lot more to say and he was uncertain whether to stay with her or not, eventually deciding he ought to. Possibly the tea helped, because she gradually recovered herself.

"It must have been his heart," she repeated, seeming oddly reconciled to the idea.

Downstairs Gilroy went through to tell the guests still at breakfast that Welch was ill. Dulcie at once insisted on going up to see him.

"His wife's with him," Gilroy said, displaying unusual firmness. "I think you should wait." She agreed reluctantly and the first animated conversation of the weekend erupted amongst everyone else.

Twenty minutes later Dr. Thompson arrived, carrying a sombre black bag, like an outsize briefcase, that contrasted oddly with his cheerful, chubby face and very active manner. After a methodical examination of Welch he confirmed that he was dead, but was cautious about the reason.

"It must be his heart," Adrienne said again, as though comforting herself with the idea.

"Was he taking any medication?" Thompson asked.

"Not regularly. He'd take a pill if he couldn't sleep. And so would I," Adrienne added. "You should have heard him snore."

"Was he a healthy person? Did he smoke a lot, drink much?"

"He liked his whisky," Adrienne admitted. "But he didn't smoke, except sometimes a cigar."

Suddenly Jim remembered two things that were missing. The first was whatever Welch had been reading, unless it had fallen on the floor. The second was the whisky glass. As the doctor continued, he went quietly to the other door, opened it and found a luxurious bathroom tiled in onyx, with a gigantic tub and a shower. Another door presumably led into the State Room. He tried the handle, but it was locked. He noticed a pair of tumblers on a glass shelf below a shaving mirror and sniffed them without touching them. There was no smell of liquor and they were clean. Standing there, he asked himself why he was doing all this. Lady Gilroy had asked him to keep an eye on the silver. That was hardly a reason for behaving like a private eye. And yet . . .

The doctor gave him a curious look as he re-entered the dressing-room, asked if that was a bathroom, went through and made up a sedative for Adrienne, using one of the tumblers. While he was there Jim managed to look around the floor by the bed and again found nothing. When Thompson returned with the sedative he told Gilroy that he would like a word in private.

"If you don't mind," he said to Adrienne, "I think it would be best if we all go downstairs." He ushered Jim and Adrienne out, then extracted the key from the inside of the bedroom door and locked it from the outside, carefully putting the key in his coat pocket.

"What d'you do that for?" Adrienne demanded. "Why shouldn't I go in? It's my husband's room! And he's in there." She began to sob again and Dr. Thompson had to take her arm and guide her down the hall.

"Can Lady Gilroy look after her?" he asked. "Somebody must do."

Fortunately Dee Dee came through from the kitchen in the east wing at this moment and took charge of Adrienne, while Jim rejoined the others and the doctor went with Gilroy to the study.

"Was this man Welch perfectly fit yesterday, so far as you know?" he demanded.

"Seemed to be." Gilroy was stunned. No one could have wished Welch out of the way more than he did, but dying was carrying things a bit far. He felt as though he had been mugged himself, and it was all too easy to spot what the doctor's next request would be.

"Since there appears to have been nothing the matter with him, I cannot possibly sign a death certificate. We must call the police."

"Do we have to?" This was exactly the wrong kind of publicity for Wittenham. The next thing they knew the grounds would be swarming with reporters.

"I'm afraid so. May I?" Thompson picked up the study's phone extension and rang a number. "As you probably know, I'm a police surgeon, but I'm not doing anything until officially asked."

"Then I shall have to tell the guests," Gilroy agreed wearily, wondering whether they would sue for refunds.

By this time breakfast was over. Dodgson discreetly chivvied everyone back to the library, Gilroy cleared his throat for an important announcement, told them all that Welch was dead and the police were on the way.

A gasp of amazement shook the room, followed by a palpable relaxation of the tension. Jemma, who had begun keeping notes in earnest for her magazine article, recorded being intrigued by people's expressions.

Dodgson and Tracy, standing respectfully apart from the guests, as the staff would have done in an Edwardian family photograph, showed silent satisfaction. Tracy's face had "Serve him right" written all over it, while the butler's displayed the relief of a long-serving worker who had not been let go after all.

The thin-lipped smile and wink that Hamish gave to Loredana were reciprocated by a tiny shrug of the shoulders from her, implying that this was none of her business, but probably a good thing. Otherwise she remained as impassive as the Ice Queen.

Only Dulcie actually spoke, and when she did it was in the strong, low tones that Jemma and her father had agreed were her business voice.

"As Mr. Welch's lawyer, I need access to papers that he was working on last night."

"I doubt the police would wish anything in his room to be touched." This was Dr. Thompson speaking.

"Then you can come with me as a witness." Dulcie's head was

tilted slightly back to challenge the doctor, who was well over six feet tall. "The document will have my fingerprints on it already. All I need to know is whether my client signed it."

"What a mystery!" Priscilla exclaimed delightedly. "Just like a thriller!"

"On the contrary." Dulcie swung round and cut her down. "This is for real and there is no mystery, simply a contract." She turned on Thompson. "Well, Doctor. Shall we go?"

Faced by this bundle of determined energy, Thompson relented and they went out, leaving the field clear for Priscilla to indulge herself.

"What's the betting he was murdered?" she cooed. "Wouldn't that be exciting!"

"Please, Mrs. Worthington." Gilroy protested.

"Oh, but he easily could have been, darling. I gave him the poisoned nightcap."

"You what!" Gilroy yelped, as everyone turned to look at her.

"He wouldn't take it in to 'Mrs. Sketchley,' so Mr. Dodgson made it up, and I took it to him instead. Horrid man."

Gilroy tried to shake off the fuzziness that this hung-over woman's remarks induced in his own head. Where did fiction end and fact begin? He had told her to get together with Dodgson and fix some skulduggery with the coffee-cups. What on earth had they actually done? He gave Dodgson a despairing glance and the butler stepped into the breach.

"If your lordship will forgive the intrusion," he wheezed, "I would like to explain. For the purposes of the plot, Mr. Welch was to take a poisoned hot drink to his 'sister.' Of course, it was not actually contaminated in any way. It was merely cocoa. I delivered it to this lady at ten in the evening."

"And I poisoned it!" Priscilla shrilled, apparently convinced that she really had.

"What is this nonsense?" Hamish demanded haughtily. "Poor old George Welch is dead and we should have some respect for him."

"Well, I put in a few sleeping tablets, that was all," Priscilla admitted sulkily, aggrieved at having her dramatics curtailed when she'd been told to keep things lively, and feeling no sorrow whatever for Welch. "He was such an old goat. He deserved to be immm-m" she stumbled over the word "immobilized" and then abandoned it. "Put out of business for the night."

"Do you know if he drank it?" Savage asked quietly, wondering why Hamish had spoken so unctuously about "poor old George."

"Of course I don't know, darling," Priscilla said cheerfully, glad to have got the secret off her chest. "It was just a joke. Jay-oh-kay-eee. I was lucky to get out of his room unraped, though, I can tell you that." She paused. "Oh, my head!"

"Where did you leave the cocoa?" Jim asked.

"On the table by his bed. That was where I went wrong. One should never go near a bed with a man like that around, should one?" She addressed the question to them all. "He put down his whisky and grabbed me; at least he tried to."

"Frankly," Hamish cut in, "I find this unnecessary and distasteful. Please excuse me." He got up and was leaving the room when Dulcie and the doctor came back, forcing him to stay.

"We have a problem," Dulcie told him curtly, then marched accusingly up to Gilroy. "The contract isn't there. Someone's taken it."

"Can't help you, I'm afraid. I certainly haven't."

Jim watched the peer's face carefully as this exchange took place and decided that Gilroy was a lot less relaxed than he was trying to sound. But it was none of his business to ask what the contract was connected with, though he could now suppose that it was what Welch had been reading in bed.

"Well, someone must have it," Dulcie insisted. "And if George did sign, then it's binding even though he's dead."

Gilroy shrugged his shoulders, but his face had paled. He could not let all these people guess what turmoil his mind was in. He should have listened to Dee Dee. He'd been a fool to agree to anything last night, when this lawyer woman had run rings around him. Furthermore, he was beginning to think that Hamish's interventions at dinner about Lloyds had been a put-up job. He scowled distractedly at Hamish, in much the same way as Adam must have given the eye to the serpent, and to his surprise the serpent reacted.

"As I said before, I find the tone of this discussion most offensive, and since the purpose of the weekend has clearly been destroyed, I propose to pack and leave."

"Not very sensible to do that until the police are here," Thompson remarked, tempted to exercise authority he did not have by ordering this curiously unpleasant man to remain where he was.

"That is only your opinion," Hamish replied coldly. He turned to Dulcie. "Are you coming, darling?"

Dulcie hesitated. She was not a criminal lawyer, but it was obvious that Thompson was right. The police would want to question everyone, even before the cause of Welch's death was known. "I'll come in a moment," she said. This time Hamish did leave the room.

"Well, I think Hamish is right," Loredana said. "The weekend's over, isn't it, Lord Gilroy?"

"Not if you don't want it to be." Gilroy's fears about refunds surfaced again. "Everything's geared up until Sunday evening." He took a chance and added, "Perhaps out of respect for the dead we ought to abandon the play-acting."

A murmur of horror came from Priscilla. The next thing she knew Gilroy would kick her out and her miserable fee would shrivel into nothing.

"But darlings, it's perfectly lovely here. Why on earth leave just because . . ." She cut herself short in the nick of time, having been about to say, ". . . because a dirty old man's kicked the bucket."

"Well, I don't want to stay if everyone else is going," Loredana said, making it rather too clear that for her only Hamish counted.

"Aren't you going to wait for Trevor?" Dulcie asked.

"Why should I, when he's so late?"

As Loredana stalked out of the library they all heard the scrunch of tyres on the gravel outside. The police had arrived. Dodgson excused himself and hurried through to the hall to let them in.

The police consisted of a young uniformed constable in a small car emblazoned with chequered flashes and the insignia of the Thames Valley Police. Twenty minutes later, having been shown the corpse and having talked briefly with Dr. Thompson, he demanded that everyone should remain in the house until the cause of George Welch's death had been established.

"I'm sure there's nothing untoward, sir," he said to Gilroy, "but we have our procedures."

Jim Savage nudged his daughter. "Lucky I haven't got a job to get back to!"

"You may not, Daddy, but I do." A note of resentment came into her voice, which her father knew only too well. As a tiny girl she had gone into fits of the sulks and she had never completely grown out of it.

Jim leaned over and whispered in her ear and Jemma's face brightened. "I hadn't thought of that," she said. "D'you really think so?"

"I'd bet on it. There's hardly a person here who didn't have something against Welch."

6

POLICE Constable Rutherford was puzzled. The police were required to "attend" any sudden death, unless a doctor had been expecting it for three days. The officer then had to compile a detailed report for the coroner, from the date of birth to the time of death. Rutherford had only done this twice before and was being doggedly methodical. But every police officer is at heart a detective, so he was puzzled because Dr. Thompson himself seemed to be.

They were in Welch's room, looking at Welch's inert body, still propped up on the pillows.

"What do you estimate the time of death was, sir?" Rutherford asked, scanning the check-list the sergeant had given him before he came.

"Between seven-fifteen and eight A.M. The body was still slightly warm when I first got here."

"What about the cause of death?"

"That'll need a post-mortem." Thompson frowned. "Since there's no visible cause, it's most likely to be one of two things. A cardiac arrest, due either to a heart attack or a brain haemorrhage, or a cerebral thrombosis."

"A stroke, sir?"

"Exactly."

"If he was conscious for long enough he'd have tried to shout for help." Thompson looked again at the relaxed expression on Welch's rubicund face. The pupils of his eyes were narrowed, which could be the effect of a drug, but they usually did become smaller at death. Whatever had overtaken the man must have done so in seconds. A heart attack was the most common reason for sudden death among middle-aged men. But . . .

"Except, sir?" A query had been implicit in Thompson's tone.

"Except that heart attacks are not usually instantaneously fatal and his wife says she never knew he had heart problems. There are nearly always early warning signs, like chest pains. Most wives would have known. They're well aware of health risks these days. And," he added breezily, "most wives of rich middle-aged men make damn sure their husbands go for medical check-ups. If they're interested in keeping them alive, that is."

"Yes, sir," Rutherford said dutifully, but sharing the doctor's puzzlement, because he had thought of something else. "They usually share a room with their husbands, too."

"She told me that the way this weekend was organized made that impossible."

"Sounds odd, sir."

"Apparently this was a murder weekend."

At this point Rutherford began to feel confused as well as puzzled. He was twenty-three years old and anxious to do everything by the book. But his training to date had not encompassed murder weekends.

"What exactly is that, sir?" he asked.

"A gimmick to promote the stately home, I imagine. You'd better ask Lord Gilroy. Now, have you a camera?"

"No, sir."

"Damn." Thompson couldn't really blame the constable for not having one. But he wanted a photographic record of exactly how the body was positioned, which meant he would have to move it as little as possible while doing a further examination to satisfy himself that he had missed nothing external. "Well," he said, "I'm going to take the rectal temperature and a blood sample." He began ferreting in his black bag, while the constable went downstairs in search of Lord Gilroy.

In the study Gilroy and Dee Dee were discussing what to do next. Adrienne had recovered sufficiently to join the Savages in the library. The rest were all in their rooms packing.

"How the hell do we entertain them if they insist on staying for the rest of the weekend?" Gilroy moaned.

"We certainly can't keep a 'murder' hunt going," Dee Dee agreed. "Not with a real corpse upstairs."

"And they can't just eat and drink all day."

"That they cannot," Dee Dee said with emphasis. "Not on our budget."

"I could show them round the estate this afternoon."

"And bore the pants off them about being paid by Europe not to farm? Much better take them down to Blenheim Palace for the afternoon. But I don't think they will stay. That lawyer isn't one to waste her time, and as for the fish-faced Hamish, he's almost as much of a pain as Welch was. I've a feeling his wife found him out last night."

"Why?"

"She wasn't fooled by his pretending he'd been in the kitchen getting coffee. Nor was I. He's the sort who phones for room service if the bedcover's crooked."

"Our rooms don't have phones, darling."

"Then ring the bell till someone comes," Dee said irritably. "You know perfectly well what I mean."

There was a knock on the door and Rutherford entered. He didn't hold aristocrats in much esteem, not when they kept selling their private lives to magazines, and he wasn't going to address Gilroy as "my lord." He stood very upright in his summer uniform of white short-sleeved shirt and dark-blue trousers, handcuffs hanging from his belt, and declined to sit down.

"There's a question I'd like to ask," he said, compromising his integrity slightly by adding, "sir."

"Fire away." Gilroy said amiably, glad to be off the subject of entertaining the guests.

"What was your murder weekend all about?"

Gilroy explained somewhat inadequately, leading Dee Dee to cut in. "Notionally Mr. Welch was involved in poisoning his sister. We gave out clues the night before and at seven-thirty this morning. Mrs. Sketchley—whom I played—was found dead by the maid. Her screams woke the whole household."

Rutherford thought about this. He might be young and inexperienced, but he was not stupid.

"So there were a lot of people around at that time."

"Everyone, except for my husband and, of course, Mr. Welch."

"If the deceased had shouted out, would someone have heard him?"

Dee Dee considered this. "I think so. Yes. We were all in the passage close to his door. Of course, there was a lot of chattering. But I think someone would have heard."

"No one thought of waking him?"

"The seven-thirty scene was strictly make-believe. Mr. Welch wasn't much interested in play-acting."

"Then why was he here?"

"Wanted to buy some land off me," Gilroy said shortly. "Signing on for the weekend gave him a good chance to haggle."

"I see," Rutherford said, deciding there was definitely more to all this than he knew. "And where would I find Mrs. Welch?"

"In the library, most likely. I'll show you." Gilroy led him out into the hall and indicated the library door.

Inside the library Jim and Jemma Savage were patiently listening to Adrienne Welch unburdening her soul on the subject of her husband.

"People didn't like George," she was saying, "I know that. Property isn't a very nice business. He had his enemies. But he was a good husband to me."

"Private faces are often very different to public ones," Jim said soothingly, remembering fraud rumours about Welch of a few years ago. "Some men can be angels to their families and devils to everyone else."

"That's right. You understand. You reely do understand." Adrienne's gratitude for this sympathy began to overflow into tears, and Jemma, who was sitting next to her on a sofa, put an arm round her shoulders. Adrienne pulled some tissues out of her bag and dabbed at her eyes. "Well, he's out of all that now." She indulged in another brief session with the tissues. "You should have heard how rude Lord Gilroy was to George. She was bad enough at dinner, but him! You'd have thought we was something the cat brought in."

"Was he doing business with the Gilroys?" Jemma prompted.

"It was supposed to be a secret. Well, it never could have been, reely. They needed cash and George needed land. The trouble was they didn't want to sell the bit we wanted."

"It's often the way." Jim nodded. "Did they agree in the end?"

"I don't know," Adrienne said helplessly. "Not when I was with them. But I think that lawyer of his persuaded them. It'll be terrible if they did, because where'd I find the money? Like that woman said, it'd be legal even though he is dead. But I don't know where the contract even is."

"Wouldn't his company buy the land?" Jim asked innocently, knowing that Welch had probably been a one-man band.

"He was the company!" Adrienne confirmed. "He could go to the bank with a deal and they'd give him loans. None of the other directors counted for a row of beans."

"So it could affect you personally?"

"It oughtn't to. I'm just worried that it might." A note of pride came into her voice. "George left me provided for, praise the Lord. Very nicely provided for. Life insurance." She smiled weakly, cheered up by this golden lining to the cloud of death. "Oh no, I'll be all right, just so long as no one lands any debts on my doorstep."

Jim was re-assuring her that her own assets could not be touched by her husband's creditors when Rutherford swung open the double doors and marched in.

Even to a cynic about the aristocracy, the Gothic library was impressive. Gloomily impressive, it was true, as if the architect had been dreaming of the ultimate in funeral parlours. But the high ranges of mahogany bookshelves lining the walls, the heavy tables and the high-backed sofas made it inconceivable to think of this as a mere information-retrieval system. Rutherford was momentarily stopped in his tracks. Then he spotted the three people sitting at the far end of the room and advanced on them.

"Mrs. Welch?" he inquired of Adrienne. "Could I have a few minutes?"

Jim got up and motioned Jemma to follow him. "We'll leave you to it," he said. "We'll be in the hall."

Sitting down rather awkwardly on the armchair Jim had vacated, Rutherford went through his routine of questions, asking finally if Welch had been taking any medications.

"Not regularly. It's like I told the doctor. He'd take an Alka Seltzer if he had a hangover. He had a high colour, but he was fit."

"And, pardon my asking, why weren't you sharing a room last night?"

"That was stupid. I have a huge bedroom, a lovely one. But Lady Gilroy insisted he slept in that little room one night 'for the murder.' "

So that explanation of Gilroy's was correct. Rutherford made careful notes. He added one last question, a question that was beyond his mandate, since he was not a detective.

"You didn't go in to wake your husband when the 'murder' happened?"

"He wasn't interested. He only came on the weekend to see how the nobs live."

As he wrote this down in his slow, neat handwriting, she wondered if it had been wise to lie about why there were here. Well, she thought, it's a white lie and he's only a very young constable.

"It was when he didn't come down to breakfast that I began worrying," she added, her voice becoming shaky. "I won't ever forget finding him there like that. Not never."

Fearful that she might break down, and inexperienced in consoling the bereaved, Rutherford thanked her and returned upstairs to the doctor.

Thompson was concluding his examination of the corpse. He had found no needle marks, for which he always looked nowadays. Due to Welch not cutting his toenails properly, the nail of one smaller toe had cut into the flesh of the next bigger one. There was absolutely nothing to explain why he was dead, though his complexion suggested he might have had high blood pressure. Perhaps it was natural of his wife to imagine he'd died of a heart attack, but Thompson was unconvinced.

"Rightly or wrongly," he told Rutherford, "I regard this as an unusual death, if not actually a suspicious one."

This remark clinched it for Rutherford. He exchanged puzzlement for decision and went straight downstairs again to telephone his police station and explain to the duty sergeant what was happening. The sergeant gave him precise orders and initiated a series of police procedures which could rapidly escalate into a murder hunt if that seemed justified.

When Hamish chanced on Rutherford in the hall and, addressing him as "Constable" in a superior way, asked if there was any reason why he and his wife should not leave Wittenham Park, he received a very firm answer. No one would be leaving until a more senior officer arrived. Rutherford then told Gilroy the same and went back upstairs to keep Welch's bedroom secure, as the sergeant had instructed him. His role as the leading investigator would very soon be over.

Jim and Jemma Savage were seated in one corner of the Great Hall, a room only fractionally less grand than the library. The staircase with its dragon newels occupied one corner, turning through ninety degrees as it ascended and then through ninety degrees again to the floor above. The front door was at the opposite end, leaving plenty of room for sofas, a substantial oak table, carefully laid out with magazines, and a writing-table with a small rack of headed stationery. Years ago the stag heads at the Lion Park had embellished the walls, or encumbered them, as Dee Dee thought. Now portraits of ancestors—almost all other people's ancestors, bought at Sotheby's and Christie's auctions—stared down superciliously as the father and daughter debated what was going on.

"The next thing will be the post-mortem," Jemma said. "Do you think Welch could have been murdered?"

"The police must think it possible."

"So who had a motive?"

"From what his wife was saying just now, she did," Jim observed. "A strong one, too. 'Nicely provided for,' she said. Only the Lord knows how many wives have slid their husbands down the eternal rubbish chute to get the life insurance."

"At least Pauline didn't try that on you!"

"Oh no? You never had to eat her spinach pancakes. Those were terminators."

"Daddy!" Jemma felt this was mildly unfair. "Just because she thought anything that was an economy could not be disgusting doesn't mean she wanted to kill you."

"Perhaps not," Jim relented. "Doesn't alter the fact that someone gets away with domestic murder every week. Adrienne Welch must be a suspect."

"And who else?"

"Who do we know had a quarrel with Welch?" Jim deliberately gave his daughter a lead.

"Gosh! Several people." Jemma consulted her notes with increasing excitement. "Welch wanted to buy part of the estate. Lady Gilroy said so quite openly. And he infuriated Lord Gilroy by saying the Lion Park would have to be closed down."

"Do we think the first row, the one we overheard before dinner, was about the land?" Jim checked his own notes. "At six thirty-one P.M. we heard Welch shout, 'You bloody well will, or else.' And the voice we think was the lawyer woman added, 'You haven't any option.' Someone was being pressurized."

"Couldn't have been Gilroy. It must have been someone else."

"But Gilroy was embarrassed when we mentioned it at dinner. And when Lady Gilroy accused Welch of blackmail she most definitely was not play-acting. Welch knew it, too. Remember how fiercely he reacted?"

"That is true, Daddy! She was just using the murder plot to have a go at him. And he was furious. He turned the colour of blueberries."

"Then we're agreed."

"The row had to be with someone else." Jemma ticked off the guests on her fingers. "The only other man around was that snobby idiot McMountdown. Why should he be involved in the land deal?"

"I'll pass on that," Jim conceded. "We don't know. So the Gilroys are prime suspects. Or rather," he hastily corrected himself, "they will be if Welch has been murdered. Which leaves the mysterious woman in a dressing-gown you saw this morning. Could that have been Lady Gilroy going into the State Bedroom? Or into Welch's room?"

"Poison in hand!" Jemma added delightedly.

"Was it her, my dear?"

"I just don't know. Several of the women had lacy night-dresses. And I'm not sure which door the woman was opening anyway."

"Very probably it was part of the 'murder plot.' Something one of us was intended to see."

"Could be," Jemma said dubiously. "But if it was acting it would have been, well, more obvious." She had an idea. "Why don't we go upstairs and experiment. You stand by Welch's bedroom door and I'll come out of mine into the passage. That might jog my memory."

Upstairs Police Constable Rutherford was standing manfully immobile in front of Welch's bedroom, his arms folded across the front of his white shirt, his legs apart. Had he been a more substantial person he would have been a serious human barrier. As it was, he merely looked as if he was trying to impersonate one. His head swivelled toward Jim and Jemma as they emerged from the wide staircase.

"Now you go along . . ." Jemma was saying, not hesitant about giving her father orders. Then she saw Rutherford. "Oh my God. What's he doing here?"

Rutherford overheard the remark and was nettled by it. "Safeguarding a possible scene of crime," he said stolidly.

Jemma shot a "What do we do next?" glance at her father and he took up the conversation.

"Would you object to my standing by the next door along for a few minutes, officer?"

"For what purpose, sir?"

"My daughter is trying to jog her memory."

Rutherford stared at them both with extreme suspicion. "Like how?" he demanded.

"I'm trying . . ." Jemma gave up petulantly. "Oh, forget it. We'll just go to our own rooms. If you've no objection."

Rutherford watched them go down the corridor, convinced that there was a lot more in this situation than met the eye, then resumed his sentry duty.

Once they were out of earshot, Jim said, "Never be bad-tempered with a cop, darling. You ought to know that."

"I wasn't," Jemma hissed at him. "Whose side are you on anyway?"

"All right." Jim gave way resignedly. "You weren't, but it still doesn't."

"Doesn't what?"

"Pay to be rude to cops."

"Oh, get lost, Daddy." Jemma went to her room.

Very soon afterwards she reappeared, darting out of her door as if disturbed. Rutherford glimpsed movement out of the corner of his eye and turned just as she retreated again. That girl was up to something, he decided. He pulled out his official notebook, recorded the time as ten forty-one, and wrote down carefully, "Miss Savage behaving in suspicious manner in corridor." He was not surprised when she came out again and entered her father's room. He would warn the inspector that they were both up to something.

In her father's room Jemma was back to being excitedly positive, their dispute forgotten. "It was that door. I'm sure it was."

"Welch's?"

"Yes, Welch's. Who else?"

"I doubt if that young constable is going to be flattered at reminding you of a woman in a night-gown."

Jemma giggled. "Daddy, you're a fool."

"And how many women were there in night-gowns or dressing-gowns at seven-thirty this morning? Lady G, the curious Priscilla, Loredana, Adrienne Welch. What about the others?"

"Loredana's was hidden by her dressing-gown. Dulcie had slung a coat over her shoulders. She wasn't wearing lace. I wasn't."

"So it was only three?"

"The night-gown I saw had lace round the bottom."

"Well, if this becomes serious," Jim said, "we'll be having a fashion parade."

"I think all the women would be suspects. Priscilla Worthington took Welch a mug of 'poisoned' cocoa. It could have been poisoned for real. She told us he tried to rape her."

"Stranger things have happened."

"He had his eye on Loredana, too. Perhaps he had a go at her."

"That still leaves his lawyer, Dulcie. Why should she want to kill her own client?"

"There you have a point, Daddy. Why should she? It's not the quickest way of getting one's fees paid."

"So, apart from the servants, that leaves only us. What motives do we have?"

"To make a story for my magazine?" Jemma laughed. "I think we're clean."

"Then I have to make a confession," Jim said, more seriously. "Welch took me aside before dinner. He was quite aggressive. 'I know who you bloody are,' he said. 'And if you know what's good for you, you'll keep out of this.' "

"He didn't! You're joking!" Jemma was horrified and instantly concerned.

"Scouts honour. There must have been some kind of scam in this land deal. I imagine that Lady Gilroy told him what my profession is, or rather was, in order to keep him under control. Something like that."

"So what did you say?"

"Told him I was never influenced by threats. Anyway, it hardly means I would want to kill him. Rather the other way around, I'd have thought."

Jemma laughed. Her father's dry humour always amused her. She answered in the same vein. "So I poisoned him to save you, Daddy." She clapped her hands. "Perfect. Everyone has a motive."

"Except the servants and the McMountdowns."

"Oh, they'll all turn out to have one."

The noise of vehicles outside interrupted them. Jim looked down from the window. An ambulance and a larger police car were in the drive.

"Things have started to happen. Let's go down again," he suggested.

As they descended the stairs, two ambulancemen with a stretcher were waiting in the hall, while a uniformed police inspector gave instructions and the rest of the guests stood in a cluster at the library end of the hall, watching. The men went upstairs. When they came down again, carrying Welch's corpse, zipped up inside a black body-bag, they were followed by a white-coated man carrying a video camera and escorted by a sergeant. The police had clearly been carrying through their procedures with exemplary speed.

Adrienne, who was being supported by Dee Dee Gilroy, burst into tears, while the rest stood in momentary silence. Not out of respect for the dead, Jemma realized, but because the bulging body-bag forced everyone to understand the reality of a death. Then subdued chattering broke out until the inspector, the two silver stars of rank glittering on the shoulder tabs of his shirt, raised his hand.

"Ladies and gentlemen." He had a burring, North Country voice, and dragged out some of the syllables. "We may not have the results of the post-mortem until tomorrow, though I'm hoping for it sooner. Until then I would be appreciative if you could make yourselves available throughout the course of the day."

"But officer," Hamish spoke up complainingly, like an indignant shareholder determined to be heard at an Annual General Meeting, "my wife and I are leaving after lunch."

"Have you anything else planned, sir?"

"Not precisely," Hamish admitted. "We have things to do at home."

"I'm afraid they will have to wait, sir." The inspector was not giving an inch. "As they would have done if this weekend had gone according to plan. A detective inspector will be here shortly. He will need to talk to everyone here."

"My God!" Dee Dee whispered to Gilroy. "You won't be able to take them to Blenheim. All they are going to do is eat and drink!"

7

As Buck Gilroy welcomed the latest police arrivals into his study, he felt he was being forced to rehearse the same scene again and again, like an actor who could never get it right. He had spent the entire morning being interviewed by policemen. First by Constable Rutherford, then Rutherford's sergeant, then the inspector with the North Country accent. Now it was an officer in a dark-grey suit, who had asked the guests "to make themselves available" with a firm politeness that suggested that he had cells ready and waiting for every one of them, Gilroy included. He had introduced himself as Detective Inspector Morton and the plain-clothes sidekick with him as Detective Sergeant Timmins.

Except that Morton was perhaps ten years the older and Timmins wore a blue blazer and slacks, they were remarkably similar in appearance: tall, broad-shouldered men with chunky faces, who would feel totally at home in a riot. They were exactly what the gangling Constable Rutherford hoped to be, but never would.

Gilroy wondered if they always worked as a team, like Barnum and Bailey or Abercrombie and Fitch. The two names had that sort of ring to them. More practically, he prayed that this was as high in the pecking order as the police representation was going to reach. In an Agatha Christie thriller the chief executive of the whole force, known as the chief constable, would have been round in seconds. In practice the chief constable was the only policeman in Oxfordshire whom Gilroy knew and the last one he wanted to see now, since that would signal a major crime to everyone, not least the press.

In the last hour or so a fearsome newspaper headline had rooted itself in Gilroy's seldom agile brain. "Murder at Wittenham Park," it read. And with it had come the realization that he had to retrieve that bloody contract. Had Welch signed it or not? If he had, was it enforceable? Either way, he was faced with disaster when the Lloyds call for cash flopped onto the mat on Monday morning. If Welch had signed, who would now pay for the land? If he hadn't, where on earth was the money to be found? Gilroy sighed to himself in this deeply unpleasant reverie. When a man stares bankruptcy in the face the last thing he wants is to be interviewed by the police equivalent of the Chicago Bears.

"You were saying, sir?" Morton prompted, taking note of the sigh and wondering why Lord Gilroy seemed so troubled.

"Oh yes. Well, the murder weekend was a scheme to make more use of the house." He explained its details. "Funny thing is that Welch was slotted as the murderer."

"Whereas it's him who's been murdered, you mean?" Sergeant Timmins suggested, deftly opening a mile-wide trap for Gilroy to fall into.

"Was he?" Gilroy's worst fears were confirmed and his expression showed it.

"You seemed to imply that, sir." Morton defended his assistant, again noticing Gilroy's agitation.

"Did I? Well I never intended to." Gilroy saw the ground opening in front of him just in time. "No, what I meant was that it's odd that the man playing the murderer should end up dead."

"Quite so," Morton said drily.

"Was he murdered? God, I do hope not."

"We have to wait for the pathologists to tell us how he died. You sound as though it matters to you?"

"It does. The publicity would be appalling."

"He was not a personal friend?"

"No." Gilroy managed to restrain himself from being more vehement.

"And when did you last see Mr. Welch?"

"After dinner last night. We had a business discussion in my study. He wanted to buy some land from us."

"At what time did that end?"

"Well . . ." Gilroy tried to reason this out. The meeting had been so inexorably painful that the last thing he wanted to do was recall it. "Dinner was over around nine. We all met in my study about half an hour later."

"There were several of you?"

"He brought his lawyer along. Mrs. McMountdown."

"For a murder weekend?"

"Welch was using the weekend to negotiate, not play cops and robbers."

"I see." Morton nodded, trusting Timmins to get all this down in writing and reflecting that Police Constable Rutherford had been correct. There must be more to this than met the eye. "And when did the meeting end?"

"Around ten or ten fifteen. That was the last time I saw him."

"And what did you do after that, sir?"

"Had a brief discussion with the lawyer about amendments to the contract and went to bed."

"So who would have been the last person to see him?"

"The lawyer would have spoken to him again. His wife might have done, although she was sleeping in another room. Otherwise I haven't a clue."

A stupidly appropriate phrase, Morton thought, thanked him for his help and asked if they could have a room to use for interviews. Gilroy offered the study, but was relieved when they declined and accepted a former staff sitting-room off the kitchens.

"And what d'you make of his lordship?" Morton asked his sergeant once they were alone.

"Worried about something, sir. And he didn't much like the deceased."

"Hated his guts, from the look on his face. Well, let's get on with it." Morton studied the guest list. "We'll start with this McMountdown woman. What a name to have to live with!"

"Don't forget Rutherford saw the father-and-daughter pair behaving suspiciously and taking notes."

"I'll see them later. Now go and fetch the lawyer."

It took very little time after Dulcie was brought in for Morton to realize that she regarded her late employer's business affairs as sacrosanct. Anticipating what was going to happen, she had dressed in a neat short-skirted fawn suit with a velvet collar. Her mop of hair was firmly brushed back and she had used her make-up sparingly.

"Did you see Mr. Welch again? After your final meeting with Lord Gilroy?" Morton asked.

"Yes." Dulcie spoke decisively. "I took some papers to his room for him to read."

"A contract for the sale of land by Lord Gilroy, I believe." Morton exceeded his brief fractionally, because he felt sure that if Welch had been murdered, the land deal would turn out to be relevant. But it was unwise of him. Dulcie cut him down.

"It would not be proper for me to comment on uncompleted business, Inspector. I'm sure you understand that."

"If it had any bearing on the deceased's death it could."

"That would be hard to imagine," Dulcie said quietly. "At all events, I discussed the documents with George, gave him my advice, and left them with him."

"What time was that?"

"Twelve minutes past eleven."

"You can be as precise as that?"

"Yes." Dulcie decided to explain why. "George was drinking whisky. For some reason he'd been brought a mug of cocoa and he offered it to me. I like a hot drink before going to bed. Then I thought I might need to do some more work, checked the time, decided it was too late, and took the mug with me."

"To your room?"

"Yes. Where else?"

"And you didn't see him again?"

"Not alive."

"Do you know if anyone did?"

"No. But there were a lot of goings-on in the night."

"Such as?"

Dulcie smiled thinly. "My apologies. That statement was hearsay.

I slept right through to when the maid started screaming at seven-thirty, though she must have knocked on my door when she left the early-morning tea outside earlier."

"So who told you about these 'goings-on'?"

"Just about everyone. They were part of the plot."

"You don't know who was moving around during the night?"

Again the thin smile. "Afraid I can't help there."

"One final question, Mrs. McMountdown. Did Mr. Welch have any reason to take his own life?"

"Not that I'm aware of. He had problems, who doesn't. But this weekend was likely to solve them."

Morton did not ask for an explanation, merely thanked her and she left.

"Bloody lawyers," Timmins remarked. "Never give away anything."

"Not if they can help it," Morton agreed. "And she does know what was going on and she didn't like it. Let's look at the guest list again." He paused as Timmins handed it across. "Nearly lunchtime. I suppose we can fit in one more."

"Why not try the father and daughter, sir? Their notes could be useful."

Morton acquiesced and a few minutes later Jim and Jemma were facing the two policemen across the battered old rectangular oak table of the servants' sitting-room.

"What were your roles in the 'murder' plot?" Morton asked genially, varying his approach. "Seems most of the guests weren't interested."

"They were beastly," said Jemma. "We were the only ones who tried, except for Priscilla Worthington. No one else even pretended to be keen."

"And you played . . . ?"

"I was the reporter and Daddy was the detective." She caught sight of the guest list that Timmins had in front of him. "But you already know that!"

"I prefer people to tell me in their own words. And when did you last see Welch, Mr. Savage?"

"Having coffee after dinner."

"Did he appear completely normal?"

"He was in a foul temper, actually." Jim said. "Swore at Mrs. Worthington and demanded a bottle of whisky in his room."

"As the detective," Morton said, unable to keep a note of cynicism out of his voice, "I assume you kept notes?"

"Fragmentary ones."

"May I see them?"

Jim fished into his coat pocket for his notebook and passed it across the table. Morton read through the few entries. "So Welch was shouting at someone before dinner. Who do you suppose that was, Mr. Savage?"

"We never discovered."

"The first clue referred to a row after dinner, not before." Jemma said.

"Hmm." Privately Morton was contemptuous of amateur detectives and had not forgotten Rutherford's description of these two's activities in the bedroom corridor. "And after dinner you overheard another conversation in Lord Gilroy's study. Quite a bit of eavesdropping, eh?"

"We were playing our parts," Savage said, starting to feel annoyed. Why was this man needling him? "This was an Agatha Christie–style weekend."

"And you continued playing them even after Mr. Welch was dead?"

"I'm afraid I don't understand you."

"You were attempting some kind of re-enactment outside Mr. Welch's room this morning."

"That was my fault," Jemma said quickly, fearful of being ridiculed but determined to retain her one piece of information. "I thought I'd seen someone outside his door earlier. But I was wrong. It was the door of the next room along."

"And who did you see?"

"It must have been Lady Gilroy. She'd been using that bedroom for the murder."

Morton was not sure that he believed this, but it fitted Rutherford's description of what they had been doing. He shifted his line of questioning.

"What is your profession, Mr. Savage?"

Savage told him, mentioning his redundancy.

"You had any prior knowledge of Mr. Welch?"

"He was under suspicion of insurance fraud a few years ago."

"Is that why you came on this weekend, then?"

"I told you, I'm retired."

"Daddy's an Agatha Christie buff," Jemma said, irritated by this attack. "Don't you listen to what people tell you?"

"Experience has taught me never to take anything at face value," Morton said quietly. "What is your profession?"

"I'm a reporter."

"I mean in real life, Miss Savage."

"In real life," Jemma said sharply, resenting Morton's attitude. "I'm a crime reporter and I'm writing up this weekend for a magazine."

"Is that so?" Morton said carefully, while Timmins's expression hardened, as if he'd just confronted a snake and was deliberating how to kill it. Morton knew there was no question of asking this girl for her notes. To do so would provoke a storm of media outrage. "Well, Miss Savage," he went on, "I'm afraid that in the present circumstances your profession confers no privileges. Not, of course, that we have any reason to think a crime has been committed."

"Then, if that's all," Jim said, rising to his feet, "we'll be getting along to lunch."

"You won't mind if I keep this?" Morton wiggled Jim Savage's notebook in the air. "Now your detective role is over."

Jim and Jemma left without saying anything more. Once outside, Jim let rip. "That man was deliberately having fun at our expense. Or trying to."

"I nearly told him to sugar off," Jemma agreed.

In the interview room Timmins let out his breath sharply. "A bloody reporter. Just our luck."

"I made a mistake there," Morton admitted. "Trouble is I never could take amateur detection seriously. So I put the girl's back up. Stupid of me. Let's go along to a pub for lunch."

As the two men walked back to the hall they discovered there was a new arrival. A lanky man in his forties was standing there looking bemused, while the woman they knew was Loredana Chancemain scourged him verbally.

"How clever of you not to be here when George died," she was saying acidly. "Now we're all stuck in this wretched place and you're free to do what you want. Really, Trevor! And it was you who was all for this weekend."

"No, darling," her husband objected weakly, "it was you who insisted on coming." Though tall and good-looking, underneath he was a mild-mannered man. He sported a small moustache and his brown hair was thinning out. His protest carried no weight at all with Loredana.

"Don't you scowl at me!" she retaliated "And what little bit of 'business' kept you in Kenya anyway? Some African 'lady,' I suppose. Why don't you just go home again? Nobody wants you here."

"Excuse me." Morton stepped up to the arguing couple and introduced himself, addressing the man. "I take it you're the missing guest, sir?"

"Only just got here," Trevor said, with more vigour than before. "What a reception!"

"How dare you say that!" Loredana shrieked, working herself up very nicely into a rage. "How dare you insult me!"

"Darling, I didn't mean—"

"You never do know what you mean." She turned this swiftly into a lament. "And you're not stuck here like the rest of us."

"I would prefer that none of the guests leave until the cause of Mr. Welch's death has been established," Morton confirmed, thinking that if this did turn into a murder inquiry he would not want the scene further contaminated by a new arrival who, on the face of it, could not be involved. "You've just returned from Kenya, sir?"

"Got into Heathrow this morning. Went home and then came straight here."

"Where all you're being is a thorough-going nuisance," Loredana cut in.

Trevor looked at her in surprise, as though he had never seen her like this before. "Listen, darling," he said, as firmly as he could, "I've just come off an overnight flight. I haven't had any sleep. And I've come straight here to be with you. How can you accuse me of being a nuisance?"

"Because you're late as usual and everything's over." She was clearly used to treating him like dirt. "Why don't you go back home?"

"Without you?"

"What do you think? Didn't you hear what the inspector said?"

"Well, at that rate I bloody well will." Trevor spoke vehemently, but with the emphasis of a weak man trying to assert himself. "She can't come with me?" he asked Morton.

"Not for the time being, sir."

Watching this confrontation from across the hall, Jim remembered an old photo of the Duchess of Windsor evidently giving the Duke absolute hell. Loredana was similarly a tigress when roused. Behind that classically high cheek-boned face there lurked a real harridan. And why was she being so foul to her husband? Presumably she didn't want him around at the moment. Why? Then he remembered the way she had been watching Hamish McMountdown at dinner last night and was astonished at the brazenness of this public performance.

"You see," she carried on, in the sharp tones of someone who has been right all along, "I can't leave and it's pointless your waiting."

At this moment Gilroy and Dee Dee appeared from the study, alerted by the sound of the altercation. Dee Dee realized who the stranger must be, having heard Loredana's last remark, and made a point of welcoming Trevor.

"Whatever else you do," she insisted, "you must stay to lunch. After that we can make decisions. I'll have the butler take your case upstairs."

"For heaven's sake—" Loredana started to argue, then realized that everyone was looking at her and changed her tune. "Please, Lady Gilroy, I'm in the middle of packing. I'd much rather my things were left undisturbed."

"Your poor husband must need to freshen up," Dee Dee said imperiously. "I will tell Dodgson to be extremely careful. Which he would be anyway."

At this Loredana herself departed upstairs, making no secret of her anger, her skirt swirling around her long legs as she turned the first corner on the stairs and disappeared.

"What a bitch!" Jemma whispered. "What can that ass Hamish see in her?"

"Lucky he's not here now," Jim commented. "She's probably as sweet as pie with him. Did you notice that she had a quite different tone of voice for her husband? About an octave higher, I'd say."

Near the front door Morton spoke briefly with Trevor, then the two policemen left. Dodgson announced that drinks were available in the library and half an hour later they all filed back through the hall to the dining-room.

Not surprisingly, lunch was a subdued occasion, with the conversation centering on what the police were doing.

"What did they ask you, darlings?" Priscilla demanded of the Savages. "I want to know what to expect." She made a show of shuddering gruesomely. "Was it the third degree?"

"They were foul to my father," Jemma said with spirit. "Tried to needle him about playing the detective."

"How very unnecessary," Hamish said. "I hope you stood up to them."

"We did."

Adrienne chimed in with sympathy, as did the Gilroys, and it became clear that on principle no one much liked the police and that Jim and Jemma earned extra credibility from their minor confrontation.

"That inspector should stick to his brief," Dulcie remarked. "He kept getting onto things that were none of his business. At least, not if George died of natural causes."

"He was questioning me about the land deal," Gilroy said, forgetting that he himself had mentioned it first himself. "Talking of which, have you found the contract yet?"

"No."

"Then where is it?"

Jim Savage listened to this exchange alertly. The land deal had been the real focal point of this weekend.

"You took it from me last night," Gilroy insisted.

"And I left it with George. But it wasn't in his room." Dulcie became aware of Jim's interest in this conversation and changed the subject, turning to Trevor. "Too bad you missed the real-life drama."

"He always does," Loredana said. "If you want to miss something, stick with Trevor."

Trevor's face reddened. If his wife continued like this he damn well would go home without her. But Dulcie came to his defence.

"He certainly missed plenty last night," she remarked to Loredana, then switched her eyes to Hamish, who was sitting next to Loredana across the table. "Didn't he, darling?"

"I don't know what you're talking about," Hamish stonewalled.

"You see," Dulcie said cattily, "one of them misses everything and the other knows nothing. What else do they have in common?"

This time it was Loredana who flushed, which her husband noticed. "I'm not feeling very well," she said. "If you'll all excuse me I'll go and lie down."

Hamish hastily got up to help with her chair and Trevor also stood up.

"I can manage, for goodness' sake," Loredana said.

Quite suddenly Trevor knew. At a later time, talking to his lawyer about the divorce, he would be unable to explain why. It was as much Dulcie's tone and her looks as what she had said. He simply knew what everyone else in the village could have told him, namely that Loredana and Hamish were having an affair.

"I'll see her upstairs," he told Hamish abruptly. "We need to have a talk."

"That's completely unnecessary," Loredana appealed to Hamish.

"For a change," Trevor said, "I'll be the judge of that." He took Loredana's arm and led her out.

"She must have had a bad night," Priscilla suggested charitably, making Dulcie wrinkle her nose as if at a bad smell. Then Dodgson brought the dessert and their conversation lapsed.

By the time Trevor came down again, they had all gone through to the library for coffee. His face was flushed and he was trembling slightly. He had told Loredana that if she wanted a divorce he would give her one. He had done it all in exactly the rushed and confused

way that was least sensible in the circumstances, when he had no evidence. Inevitably she had slapped his face and told him he would
pay for this.

"I'll be leaving now," he told Lady Gilroy, as the others
unashamedly stared at his distraught appearance. "Thank you very
much for lunch."

"My dear man, you don't have to go so soon. And what about
your wife?"

"Damn my wife," he said with explosive candour. "She can
come when the police have finished their questions."

"Well, that's entirely up to you," Dee Dee said, maintaining neu-
tality. "Dodgson will bring your case down again."

"I brought it myself. Loredana doesn't want to be disturbed."

"Then I can only wish you a safe journey."

Trevor shook hands awkwardly and departed.

"What on earth's got into him?" Hamish asked. "He doesn't
normally behave like that."

"I think," Dulcie suggested, "that he's woken up at last."

Hamish caught her eye and thought better of asking how, which
Jim noticed. Then they all dispersed to kill time while waiting to be
interviewed. There never had been much of a party atmosphere
about the "murder weekend," and it was now lost completely.

During the afternoon Morton interviewed everyone else and
then summarized his conclusions with Timmins. The last people to
see Welch alive had apparently been Gilroy, then Priscilla when she
brought him the unwanted cocoa, and finally Dulcie. The maid,
Tracy, had knocked on his door at around 7:05 A.M. and called out,
"Early-morning tea," but scurried off again so quickly that she
didn't know if he had answered or not. Assuming that the doctor
was correct, he had died in the ensuing hour or less.

Then, shortly after four, there came a phone call from the
pathologist.

"Inspector Morton? Welch did not die naturally. There's a lot of
congestion of the lungs and liver. I should say he died of respiratory
failure."

"Caused by?"

"We don't know yet. We're sending samples to the forensic lab. Blood, urine, stomach contents. The usual."

"Some kind of poison, you mean?"

"An opiate would be my guess. But at this stage it is only a guess."

Morton put the phone down. "Let's get the circus running, Fred," he said to the sergeant. "One of the people in this house is a murderer. We don't want the scent to get cold."

8

"DARLINGS, I can't believe this is happening," Priscilla shrilled. "What are they doing to us?" They were all having pre-dinner drinks in a sparsely furnished games room in the east wing and feeling the effects of the way the police had swung into action. Whatever they might think individually of Inspector Morton, they had to recognize that he was no slouch. He had politely but firmly organized searches of their rooms and then, again politely, asked them to transfer their belongings to the former servants' quarters in the east wing dating from the days when Wittenham Park employed twenty household staff. Now Priscilla was voicing the outrage most of them felt, fuelled by a stiff gin and tonic.

"Darlings," she appealed to everyone, her arms outstretched theatrically, as though drawing the audience to her, "what have we done to deserve this?"

"It's completely unnecessary," Hamish agreed censoriously. "Surely searching our rooms . . ."

"Anyone would think we were criminals!"

". . . was enough." Hamish disliked being interrupted. "But why force us all to move?"

"It's absurd," Loredana echoed. "And the poky little attic they've put me in has the hardest-possible bed."

Dulcie smiled. She couldn't help it. The thought of Loredana being evicted from the four-postered silken glories of the Chinese Room and consigned to a disused maid's room was most appealing. In fact, she and the Savages were the only ones who had not reacted violently to Inspector Morton's request. Dulcie understood that Morton wanted every potential suspect's room made sterile, as well as searched. If he could have transferred them to a different building he would have done so. But the gamekeeper's cottage was too small and there was nowhere else, except for the maze of rooms on the servants' side of the green baize doors. Nor had he made an exception for the owners. Lord and Lady Gilroy were suffering like everyone else.

"Just like Agatha Christie," Jim Savage remarked, "except that there won't be a climax with everyone sitting around and the finger being pointed at one of them."

"Isn't that how they do things?" Gilroy inquired. He'd read so much Agatha Christie in preparation for this weekend that he regarded her words as Holy Writ.

"No way," Jemma said. "Don't you watch telly, Lord Gilroy? They'll have inquiry teams ferreting out our backgrounds and talking to our neighbours. They'll be running our names through their computers. And they'll never ever interview us together."

"Well, I'll be damned," Gilroy said, looking as confused as if he'd just sold a car and had it returned five minutes later. "I had no idea."

"She knows," Jim said with a touch of pride, wondering how Gilroy could possibly be so ignorant. "She's a crime reporter."

"You think we're all suspects?" Dee Dee asked anxiously.

The irony of organizing a murder weekend and then being suspected of murder oneself was not lost on her. This was absolutely the last time she was going to have anything to do with one of Buck's little schemes. Could this one misfiring be grounds for divorce? In California she was sure it could. Anything could in California, and this weekend must constitute mental cruelty of the worst kind.

"I'm sure we're all suspects," Dulcie assured her cheerfully. "Unless there was an intruder, one of us must have done for George."

"Well, I object," Loredana complained. "I won't be slandered! And I don't believe the police can keep us here either."

"What do you think, darling?" Hamish asked Dulcie. "Surely Loredana's right?"

"Completely," Dulcie said coldly, as though acknowledging that the village idiot had made a clever remark. "And the inspector will assume that anyone who does leave is frightened of being questioned."

"He should have said he couldn't force us to stay," said Loredana in her spoilt-child voice. "Why didn't he?"

"He did," Dulcie said contemptuously. "If you were listening. He said that he would be grateful for our assistance and it would help his inquiries if we stayed." She had noticed that, possibly because he was facing both a reporter and lawyer, Morton had been both correct and tactful.

"Well, it's most unfair. Do we look like murderers?"

This time no one reacted. She was beginning to get on everyone's nerves. But Jim looked around the assembled company and was forced to agree, though he did not say so. How could you identify a murderer—or a murderess—among this lot?

Lord and Lady Gilroy had abandoned wearing formal evening clothes for a dinner that would be held in the servants' hall, with its scrubbed table and benches. However, Buck still wore a dark suit and Dee Dee a long blue dress, since their position as hosts was unchanged, though it had occurred to them that if the police investigation lasted beyond tomorrow, Sunday, they ought to be putting on biblical sackcloth, and ashes in their hair. This damn murder was going to cost them a packet, unless they could start charging for the drinks and food. And if they did, would any of their enforced guests pay? Probably not, was Dee Dee's guess.

Savage sensed the tension between them and Jemma whispered to him, "They've got something on their minds."

"I think we all have."

Dulcie was watching Loredana, who must have brought enough clothes for a fortnight at least. She was in a different dress every time she appeared. Tonight it resembled a skimpy, slinky Versace creation in lurid colours, which Hamish—still in his blazer and flannels—made no secret of admiring.

How in hell, thought Dulcie, could Trevor afford Versace for his wife? She herself, being highly paid, didn't take a dress allowance from Hamish. But Loredana had no money of her own. Hmm. She could guess who'd paid for that number. She smoothed down her own demure black trouser suit and took a cool look at the others.

Adrienne was red-eyed and jumpy, wearing the same spotted silk dress as last night. She took a strong whisky from the butler, Priscilla was going through the gin and tonics fast. Jim now knew that she was an actress, employed to jolly things along, but the turn of events had evidently upset her. Slightly to his surprise she came across to him, after Dodgson had come round with the drinks-tray again, and asked if they could talk for a moment. They went through into the servants' hall to sit at the end of the long table, which was now laid for dinner.

"Is something troubling you?" Jim asked. It was fairly obvious something was. Priscilla's hand trembled as she held her gin and tonic.

"You know how I took the drugged cocoa up to Mr. Welch?" she began.

Jim nodded, remembering the histrionics of this morning, when she claimed Welch had tried to grab her.

"Well, he never drank it."

"How do you know?"

"He offered me twenty pounds if I'd fetch him some more whisky. So I went down to the kitchen and couldn't find the cupboard and then the butler appeared and asked what I was doing. So I told him there was something in it for him if he helped and in the end I took it up. But it all took an age."

"I thought Welch made a pass at you and you only just escaped?"

"That was when I took him the whisky, not the cocoa. He wanted me to join him for a drink, but whisky does horrible things to me on top of gin, so I refused."

Jim tried to recall what she had said this morning. Surely she had put the cocoa on a table by Welch's bed? "And the second time the cocoa wasn't there?"

"That's right! I told him. 'If you'd had that cocoa you'd have calmed down by now,' I said. 'Drink that muck!' he said. 'Who d'you think I am? I gave it to Dulcie. Now, come on girl, 'ow about a little bit of nooky?' What a nerve!" Priscilla sat up straighter, looking suitably indignant. "That was when he tried to pull me onto the bed."

"And you had to run for it?"

"I never got the twenty pounds either."

"What time d'you think that was?"

"It must have been nearly half past eleven."

"Did you tell the police?"

"No." Priscilla fidgeted with her glass. "I was afraid that would make me the last person to have seen him alive. But it means something more important too." She leaned forward across the table. "It couldn't have been the cocoa, because look at Dulcie! She drank it and she's as right as rain."

"You didn't take the whisky glass?"

"I felt like it! That would have served him right. But I just had to run." Having got all this off her chest, Priscilla relaxed. "So you see, I'm not guilty." She smiled warmly. "I feel so much better for telling you."

"You really ought to tell the police." Jim marvelled that it had not occurred to her that someone could have put poison in the whisky decanter. Such innocence in an actress of fifty was rather touching. Or was it suspicious?

"Perhaps I will," Priscilla said. "If they ask me. After they've found the murderer."

They were interrupted by Dodgson entering and standing by the door, hovering as if he were waiting for them to leave. Priscilla was embarrassed, sure she'd been overheard, then decided she'd said enough anyway, thanked Savage, gave Dodgson a filthy look and departed.

But Dodgson still stood there, until Savage asked if he wanted something.

"I'd like a word, sir. If it's not inconvenient."

"Come and sit down then." Savage was surprised, but tried not to show it. Something seemed to have suddenly made him the popular choice as Father Confessor, though what he didn't know.

Dodgson perched himself where Priscilla had been, cleared his throat with a dry, rasping noise, and unburdened his soul.

"Did that woman tell you about the whisky, sir?" Evidently

Priscilla didn't merit the description "lady." Dodgson was very much the old-style retainer, whose social sensibilities were more acute than his employer's.

"She mentioned Mr. Welch asking her to fetch some," Savage agreed cautiously. "I suppose she should have refused."

"She was offered inducements," Dodgson said, in the acid tone of one who had failed to receive his cut. "But that isn't what's worrying me, sir."

"Oh?"

"No, sir. It was his lordship's instructions to give them whatever drinks they asked for. Not," he added, "that her ladyship approved."

"I see," Savage said, completely failing to, unless the purpose of this interview was to bad-mouth the Gilroys.

"It's that I need the decanters, sir."

It took Savage a moment to appreciate that Dodgson had said "decanters," in the plural. Then he realized that the second supply of whisky would never have been sent up in a bottle, and so there must have been two.

"Well," he said, clearly remembering the small cut-glass decanter that had been on top of the chest of drawers in Welch's room, "I only saw one, which presumably the police will by now have sent for tests."

"For poison, you mean, sir?" The butler's thin voice was apprehensive. "I can't deny I took him up the first decanter. Filled it with Bells."

"Was the second one identical?"

"Not exactly, sir. We did have a set of half-size ones for guests, but some got broken and others was bought. I'd know which was which myself."

"But I might not?"

"Most likely not, sir."

"Was it the same whisky?"

"Yes, sir. I gave him the rest of the Bells. The question is, where's the decanter, because I could need it."

"The maid couldn't have taken it?"

"Tracy, sir? No, sir. She brought down the early-morning tea-trays. Mr. Welch's was outside his room. But when she went later to clear up, the doctor wouldn't let her in."

Savage pondered this. The second decanter could have been out of sight in the room, on the floor, for instance, except that he himself had looked under the bed. Someone would have to tell Inspector Morton, since the whisky was a substance Welch had been witnessed taking shortly before his death. And the glass was still unaccounted for. Whether he had drunk the early-morning tea was presumably known to the pathologist and possibly to the maid. He asked Dodgson about the tea-things.

"They've all been washed up, sir. Them and the breakfast dishes. That police sergeant was quite annoyed."

"What about the whisky glass?"

"Must still be in the room, sir. I keep a check on the glasses. His lordship's very particular about guests' having proper tumblers for their drinks."

"Even these guests?"

"I have my orders, sir," Dodgson said with disapproval in his slightly quavering voice, as if changing the rules for this weekend ought not to have slipped his master's mind.

So that was that, though the glass was still missing. "Tell me something, Dodgson," Savage asked. "If Mr. Welch had bought part of the estate, would you have lost your job?"

It was a question designed to put the butler on the defensive, which it did.

"Can't think of a reason for that, sir."

"But if Lord Gilroy had sold up completely, you would have done?"

"He wouldn't ever do that, sir!" The butler sounded horrified. "He's keeping it for his son."

"Well." Savage realized that he was being a little too much of an interrogator. "Was there anything else?"

"No, sir. I mean, nothing was put in the whisky I took up to him or in the lot I gave Mrs. Worthington." He sounded distressed again as the immediate worry came back to him. "His lordship'll give me hell if there's a decanter gone."

"I'll ask the inspector about it." Savage suddenly felt sorry for the old man. He must be past retirement age and probably had nowhere else to go.

"Thank you, sir." Dodgson walked stiffly back towards the kitchens, leaving Savage barely time to think over what he had said before Jemma came in.

"What have you been doing, Daddy?" she exclaimed. "Everybody's asking."

"Listening to people proclaim their innocence, my dear."

"Priscilla, you mean? I'm sure she drinks too much."

"She's got the shakes. Or something very like it. Anyway, she let out one interesting piece of intelligence. She went to Welch's room twice last night, the second time much later." Savage retailed the conversation about the whisky.

"Which means that she could have poisoned him?"

"She had the opportunity. But why should an out-of-work actress want to kill a man she'd never met before?"

Jemma thought about this. "Hardly because he tried to assault her. Anyway, that was on her second visit," she agreed. "So why did she pretend she'd only been to his room once?"

"There you have me." There was no sense in it. "Except for her not wanting to be the last person to have seen him alive."

"I've been thinking about that. This morning there was plenty of time after we'd all been woken up for someone to go into Welch's room. It was almost an hour and a half before we went down to breakfast and nearer nine-thirty before Mrs. Welch went up to look for him."

"And Lord and Lady Gilroy weren't at breakfast," Savage mused. "On the other hand, I overheard someone say that death occurred between seven-fifteen and eight."

"I didn't know that!" Jemma exclaimed in annoyance. "Why didn't you tell me!"

"Sorry, darling."

"Well, you should tell me things." She was still petulant. "Anyway, there's something all the others want you to do for them, Lady Gilroy included."

"There is?" Now it was Savage's turn to be alarmed. Anything that united the Gilroys and their guests must have a catch in it.

"They want you to talk the inspector into letting us use the library again. It is pretty miserable in that games room and, as Dulcie says, he's no right to keep us here at all."

Savage frowned. He had a feeling his daughter might have "volunteered" him, as they used to say in the army. Like most daughters, she had very little hesitation about letting her parent in for things, from mending a fuse onwards. Which was not a bad comparison, given Inspector Morton's high-voltage rating.

"You've been elected. You're the only person they all trust."

"Because I didn't get on with Morton, I suppose?"

"Go on. You can't refuse."

Jemma took him by the arm and led him firmly through to the Great Hall, then pointed him towards the nearest of several policemen and set him going, as if he were automated.

The policeman escorted him through to the makeshift interview-room off the kitchen, which Savage realized was very close to the room he had just left, and asked him to wait outside in the passage. Standing there, he reflected that the domestic geography, apart from the main rooms, did not matter much. But the whole scenario had a feeling of clinging unreality, as if Welch's death were an event he had read about and which was never meant to involve him at all, yet was increasingly doing so.

However, Morton was real enough, sitting at the scrubbed table and motioning him to an upright kitchen chair.

"Well, sir. What can I do for you?" the inspector inquired somewhat brusquely, as if he didn't relish his time being wasted.

"There's something you ought perhaps to know," Savage said firmly and explained about Priscilla and the whisky.

Morton listened attentively, then asked, "Why did she tell you this?"

"She seemed anxious to get it off her chest. I encouraged her to tell you herself."

"Which she didn't want to do?"

"Quite right." Savage almost laughed, really because the inspector had got it right the first time. Then, feeling this made him seem like an informer, he added, "Normally I don't break confidences."

"Nor do I." Morton grunted. "Never reveal sources either."

"But the second decanter could be important."

"We'll decide on that." Morton's instinctive dislike of amateurs resurfaced. He instantly regretted it and added more emolliently, "Thank you for telling me. Has anyone else confided in you?"

This gave Savage the opening he needed. "Yes," he said with a decisiveness to match the inspector's. "They have. They would all like the use of the library again."

"Why? There may be evidence there."

"The present room is very cramped. They're willing to stay and help with your investigation . . ."—this was a definite smoothing over of their actual attitudes—". . . rather than insist on their right to leave. But they also paid a lot of money for this weekend."

Morton tapped meditatively on the table with the Biro he was holding. It was a cliché of a movement, intended to imply that he was taking the idea seriously. Which he was, because he had to. Murder cases went cold very fast. If he didn't get a lead in the first three or four days, he might wait months for one, and it would be a lot easier to get that lead with his group of suspects readily available.

"When your searches are complete," Savage prompted.

"All right then." Morton gave way. In fact, they'd been over the library very thoroughly already and found only the "clues" that Welch and McMountdown had thrown away. "You can go back in there tonight, after you've eaten." That would allow time to set up a listening device, which he had not done in the games room. There might be a useful percentage in the change.

Savage thanked him and returned to something of a hero's welcome from the others.

"How clever of you!" Loredana cooed. "This horrid place was really getting on my nerves."

"Wish I could get my study back," Gilroy remarked. He was finding the whole performance extremely irksome, though, as Dee Dee had observed, there was no hope for the study because of the rows that been overheard going on there.

"I wish we could bloody well leave," McMountdown said irritably.

"Well, we hardly can do now," Jim remarked, annoyed at

Hamish's persistently negative attitude. "Not when he's just given ground."

The realization that by asking for the library back they had all committed themselves to remaining did nothing to help the conversation. When Dulcie joked that the situation was getting more and more like something out of Agatha Christie, nobody laughed.

They were all longing for Dodgson to announce dinner when Inspector Morton entered, said "Good evening, all," and walked across to Gilroy. In fact, he had several things to talk to the peer about, one of which was that a bottle of morphine had been discovered in the medicine cupboard, and morphine, as even the most dim-witted lord ought to know, was a deadly opiate. But at this moment there was a more urgent problem.

"May I have a word, sir," he said quietly, drawing Gilroy aside. "There's been an accident down at the Lion Park."

Gilroy blanched. Today had been just one piece of bad news after another. He told Dee Dee to start the meal without him and left hurriedly with Morton, while their guests crowded round to ask her what was going on.

9

IT WAS A perfect summer evening to go for a stroll before dinner. The grass was not yet wet with dew. The sky was a blue that was not yet darkening, and the late sun bathed the stone façade of Wittenham Park in gold, making it look almost distinguished. If Gilroy had been selling the place, this would have been the moment to snap the estate agent's photos. Only a single detail was wrong.

In one place the grass was wet. Not with dew, but blood. Ted Matthews's body lay on its back in the Lion Park's enclosure. His right forearm was attached to the elbow only by skeins of tissue and tendon, the other torn to the bone, his old safari jacket was ripped and soaked in blood, and his head lacked a recognizable face.

"Jesus!" Morton muttered. "Poor bastard."

Gilroy gazed down at the corpse, temporarily too shocked to speak, while the ranger who had found it explained and two others stood by, holding rifles and keeping an eye open for the lions. The ranger was a young Oxfordshire man dressed in the big-game-hunter-style gear that Mathews himself had refused to wear, and he spoke with a strong local farming accent. His name was Gary.

"Ted meant to go off around five, sir, before Caesar woke up proper. The lions all snooze in the afternoons. But then a detective comes down to ask what 'e knows about the deceased up at the house and one way and t'other 'twas six before he had the dart and all that ready and we could get on with it."

"What dart?" Morton asked.

"It's a tranquillizer, sir. Ted makes up what he calls his 'cocktail,' he loads the dart in the gun and off we all go. He takes his vehicle and we need two others at least."

Morton was looking puzzled and Gilroy found his voice sufficiently to explain. "The problem is, Inspector, when you tranquillize one of these brutes you have to protect it from the rest of the pride. Otherwise while it's wandering around groggy, the others attack it."

"Friendly lot," Morton commented, then looked down again at Matthews's mutilated body. "Jesus," he murmured again. "I've never seen anything like that. Have you called a doctor?"

"He's on his way, sir," Gary said. "Not that he'll be much good. Can we take Ted's body away now, sir?"

"Why didn't you before?"

"We didn't like to until you was here, sir. Even though we've had to chase the other lions off a couple of times."

The rest of the pride were some distance away, moving around in a restless and disturbed way, watched by yet another ranger in a third vehicle. Morton realized that this was not exactly the safest place to be with a fresh corpse. Gary's extreme caution must have been a reaction to the investigation going on up at the house.

All the estate workers would have heard how nothing there was allowed to be moved, not even the body, though this was different. No human could have inflicted these wounds. It was a killing all right, and a savage one, but not a homicide.

"You'd better take him back to the workshop," Morton said.

"Best use the lion stretcher, then." Gary and another ranger fetched an unusually large canvas-and-wood stretcher out of the Land Rover's trailer and carefully lifted the body into it, folding the tattered arms across the abdomen. Morton noticed the blood was only just beginning to congeal. It left a wide stain on the grass. For the first time in many years, he felt sick.

They drove back in a small convoy, out through the gate in the electrified fence, and then to the workshop, with Gilroy thankful that the park had been closed early on account of the darting and there were no visitors around.

"So what exactly happened?" Morton demanded, when the corpse had been laid down on the floor of the room where Ted had prepared for his fatal mission.

THEY had driven out from the park's offices around six-thirty. Ted was in his own Land Rover, the darting rifle secure in its clamp. He was towing a high-sided trailer, on which to lift the sedated lion, and had the specially fabricated stretcher in the back of his truck. A grown lion weighed all of five hundred pounds and the men would have to roll the lion sideways onto the stretcher before lifting it into the trailer. Then they would take it back to a cage and deal with the injured foot. The operation required three or four men.

Gary had gone in a second vehicle, two more rangers in a third. They were aggravated at running late, thanks to the detective, and to be missing good drinking time in the local pub. They had hand-held walkie-talkies and they only had to drive along the park's winding roads for a few minutes to locate the pride. A male, two females, and several cubs were out in the open, lazily enjoying the last warmth of the sun, while Caesar lay apart from them beneath his favourite tree, occasionally licking his front paw.

They all looked somnolent and inactive, but Ted knew this was an illusion. In the wild they only killed every few days, and they had not been fed today.

"Are there any others around?" he asked over the radio.

"Can't see any," Gary reported.

"Then go between Caesar and the pride and we'll get going."

The rangers had driven off the road and positioned themselves on the grass, ready to head off any move by the other lions. Not that things would happen fast. The drug could take half an hour to act. They were facing the pride, their backs to Ted, but they knew what he would be doing.

Ted manoeuvred to within a few yards of Caesar and stopped, keeping his engine running, while he checked the rifle and loaded the steel cylinder of the dart. He had made up the dart himself with great care. The "cocktail" he had mixed up in one of his laboratory vials consisted of four millilitres of an opiate powder called

Rompen and one millilitre of a liquid named Vetallar, plus a tiny amount of water, which produced a colourless solution of great potency. It would only need a drop, if he had a cut on his hand, to put him in serious danger of death, and the substance would have to be washed away with copious quantities of water immediately, before he injected himself with what the veterinary journals cheerfully called "an antagonist."

This concoction went into a cylinder only a quarter inch thick, fitted with an explosive charge and a plunger. The final item, the hypodermic needle, was then screwed into the cylinder's top end, before the dart was fired like a low-velocity bullet. Firing a hypodermic into a lion's thigh was not the most elegant way to deal with the King of Beasts. The one certainty was that Caesar was not going to like it.

What happened after that could vary. The lion might career off, he might charge the Land Rover, he might react with fury at the dart itself and try to pull it out with his teeth, he might do anything. And Ted would proceed very cautiously until Caesar was definitely sedated. As his mentor in South Africa used to say, "There are good lions and bad lions, but no safe lions."

Ted wound down the window and took aim at the fleshy, muscular part of Caesar's hind leg. Since the lion was recumbent, it was an angle shot. Caesar raised his great, dark-maned head and looked at him indolently as Ted fired.

There wasn't much of a bang. The rifle was only an adapted .22-caliber. But Caesar took off as if the Concorde had broken the sound barrier behind him. Growling, his tail thrashing, he charged the Land Rover, the dart firmly embedded in his rump. Ted hastily wound up the window. At the last moment Caesar sprang clear over the vehicle, walked around it growling angrily, then loped away.

The Lion Park wasn't densely wooded or large enough for him to vanish and Ted followed at a distance in the Land Rover, until Caesar sat down. Ted thought he was trying to extract the dart. Then he realized it was no longer embedded in the skin and must have dropped off along the way. At last, Caesar lay down, looking sleepy. It was thirty-five minutes since he'd been darted. Taking a normal rifle with him, Ted got out of the vehicle and approached cautiously. When he was satisfied that the lion was out for the count, he would radio the others, who were keeping the rest of the pride away.

Caesar stirred and came to when Ted was only four yards away. He lolloped groggily to his feet, then suddenly gathered himself and sprang, knocking Ted onto his back. There was no time to fire, only to fight with legs and arms against the lion's crushing, clawing biting weight.

EVEN though Inspector Morton's words about the Lion Park had been sotto voce, the way Gilroy left the room so rapidly with him caused immediate comment, from the self-centered to the curious.

"I suppose we'll have to wait for dinner until he's back, damn it," Hamish complained to no one in particular, still smarting from having had his belongings searched earlier.

"Not at all," Dee Dee said. "We shall dine at eight, with or without my husband."

"What's happened?" Loredana asked. All of them except the Savages were together in the library. Loredana had been making stilted conversation with Priscilla, whose principal concern was catching the butler's eye for more gin.

"There's a small problem down at the Lion Park," Dee Dee said.

"Nothing serious?" Loredana sounded concerned.

"I hope not."

"Your keeper is such a nice man."

"Aren't all men nice?" Dulcie asked innocently.

"What a silly thing to say." Loredana gave her an icy look. "Trevor can be an appalling bore. Men are just a necessary nuisance, in my opinion."

"Well, you're the expert."

Sitting a little way away, Jim and Jemma listened to this exchange.

"There's going to be a show-down there before long," Jim commented softly. "I might just have a word with Mrs. McMountdown." He got up, leaving his daughter to read a glossy magazine, and went across.

"Mind if I join you?"

"Please do," Dee Dee said, making room on the sofa. Savage was one of the very few people on this weekend whom she liked and, better, still trusted. Then it occurred to her that with him around she could temporarily cease shepherding Adrienne and get on with more important things, like working out cheaper menus with the cook, and she left them.

After a little small talk Savage casually asked Dulcie, "Had any luck finding that contract?"

He could hardly have grabbed everyone's attention faster if he had sprouted donkey's ears and begun braying. Adrienne looked flustered and Dulcie drew in her breath sharply, as if this were an unexpected lapse of taste. Even Hamish looked interested, while Loredana abandoned her stilted conversation with Priscilla.

"Since you ask, the answer is no," Dulcie said. "But why do you ask?"

"You've mentioned it several times," Jim said, as if defensively. "I merely had a sudden thought about where it might be."

"It was nowhere in George's room," Adrienne said, as she had many times before.

"Oh, no. I'm sure you're right about that. And I don't think the police have it either."

"Well, spill the beans then, old chap," Hamish said. "Don't keep us all in suspense."

"Your wife might prefer to hear my ideas in private." Jim smiled confidentially at Dulcie.

"I think I might," Dulcie agreed, giving her husband a stony look.

"Why don't we go for a short stroll before dinner? It's a beautiful evening."

"If that's allowed."

"We can but try."

Jim led her through to the hall, where they ran into Sergeant Timmins, who had just received the first results of inquiries about the Savages. Their neighbours all regarded Jim as reliable, if quiet.

His former employers gave him good references. There was nothing conclusive about all this, but it inclined Timmins to respond positively. In any case Morton had emphasized that if the guests' freedom was too curtailed, they might well insist on their rights and leave. Both officers remained equally wary of the lawyer. So Timmins wished them a pleasant evening and they walked out onto the lawns that led down to the lake and the landscape of the late George Welch's development dreams.

When they returned twenty minutes later, Dulcie had the expression of someone to whom a truth has been revealed. Not an eternal truth, but a significant one. She now knew that she'd slept like a log last night because she'd been doped. Furthermore, Savage had explained his theory about the contract.

"Let's hope you're right," she said, before they rejoined the others, "and at least I now know why I'm the only person who heard nothing during the night. Whatever that woman put in the cocoa was powerful stuff."

As they re-entered the library Dodgson, who had been waiting for them, announced dinner and they all trooped through to the servants' hall. No matter what anyone might do to improve the room—and Dodgson had done his best with linen and silver—the servants' hall remained a gloomy, high-ceilinged cavern. Its cream paint was peeling, and below the dado-rail the walls were an ugly tone of chocolate. The ceiling lights had white plastic shades, like an old-fashioned railway waiting-room. The builder of Wittenham Park had seen no reason for the staff either to be or feel comfortable. Gilroy's grandfather had not been a mine owner for nothing, and Gilroy had not bothered to redecorate a room that was very seldom used. Few of his acquaintances travelled with a valet or a lady's-maid these days.

It was a relief when the meal was over and Dodgson told them coffee and liqueurs were available in the library.

Jim Savage, however, told Jemma he wanted to talk to the maid and went through to the kitchen. As he had expected, Tracy was clearing dishes into a catering-sized washing-up machine.

"Hullo, sir," she said brightly, turning around with a plate in her hand. "Isn't that dreadful about poor Ted?"

For a moment Jim couldn't think who Ted was, but was reminded when she went on with morbid enthusiasm.

"Imagine being torn to pieces by a lion! He was such a nice man, too."

"He what? You mean the lion keeper? What happened?"

To his horror Tracy related what she knew, adding, "Can't have been drugged can it? Not properly. No way."

"The experts will find out soon enough." Jim re-assured her, thinking that two deaths in twenty-four hours seemed to be extraordinary. "Have they had trouble with the lions before?"

"Ooh yes. One of Ted's men got mauled last year. I don't go anywhere near the place myself. They had to shoot the lion." She resumed stacking plates and asked over her shoulder, "You looking for Mr. Dodgson?"

"No." He put the lion park tragedy out of his mind. "In fact, I wanted to ask you something. This morning were all the early morning teacups washed up?"

"I put them in the machine myself."

"Including Mr. Welch's? Did you go into his room to fetch the tray?"

"No way! Not after what he'd tried to do yesterday."

"So where was it?"

"Outside his door."

"And the cup had been used? I mean, he'd drunk his tea?"

She had to think about this. "He must have done because I gave him the nasty old blue teapot set and the cup was dirty."

"What time d'you think you collected the trays?"

"I waited till they'd all gone down to breakfast."

"So it was after nine o'clock?"

"Oh yes." She remembered something. "Except that tall, thin lady, the one who thinks she's God Almighty. She brought her own tray down at about twenty to nine."

"Tall and thin?" He realized she must be talking about Loredana. "The lady in the Chinese Room whose husband didn't come?"

"That's her. She made a big thing about how she wanted to save us work! What difference does one tray make, I ask you? And you should see her room. Enough bottles for a perfume shop." Tracy suddenly stopped her brief tirade and looked at him curiously. Inspector Morton had been asking her very similar questions and policemen had been going through everything, even the dustbins. "You're not a detective, are you?"

He laughed gently. "No. Just interested. I was supposed to play the detective this weekend, but that was before Mr. Welch died. My daughter writes for a crime magazine."

"Are you serious?" Tracy was enthralled. "Can I talk to her?"

"I'm sure she'd like that. I'll tell her."

When Jim rejoined the others his mind was still concentrated on what Tracy had said and he felt a definite sense of progress. He told Jemma about the lion quietly, then outlined his theory. Unless he had got the sequence of events completely wrong George Welch had placed his early-morning tea-tray outside his room shortly before he died. If whatever poisoned him had been fast-acting, that was exceptionally unlikely. Nor was it in Welch's character to put a tea-tray, or anything else, out for collection by the maid. He was too bad-mannered and selfish. So if he hadn't put it out, who had?

"Could have been his wife," Jemma suggested. "Who else would have wanted to go into his room?"

"Whoever wanted him dead?"

"You mean we're back to square one? Come on, Daddy. Who had the motive, who had the means and who had the opportunity? That's what we need to know. That's what our heavy-handed inspector will be asking himself."

"Then it's what I'd better ask myself again," Savage said, "which means rewriting my notes."

While he did so, Jemma picked up a magazine to flip through.

"How beastly of someone!" she said after a few minutes, disturbing her father to show him the magazine. "The horoscope page has been torn out. Just when we needed it."

Having learned to react immediately to things his daughter said, Jim put aside his notebook and looked obediently at the page. Only a section of it had been removed. It was still headed, "Your stars this June." The missing parts covered from Pisces to Leo.

"Amazing how obsessed some people are by the stars," he commented and tried to resume his note-taking.

"Daddy! Haven't you got any imagination? Someone wanted to know if this was a propitious time."

"That could apply to just about everyone here, from Lord Gilroy wondering about contracts, or the actress worrying about her next job." He examined the page more carefully. The missing paper had not been roughly torn, but quite neatly removed, perhaps with a slightly blunt knife. "Well," he said, "that's one more thing to keep an eye open for."

They were interrupted by Hamish, who joined them apparently casually, but soon asked if they had any idea where the missing contract was. "My wife's very concerned about it," he explained.

"Does it affect you?" Jim asked.

"Only through her."

Why did Hamish sound evasive, when it was he who had raised the subject? Jim's thoughts went back to the row they had overheard before dinner last night. Welch had bellowed out, "You bloody well will, or else." And another voice, which might have been Dulcie's, had added, "You haven't any option." So was it Hamish who'd had no option? And then, during dinner, he had forced the subject of Lloyds losses into the conversation. Was that what he had been told to do? And it had a bearing on the contract, because Gilroy's losses might make him feel compelled to raise money through the sale of land. Jim decided to cast a metaphorical fly over these deep waters.

"I imagine quite a few people will be glad to know George Welch is dead," he suggested.

Hamish smiled his thin, inward smile. "No one would disagree with that."

"A bit of a bastard in business?"

"As tough as they come."

"But your wife knew how to handle him?"

"My wife is quite a strong character," Hamish admitted. It sounded to both Jim and Jemma that there were times when he wished she weren't. "But not always. He could be incredibly rude."

At that moment Gilroy walked in, looking harassed and slightly dishevelled. Everybody looked up. He hesitated, then addressed them.

"I'm sorry to tell you that Ted, our Lion Park keeper, has been killed by one of the lions."

"Oh no!" Loredana burst out emotionally. "How horrible. He was such a nice man. What happened?"

"A lion he thought was sedated attacked him. The lion has had to be shot." Gilroy almost mentioned the thousands of pounds that an adult male lion was worth, and that he had now lost, but thought better of it. "There will be a full investigation."

That was all he felt it necessary to say. During the flurry of talk that followed he went across to his wife and they went through to the servants' hall to find him some food.

Next Adrienne excused herself, saying that she hoped never to have another day like this in her life, and was escorted upstairs by Priscilla Worthington. Dee Dee had suggested, virtually ordered, Priscilla to look after the newly widowed woman.

Across the room Loredana was telling Hamish and an unreceptive Dulcie that she couldn't believe such a tragedy had happened, though she knew, from having been on safari herself, that lions could never be trusted.

"Hamish, I'm exhausted," Dulcie said eventually, cutting brutally into the flow of Loredana's safari knowledge. "For heaven's sake, let's go to bed."

After they had gone, Jim found himself yawning and earning an instant reprimand.

"Daddy! Please! I can't bear your falling asleep after dinner."

"Sorry, darling." Jim made an effort to sit upright, but knew it was a lost cause. "I think I'll go up too."

"Well, that is sociable! Who gets to entertain me?"

"Loredana?" Jim suggested wickedly, getting up. "See you in the morning, darling."

When he reached his small room and opened the door, he had a sixth-sense feeling that there had been an intruder. Seconds later he realized that there had. A thick white envelope was lying on his bedcover. He picked it up, saw there was nothing written on the outside and that it was unsealed, then extracted the contents and gave a low whistle, of which his daughter would have deeply disapproved. He was holding the missing contract of sale for five hundred acres of Whittenham Park. He flipped through the typed pages, some with changes written in by hand. Two signatories were named. Above the words, "Baron Gilroy of Wittenham," there was no signature. Above the name, "George Ernest Welch," there was another blank space. Neither had signed.

10

INSPECTOR Morton had the contract document inside a transparent plastic exhibit bag, labelled with the details of where and when it had been found. Jim Savage had brought it down before breakfast, after showing it to Dulcie Mc-Mountdown, who had at first objected to its being given to the police, then seen the wisdom of it. Morton was grateful. Contrary to his expectations, Savage was being sensible and co-operative. He felt certain that the contract was central to his investigation, although why it should have been dumped in Savage's room was a mystery.

"I had a feeling it might be," Savage had said non-committally.

"Why?"

"Because the others see me as neutral."

"There's no neutrality between the law and a murderer," Morton growled.

"But I am not the law. And not everyone thinks as correctly as that."

Morton had been forced to agree with this. Now he was seated at the table in his interview-room looking across at one person who unquestionably did think logically and correctly: Dulcie Mc-Mountdown. The time was 10 A.M. on Sunday, of which he made a note. The document in its plastic bag lay between them, inanimate, yet able to speak volumes, if it only had a voice.

"Was there anything significant about the contract, Mrs. Mc-Mountdown?"

"Yes. George Welch had not signed it."

"And why do you think he hadn't?"

"On the last occasion I spoke to him he was uncertain about all the amendments. They gave certain advantages to Lord Gilroy." Dulcie spoke calmly and circumspectly. She could not reason out how this document figured in Welch's death, but she was as convinced as Morton that it did. Not that he had said so, she merely sensed it. "I advised Mr. Welch that there were limits beyond which we could not push Lord Gilroy over the land sale."

"So he died before he was ready to sign?"

"Presumably." Actually this was jumping to conclusions. Depending on how George was poisoned, he might have been killed before he could sign. She decided to speculate gently. "When I last saw him on Friday night, he'd drunk quite a lot of whisky. He might have fallen asleep. He might have decided to go over the amendments again in the morning. After all, Lord Gilroy had agreed to sign if this draft was accepted."

"Gilroy's word is his bond?"

"In today's world, nobody's is." Remembering the stormy meetings they'd had, Dulcie's plan had been to get them both round the table in the morning and have both sign then and there.

"Did anyone visit Mr. Welch after you that night?" Morton wondered if she knew that Mrs. Worthington had brought him yet more whisky at 11:30 P.M.

"Not that I know of. Did they?"

"When Mrs. Worthington brought him the cocoa he told her to ask the butler for more whisky." He carefully did not specify who took up the liquor.

"That damn cocoa!" Dulcie said with feeling. "You know I ended up drinking it, and it was doped?"

Morton nodded. "In other words, you know very little about what went on during the night?" Was there a flash of anger in her blue eyes? He thought so. But her answer was as guarded as it could be.

"That is quite right. I had to force myself awake when the maid began screaming."

"As part of the 'murder' plot?"

Dulcie heard the disdain in his voice and decided to be frank. "The only people who cared about the plot in the least were the

Savages and Priscilla Worthington. The contract was the real issue for most of us."

"Including Mrs. Chancemain?"

"She and her husband were invited purely to make up the numbers." Again that flash of annoyance. "Loredana was a hanger-on."

Morton was now quite aware of Loredana's activities, but in his estimation they were indeed peripheral. He returned to the subject of the contract.

"Was Lord Gilroy unhappy with the land deal?"

So, Dulcie thought, he's begun to suspect Gilroy. Personally she could not imagine a man less likely to murder anyone competently than the third Baron G of W.

"He would have preferred to sell land for a golf course," she said. "The amendments to the contract represented a compromise. But he's not my client. I can't speak for him."

"But he was unhappy about it?" Morton persisted.

"He didn't have much alternative. Thanks to Lloyds he's very short of money."

Morton stretched his shoulders. He'd been sitting at this table too long and his muscles ached. "Forgive me," he said. "I'm not a desk-job man. Thank you for your help. There's just one other thing." He tapped the exhibit bag with his Biro. "You've handled this, so I'd like to have your fingerprints taken for elimination purposes. I'll be taking everyone else's."

Dulcie agreed readily enough, reflecting with pleasure that Hamish would not like the procedure one little bit. But she did not want to lose sight of the document. Even though it was on the computer at her office, the amendments were not. "Mr. Welch's partners might want to proceed. We might still need the contract."

"Hmm." This had not occurred to Morton. "Who would inherit his money?"

"His wife, I suppose." Dulcie did not remark that there were more likely to be debts than assets. "Another firm holds his will. I was his commercial lawyer."

Morton asked for the firm's name and thanked her again. When she had been fingerprinted, Timmins came back to the interview room.

"Have an officer get onto these solicitors, will you?" Morton asked. "Track them down at home. Find out what's in Welch's will. Who stood to gain what. And ask Lord Gilroy to come through."

Buck Gilroy had been having a tough morning. Breakfast had hardly begun when the first national tabloid had been on the line about Ted's death. A TV crew had just turned up at the Lion Park. He needed Morton's help.

"How can we control them?" he demanded plaintively as soon as he sat down.

"Tell them the body's at the mortuary and a full investigation is being made."

"Can't you say that because of Welch's death no one can be interviewed?"

"So far as I'm concerned the two events are unconnected." Not for the first time Morton wondered how the strength of character which had earned Gilroy's grandfather a peerage could have been so totally lost in a mere two generations. "In my experience," he added, "it's better to talk to them, even if you say very little."

"I suppose so." All Gilroy's fears of bad publicity resurfaced. "They'll be calling this 'The House of Horrors' next."

Morton shrugged his broad shoulders. He couldn't care less what they called Wittenham Park, or Lord Gilroy himself, as long as the media didn't get in his own way.

"Matthews's death is not what I wanted to talk about," he said. "What I'm interested in is the morphine in your medicine cupboard." His desk now had a different exhibit standing on it. Inside another transparent bag was a small brown bottle labelled "Oramorph." "Morphine is a dangerous drug and ought not to be kept in an unlocked cupboard. Why have you got it anyway?"

"Completely forgot I had." Gilroy was bemused. "We got it when someone staying with us was in a lot of pain. Fellow called Jack Anderson."

"When was that?"

"Three years. Four years. You should ask my wife."

"And when was it last used?"

"When Jack was here. He was taken to hospital and it got left behind."

"So it's been here ever since?"

"Yes." Gilroy found this sudden interrogation unnerving. What on earth was the man getting at? "There are all sorts of medicines in there. We ought to have a clear-out."

"You do realize that Mr. Welch died from an opiate overdose and that morphine is an opiate?"

"It is?" Gilroy was almost struck dumb as he realized that he was being suspected of involvement in the murder. "Well, I mean, they used it in the army if you were wounded. It's a pain-killer. That's what Jack used it for."

"It can also kill," Morton said flatly. "I shall be testing the bottle for fingerprints and I hope you and your staff will co-operate."

"Whatever you say." He didn't much like having his fingerprints taken, as if he were a common criminal. Dee Dee would be appalled. But he could see that it was essential to be helpful. "I shouldn't think that bottle's been touched for years."

"Then there won't be anything to worry about, will there?" Morton said with an edge in his voice. "By the way, did you have a row with Welch over the contract?

"A bit of one. He was piling on the pressure."

"And you had to sell?"

"It's all to do with Lloyds. I'll know for sure on Monday. But, between ourselves, he was insisting on a deal today."

"I see." Morton thanked Gilroy and ushered him out before calling Timmins in again.

"You know something, Sergeant?" he said reflectively. "Lord Gilroy loathed Welch and he hated this deal he was being hijacked into. What do you think?"

"He hadn't signed anything, had he, sir?"

"His wife was in the room next to Welch. She could have slipped something into Welch's drink."

"Or that death-warmed-up butler could have done, sir. By the way, I've sent the empty bottle of Bells from the dustbins for analysis."

"It won't tell us anything," Morton said with certainty. "What we need to find is that second decanter. But you've a point there over the butler. Suppose he thought Gilroy had signed and he was going to lose his job? That would be a motive."

UPSTAIRS Jemma was sitting in her father's room, relating how when she was on her way to bed last night she had overheard yet another quarrel, although not before she'd been subjected to a more than patronizing conversation with Loredana.

"One at a time! Which came first?" Jim asked.

"Oh, Daddy. Don't be so silly. I was talking to Loredana downstairs after you left."

"And what did she have to say?"

"That was the funny thing. I'm not sure that what she was saying was what she was actually talking about."

"Admirably clear, darling. Do you make this kind of remark to your editor? Or is he psychic?"

Jemma lifted her foot and kicked her father sharply on the ankle, so that he grimaced. "You're lucky I'm wearing trainers. You deserve boots."

"All right, then." Jim gave way. "What was she saying?"

"She was talking about that poor man Ted and the lion and how it must have been fate and it was probably in his stars that death was round the corner in some form. Nothing he could have done would have prevented it, even if he'd been warned."

"About the lion or his stars?"

"I think she meant his horoscope, because she said that if anyone had read Welch's, they might have known he was going to die soon."

"So she was actually saying that we are powerless in the hands of the gods?"

"I think so. But she doesn't seem that sort of person. Especially not when she's carrying on with someone else's husband. Suppose Dulcie had the stars on her side?" Jemma laughed. "Hamish is such a cold fish, she probably has. Anyway, after that Loredana did a bit of a number on me. How bored I must be and if she could do anything for me."

"Which meant there were things you could do for her?"

"Got it in one. She wanted me to pretend that I'd seen Hamish going down to the kitchen this morning and that he must have come from his own room."

"And?"

"I played dumb and said I was sure no one would ever ask me. Then I came upstairs and heard the row between Hamish and Dulcie."

"Ah. Event number two."

"Daddy!" Jemma lifted a finger in warning. "One more crack out of you and I'll"—she hesitated while deciding what to threaten—"I'll keep everything to myself."

Jim raised his hands in mock surrender. "I give in! What was going on between Dulcie and her husband?"

"She was giving him hell."

"You heard it?"

"What do you think? I can hear it now. And it answers one of our big questions."

"DON'T THINK you're going to sneak out and spend the night with her again, either!" Dulcie had been so angry that Jemma had caught every syllable. "Because you're not!"

"What d'you mean, 'again'?" Hamish was arguing back, but weakly.

"You didn't sleep here last night. Nor did you go to the kitchen from here."

"Don't be absurd, darling."

"You're a bad liar, Hamish. I was out for the count and when I did wake up you weren't there and your bed was cold."

"You're imagining things."

"I told you last night." Dulcie had become seriously incensed. "I've had enough. For months I've watched you come back across the square in the early morning, when Trevor's been away, and I've pretended to be asleep when you came back into the room." Suddenly she had begun to cry. "I've pretended too often. And now you have the nerve to screw her here! Oh God, Hamish, how could you. I loved you once, but I don't any more. It's over."

"But Dulcie, darling, everything's changed now."

"Nothing's changed. You're an unfaithful bastard and I've been humiliated enough."

"Dulcie, please . . ."

AT THIS moment Adrienne had come along the passage in her dressing-gown and Jemma was forced to move out of the way. She noticed the flare of lace beneath the gown as Adrienne opened the lavatory door and was instantly reminded of the mystery woman on Saturday morning. Then she continued on to her own room.

"And that was all you heard?" Jim asked. "Hardly earns you a master's in eavesdropping. I don't know whether to be proud of you or ashamed."

"And you said that domestic geography didn't matter! If I hadn't passed their door I would never have heard anything."

"All right," Jim conceded. "But what does it all signify? We already guessed that Hamish and Loredana are having an affair."

"It would give them both an alibi."

"With a little help from Priscilla drugging the cocoa." Jim chuckled. "This is becoming more like a farce than a murder."

"So why does Loredana ask me to pretend that Hamish didn't go from her room to the kitchen in the morning?" Jemma argued. "That would destroy the alibi."

"Perhaps they don't care. Perhaps they have nothing to do with Welch's death. It's hard to see how Loredana could be connected. She'd never met the man before."

Jemma tried to reason this out. "Wait a minute. Let's start with Dulcie. She was Welch's lawyer. And your hunch was right, even though she denied it. She definitely was the third person in that row before dinner on Friday."

"Well, thank you, my love. It's nice to have recognition."

"Last night she was speaking in the same low, angry voice. You could almost mistake it for a man's. She was telling Hamish he had no option but to do something for Welch."

"So what did Hamish do?" Jim went over the dinner conversation in his mind, then snapped his fingers. "Got it. He laid it on the line to Gilroy about the next round of Lloyds losses. And sure enough, Gilroy got worried."

"And felt he would have to sell the land to Welch. Easy peasy. Except, as my news editor would ask, why didn't he sign the contract? It doesn't make sense."

"An awful lot of things don't," Jim admitted. "Why did Welch invite Loredana and her husband? Purely to make sure he dominated the weekend? On the face of it, Dulcie ought to have objected like hell."

"Not if Hamish was essential to Welch's plan, Daddy. Loredana also told me what friends the four of them were. She really laid it on thick. Some friends!"

"Perhaps they often did things together and Loredana's husband hadn't an inkling of what was going on behind his back."

"Come on, Daddy!"

"It's the oldest story in the world. Well, perhaps the second-oldest. The cuckold. 'Cuckoo cuckoo, a merry note,' " Jim briefly quoted Shakespeare. "I can just imagine it. Dulcie's away on her legal business and Loredana tells her devoted idiot, 'Poor old Hamish is on his own again, we must have him for supper.' They must both have been killing themselves laughing."

"Doesn't mean they're killers, though," Jemma said.

"Not at all. Just creatures of habit. They're used to playing games with other people. Loredana probably can't stop, she finds it too entertaining. Like stringing you along. She'll be having a go at me next, I expect."

"Daddy." Jemma abruptly became firm. "This is getting us nowhere. Why should Hamish have said that everything's changed?"

"Presumably he meant the pressure from Welch was off. 'As tough as they come,' he called him last night. But what did he stand to gain? We don't know. Whereas Adrienne?"

"Adrienne is recovering amazingly quickly," Jemma observed. "She's not even wearing black."

"Maybe she didn't come prepared," Jim said sardonically. "It would be rather obvious if she'd packed mourning-gear in advance. But you're right. There is an interesting woman. Within an hour of my saying last night that I had a good idea where the contract was, hey, presto, it appears on my bed. I wish I could do the same with the missing decanter. If it's not full of whisky, it might easily appear to be something else, a vase of flowers, for example. Morton might be quite impressed."

"He doesn't much like us, does he?"

"Can you blame him? What real detective wants an amateur sleuth and a crime reporter on his patch? But I wish he could see it from our side of the fence. How on earth would he occupy his time if he was cooped up here?"

"He could always let us go home."

"Not a hope, my love. Morton is a very methodical man. Now let's go downstairs. Your astute father has a feeling that something dramatic is about to happen."

When they reached the Great Hall, Jim's prediction proved accurate. A TV crew, with arc lights and cameras, was in action in the drive outside, while Priscilla gave one of the performances of her life from the front steps, as though she were the chatelaine of Wittenham.

"That poor dear keeper," they heard her declaiming, "such a terrible way to die. Torn to pieces by a lion. It could be ancient Rome. And as for Mr. Welch's death! It's like a House of Horrors."

Lady Gilroy was watching through the open windows with frozen detachment.

"How did the agency find that woman?" she asked. "She's crazy. Anyone would think she owned the place."

From outside came Priscilla's silvery tones, mixing theatrical despair with brave honesty. "The police are investigating. They're marvellous. I don't know what we would do without them. Of course, as a tourist attraction we're ruined."

"Oh shoot!" Dee Dee muttered. "I guess anything's better than our being interviewed. Buck's practically gone into hiding. But how do we get her offstage again?"

"May I try?" Jim suggested.

"Can you?" Dee grasped at his offer as if it were the last lifebelt on the *Titanic*.

"Come on, Jemma," Jim said. "We're the men in white coats, okay?"

He led his daughter out of the front door and down the steps, straight into the TV cameras' vision.

"Hey," the interviewer shouted, "get outta the way. Can't you see we're shooting?"

"Time for your medicine, Mrs. Worthington," Jim said, grasping Priscilla's elbow, "you can't have forgotten." He propelled her away from the cameras and back towards the front steps.

"What the hell's going on?" demanded the interviewer.

Jim waved cheerfully as he and Jemma marched Priscilla back into the house. "Sorry, boys. You had the wrong lady."

Once they were inside the house, Jim released Priscilla and told her, "You're being extremely naughty. Why?"

"Oh, but darlings." Priscilla was unrepentant. "They so wanted an interview. Nobody else was around."

"Apart from the entire household," Dee Dee said savagely. "Mrs. Worthington, you're fired."

"You mean I can go?"

"Unfortunately not," Jim said. "We're all in the same boat."

"Then stuff the lot of you," Priscilla said with spirit. "Can't pay, won't go." She left them a little unsteadily, heading for the library.

"What do we do with her?" Dee Dee asked, "Trust my husband to hire a weirdo."

"There's nothing you can do until Morton lets us all off the hook."

"So we have a murderer and a madwoman on the loose together." Dee Dee groaned. "There are moments when I feel I'm losing my grip on reality."

"They could be the same person," Jemma suggested.

"I doubt it," Jim said, then turned to what had been on his mind before this TV extravaganza. "Does anyone know what went wrong with the lion?"

"There's a vet at the Lion Park now," Dee Dee said, her mind on other things, specifically on finding her husband and delivering a few choice words about his responsibilities.

"Would you mind if I go down there?" Jim asked, aware that Lady Gilroy was barely listening.

"Sure. Go ahead. Anything you like."

"Feel like a walk?" Jim asked his daughter, who looked doubtful.

"I think I'll stick around here," Jemma said.

"The inspector's sure to liven up your day," Dee Dee said, coming back into the conversation. "He likes to question everyone. Often. Anyway, it's time for elevenses."

"Elevenses," was an old country-house tradition, which Dee Dee had revived at Wittenham, basically coffee or tea and biscuits or cake, half-way between breakfast and lunch. Today it would be a useful way of killing time as everyone waited. And waited.

Dee Dee rang a bell and Dodgson appeared with a tray, as if he had been waiting for the summons. Jemma noticed that he was looking more than usually lugubrious. There seemed to be no spring in his step at all. However, her speculation as to the reason was cut short by Adrienne arriving, full of indignation about Inspector Morton.

"It's not as though everybody doesn't know George left me well provided for," she complained. "But that man makes it sound like a crime. He must have had detectives talking to the neighbours too. How else would he know George liked going to the pub?" She shook her head vexedly "Or that he'd taken a fancy to the barmaid?"

"They'll have sent out a 'victim-inquiry team,'" Jemma said knowledgeably. "They'll have interviewed your neighbours."

"Without so much as a 'by your leave' from me, I suppose," Adrienne snapped, then burst into tears and stood with her shoulders hunched, sobbing. "All I've ever done was defend him, no matter what he did to me."

"Don't worry, they'll know that." Dee put aside her own problems and stepped forward to comfort her. "Sit down and have some tea."

As Adrienne sat trembling on a sofa, trying to wipe away her tears with a tiny handkerchief, Priscilla reappeared.

"Oh, the poor darling," she exclaimed at once. "I don't blame her for being in a state."

"How can you possibly know what's been happening to her?" Dee Dee reacted furiously, "when you've been queening it in front of the cameras?"

"But I saw her going to Morton's room. He put me through the hoop too."

"I'm delighted to hear it."

Priscilla disregarded this. She had another little drama to unfold and she was not about to be upstaged. "They even dragged up a load of old gossip about my being a pyromaniac," she said, hopeful of causing consternation and fully succeeding.

"A what?" Dee Dee almost screamed, totally forgetting Adrienne as the spectre of the house being set on fire rose before her. That really would set the seal on the weekend. And this madwoman was probably capable of imagining that she had murdered Welch and of then setting the place on fire to destroy the evidence. "What did you just say?"

"It was a total lie, darling. It was nothing to do with me that the theatre caught fire. If I'd had the money I'd have sued them for sacking me. What I mean is, the police drag up everything."

"I put up with more than a woman can bear from George," Adrienne moaned from the sofa, trying to regain everyone's attention. "Reely I did."

To Jemma's surprise, Hamish reacted to this blatant piece of self-pity. He deserted Loredana, with whom he had just come in, and went straight across, sat down on an adjacent chair, and listened attentively to Adrienne's various woes. Loredana was evidently not amused and manoeuvred herself into a conversation with Dee Dee.

When Dulcie returned, Jemma decided she was definitely surplus to requirements and set out for what she called a "think walk." This took her through the Great Hall, past the guardian policeman and the police van in the drive, to the park. She found it clarified her mind to take walks alone, and she had plenty to think about.

For a start there was something about Adrienne's dramatic collapse that didn't quite ring true. One minute she was behaving with a self-control that few women could genuinely feel, the next she was overplaying the bereavement role.

As Jim had remarked, it was a well-known fact that the majority of murders are domestic ones; and many of those are never revealed for what they are. If one was looking for motive and opportunity, then Adrienne qualified richly on both counts. When she left the breakfast table on Saturday morning, saying it was odd for her husband not to have appeared, everyone assumed that she had not yet been to his room. But she could have gone there any time between the mock murder and breakfast. As she walked in the bright sunshine, Jemma decided to talk this over with her father and wondered what he was doing.

Jim was doing little except listen to others at the Lion Park, where the great tawny cadaver of Caesar lay stretched out on the laboratory floor, already giving off a sickly smell. The specialist vet had just finished examining the body and was questioning the staff. He was a small, dark-haired, rather pugnacious man, who was working with his shirt-sleeves rolled up, revealing muscular forearms.

"You say that Ted made up the tranquillizer solution himself?" he was asking.

"That's right, sir," Gary confirmed. "He did it in his workshop. Very particular he was about the amounts, too. They had to be just right."

The vet grunted. "Sounds to me as though the lion wasn't fully tranquillized."

"Wouldn't be like Ted to make that kind of mistake, sir."

"Can you tell from a blood test?" Jim asked.

The vet eyed him suspiciously. "Do you work for his lordship?"

"No, no. So sorry. I'm just a visitor up at the house." Jim made a show of being apologetic. "It's simple curiosity."

"I see." The vet was wary of the strangers who invariably gathered round after any incident with animals, then decided that this one looked honest enough. And if he was staying with the Gilroys, he was not a total outsider. "A toxicologist could tell, but it's an expensive series of tests. I doubt if Lord Gilroy would want to spend the money. When all's said and done, the lion's dead, and so, tragically, is Ted. What would be the point of proving he made a mistake?"

"He wouldn't have done, sir," Gary insisted. "Meself I reckon the dart fell out and he didn't see it had."

"Has it been found yet?"

"No, sir. No one's had time to look properly. Could be anywhere."

"Excuse my asking," Jim interrupted, "but what's the significance of the dart falling out?"

"If it hit a bone, for instance," the vet said, "it could fail to inject the tranquillizer at all, although"—he bent down over the lion's haunches and pointed to a puncture in the hide—"it wasn't in a bad place. But it unquestionably did fall out. Darting isn't a very exact science, not like injecting a human."

Jim looked down at the lion. Was he imagining blood caked on the fur around its mouth? He shuddered. What had Ted told them? There were good lions and bad lions, but no safe lions. The last time he'd seen this one it had been busy mating. It hadn't looked particularly noble then and it didn't now, which confusingly reminded him of Adrienne's revulsion at seeing the sex act. Why had that upset her? Probably the thought of her husband's activities with other women.

As the vet continued his discussion, Jim looked around the laboratory, at the benches, the shelves of medicaments and small bottles for injection fluids. Although he knew nothing of veterinary science, the set-up here seemed totally professional.

He was still thinking about that when he walked back to the house. Two deaths in twenty-four hours—it was an extraordinary coincidence. Yet Inspector Morton didn't seem to think so. Perhaps the inspector was shrewder than he appeared.

Up at the house, Morton himself was closeted in his interview-room and not feeling shrewd at all. He had now assembled files on everyone in the house. Their names had been run through the police national computer. Altogether the inquiry teams had collated an astonishing amount of scandal; at least an amount that would have been astonishing to anyone unfamiliar with the perversities of other people's lives.

There was dirt on practically everyone, from Jemma's rock-band boy-friend to Priscilla's pyromania. Gilroy had lost his licence for speeding two years ago. Dee Dee was occasionally seen at Annabel's night-club in London with another man. Welch had been suspected of insurance fraud and the man who had blacklisted him was Savage. Loredana was the talk of her village. Dulcie was seen as hard-nosed under a veil of femininity. Local gossip in Wittenham about the servants was multifarious. But Morton was still waiting for news of Welch's will, and none of this miscellany of information left him with a prime suspect. Who was really linked to whom, who had the motive, and who had had the opportunity to murder George Welch?

Morton had made a list, headed by Adrienne, of those who had the most to gain. Next came the Gilroys and their servants. Or possibly the servants first, since they might lose their jobs. Priscilla seemed enough of an oddball to do anything. Hamish McMountdown, he felt, was basically self-interested and untrustworthy. Then there was Dulcie. For what possible reason should she kill her client in the middle of a negotiation? He felt sure a lawyer must have murdered a client before now, if only out of exasperation, but surely not on this occasion.

That left Loredana and the Savages, of whom only Savage had any previous links with Welch. He had one or two things to have out with Savage, notably the inadequately explained behaviour in the passage recorded by Constable Rutherford. Well, he would do that soon. In the meantime what he needed was more information. Faced with this necessity, he resorted to a device that might not directly solve a crime, and might seem out of place here, but that often threw up clues.

When the group finally assembled for Sunday lunch, Morton gathered them together in the library and announced that he would be staging a re-enactment of early Saturday morning. He did not want to wait another day—which drew a few sighs of relief—so it would be held this afternoon. Would everyone try to recall exactly what they had done and repeat it as close to the correct time sequence as possible?

He was not delighted at Gilroy's reaction.

"Oh my God!" the noble peer exclaimed. "Where was I at seven yesterday morning?"

"In bed, you idiot," Dee Dee hissed. "And fast asleep."

11

JIM SAVAGE watched with quiet amusement as Morton outlined the re-enactment requirements. The inspector stood in front of the great stone fireplace, with the guests in a half-circle around him, fully prepared to argue and cajole. The question now was who would fail to do what they had actually done on Saturday morning before George Welch was found dead.

"Who's going to cheat?" Jemma whispered. "Want any bets?"

"Shush." Jim put his finger to his lips, as Morton eyed them with annoyance.

Morton was having a hard time. In spite of his request being politely phrased, it provoked vociferous feelings, especially when he suggested that since the idea was to jog people's memories, everyone should wear what they had worn early on Saturday; which meant their night-clothes.

"But that's absurd in the middle of the afternoon!" Loredana protested. "D'you want us all to look complete idiots?"

For once Dee Dee agreed with her. "Are you serious, Inspector?" she asked. "Surely it's enough to know where people were at specific times?"

"In the interests of authenticity it would be better." This closed circle of guests was a far cry from the re-enactment of a countryside murder, where police dressed like the victims walked a lane, or crossed a street, and the time of day was crucial if the memories of passers-by were to be stimulated. But he stuck to his decision. "Somebody may remember something."

"Which identifies the murderer, darlings!" Priscilla chimed in. "How thrilling!"

"As one of us, you mean?" Hamish said coldly.

"Oh, I quite forgot about that." Priscilla looked abashed, which was rare for her. "Silly me!"

"Surely, Inspector," Hamish persisted, "it could have been an outsider? Are you sure there was no one else in the house?"

This was a point that had exercised Morton considerably. But there had been no known break-in during the night, and once the staff were up it would have been hard for an intruder to reach Welch's room unobserved.

Gilroy decided to defend Morton. "We have quite an alarm system," he said, "both for burglars and fires."

"Thank you, sir," Morton said. "Nothing can be ruled out, but there is no evidence. Now as to the timing. We could always wait until seven tomorrow morning."

"Which would mean hanging around another day," Hamish commented in his flat, expressionless way. "Which raises the question of when on earth you're going to let us leave."

"I'm hoping for your collaboration until I have all the information I can reasonably hope for."

Morton knew that he would have to let them go after another day. This was Sunday and up until this evening they would have been here anyway. Mentally he was giving himself until Monday night or, at worst, Tuesday morning, either to make an arrest or accept that the case had gone cold. Tomorrow he ought to have the blood-test results and the poison would be identified. So he was feeling under pressure, though his expression never showed it.

"We ought to do as the inspector suggests," Jim said. "After all, what else have we got to occupy ourselves with?"

"Hear, hear," Dulcie echoed him in her commonsensical voice. "All we're achieving"—here she looked pointedly at Hamish—"is to get more and more irritable."

This was unquestionably true as far as her husband and Loredana were concerned, Jemma thought, and probably true of the Gilroys. Being confined had a very demoralizing effect on people, even in these relatively luxurious circumstances, although Lord Gilroy was displaying unexpected sang-froid under pressure. Perhaps he wasn't quite the buffoon he made himself out to be.

"Then I'll tell the servants," Dee Dee said, making the decision for all of them. "When d'you want to start, Mr. Morton?"

"Does half an hour give you all enough time?" There was grudging assent. "Good. Then can we all be upstairs on the main landing at three forty-five, which will represent six forty-five on Saturday. And please dress exactly as you did then."

Before they assembled, Morton positioned a constable in what had been Welch's room to note down everything he heard. Then the charade was ready to begin.

Jim Savage supposed, as he pulled on his pyjamas over his underwear, that Morton knew it would be a charade, given the temperaments of those involved. At the same time he was sure it would help prove or disprove his own theory about the murder. It was a theory that he was deliberately not discussing with Jemma. If she came to the same conclusion he would be delighted. But he did not want to propel her into it, and anyway she was developing her own ideas. Eventually they would combine them, though whether the police would be interested was another question. Morton had made his attitude abundantly clear several times. It was the Savages' duty to pass any relevant facts to him. He was under no obligation to tell them anything.

After he had put on his dressing-gown, Jim slipped his new red notebook into a pocket—it was as well he'd brought several—and the two of them went from the servants' wing to the main house again. Jemma was wearing a yellow kimono with deep sleeves.

"Surely that's not what you had on yesterday?" Jim asked.

"Dead right, Daddy. I want to see if anyone notices."

As they reached the corridor Gilroy appeared, looking surprisingly suave in a blue-and-white-spotted dressing-gown and royal-blue velvet slippers embroidered with a coronet. Dee had on the same red satin housecoat that Jemma recalled. And the same white ruffle of lace showed beneath its hem.

"Now, Lady Gilroy," Morton asked, beginning a routine that he intended to follow with everyone, "what was your first action on Saturday morning?"

"At about seven I came through from our suite in the west wing to the State Room"—Dee Dee indicated its door—"to play the part of Mrs. Sketchley. The maid arrived with the morning tea as I got there. So I took the tray in and waited."

"And Lord Gilroy?"

"He was asleep when I left him. His tea was taken separately."

"Actually," Gilroy said, "I never saw any of the action. This was what I was wearing, of course." He surveyed his apparel with satisfaction. The monogrammed and crested slippers were a particular joy to him, specially made by a shop on Jermyn Street, London's top location for gents' outfitters.

"You took no part?" Morton asked, kicking himself for having invited someone irrelevant to participate and feeling sick at the sight of the slippers.

" 'Fraid not."

"You'd better go back to your suite then. Both of you. And Lady Gilroy, we'll say the notional time now is six forty-five." He made a show of setting his watch, which the others followed. "Just before seven the maid will start taking round trays and at seven you come through."

"And what d'you want me to do?" Gilroy was not giving up.

"Whatever you actually did."

"Oh. Right. Well, I didn't hear my wife go out, woke up when I heard the screams, thought, thank God that's underway, and went back to sleep."

"Then do just that, sir."

The Gilroys departed regally. Morton turned to Savage and was about to go through the same procedure when Jim asked if he could hang around. "If you don't mind, we'd like to watch the others. That's what we were doing yesterday."

"Have a theory, have you?"

"Hardly as much as that, Inspector."

Before Morton could challenge this, Hamish and Dulcie came up the stairs. Dulcie had a short fawn coat on over her lace-frilled night-dress, while the striped legs of Hamish's pyjamas protruded from beneath a lightweight woollen gown held in with a tasselled cord. It struck Jemma that he looked remarkably unglamorous. She would have been far from thrilled if a lover had visited her in that gear. However, both he and Dulcie were unquestionably wearing what they'd worn yesterday. They were dispatched to the Pink Room, on the other side of the State Bedroom from Welch.

"This is a pantomime," Dulcie muttered as they departed, and Jemma had to agree with her. For a group of adults to be wandering around in mid-afternoon in their nightwear, stone-cold sober, was surreal.

"Maybe," Morton said angrily. "But give it a chance."

Next came Priscilla, again in a lace-edged night-gown, though with a blue ribbon threaded through the lace. Probably not the one I saw outside Welch's door, Jemma decided, although she might not have spotted the strand of blue from a distance. She was still puzzling over that glimpse of a woman at about seven-ten on Saturday morning, and still keeping it to herself. Priscilla had slept in a small bedroom beyond the Chinese Room, so off she went, after a few gushing remarks.

Finally Loredana herself appeared in a slinky cream silk gown which hid her night-dress, and which Jemma thought she remembered. She took a quick look at Jemma and said at once, "But you weren't wearing that, were you?"

"Is that right?" Morton intervened.

Jemma nodded. "I wanted to see how observant people are. I'll go and change."

"How silly!" Loredana commented nastily. "As if we haven't all got eyes in our heads. It's time your daughter grew up, Mr. Savage." She walked off vexedly to the Chinese Room.

"I think she was trying out an idea," Jim apologized.

Morton was tempted to add, "and wasting police time," but refrained. He and Jim were now alone at the head of the great staircase and an incongruous pair they made, with Morton in his blazer and dark trousers and Jim in a frayed brown woollen dressing-gown that ought to have been replaced several Christmases ago. Jemma sometimes commented that if he dressed like that it was no wonder Pauline had left him, but he refused to throw it away. None the less he felt pretty stupid standing there in it now. In fact, he wondered if it wasn't part of Morton's plan to make them all feel embarrassed and likely to say things they did not intend.

"So what did you do first thing yesterday morning?" Morton demanded.

Jim had no problem recollecting this. "I woke up, heard footsteps in the passage, which was probably the maid. Then I went to the bathroom across the passage and saw her delivering tea-trays."

"What time was that?"

"Perhaps seven-oh-five or seven-oh-six. You must remember, Inspector, that none of us knew when the action would start."

This was a point that had not been emphasized before. Of course the Gilroys had known when the screaming would begin. So had the maid. But not anyone else. Yet, as Morton now appreciated, it had somehow become accepted as a fixed point in the morning's action, around which Welch's murder might have been planned.

"But you knew when the tea would be brought?" Morton argued.

"Yes. But not when the 'murder' would be discovered."

Morton grunted acknowledgement of this, asked Jim to go his room, and went downstairs to make sure the maid was ready to start.

He found Tracy in fierce argument with Dodgson.

"They're not going to drink the tea, so what's the point in making it?"

"It's a re-enactment," Dodgson was insisting in his high-pitched voice. "If the police want it like it was, then we do like it was. Anyway, I made the tea, didn't I?"

"You did?" Morton said, catching the words as he came into the kitchen.

"Who's that?" Dodgson started as though addressed by a ghost. "Oh, it's you, sir. Yes. I'm just reminding Tracy here that I made each teapot myself and she took them up in turn."

"And who had which tray?"

Tracy gazed along the row of nine trays. "Well"—she pointed to the most elegant, flower-patterned teaset—"that's always Lord and Lady Gilroy's. Then there was a separate one for Lady Gilroy as Mrs. Sketchley. The Wedgwood ones always go to the Chinese

Room. Welch had the ugly blue." She pointed to the most ordinary of the tea-sets, a small chunky blue pot and a far from elegant cup and saucer. "Wouldn't give him anything better."

"Common as dirt, that man," Dodgson added, quivering slightly, so that Morton wondered if he had some ailment.

"And had it been used when you brought it down again?"

"Yes." Tracy was positive about this. "The cup was dirty, though he hadn't drunk much tea. Like I told that Mr. Savage."

"Told him what?" Morton reacted with annoyance.

"I was telling him about the teacups and how I thought they'd all been used, but one hadn't."

"You realize that evidence ought to be given to the police?"

"Well, it isn't evidence, is it?" Tracy didn't like being criticized.

"All material facts are evidence. Who did not drink their tea?"

This puzzled her. She had to look carefully along the line of trays. "I can't honestly remember," she confessed at last. "But one cup was clean."

"Not Welch's?"

"Nope. Not his."

"And what else happened?"

"That schmuck McMountdown came wanting coffee, 'cos he doesn't drink tea." Tracy made a face. "He and that woman he's having it off with make a right pair; as selfish as you like, the both of them."

Morton picked up on this fast and began finding out just how much the two servants knew about Hamish's affair with Loredana. But Tracy could not say for sure whether Hamish had spent the night in Loredana's room or not. When she'd left the tray outside the Chinese Room, it had been Loredana's voice that called out "Thank you," though she did recall that Hamish had come down the back stairs, which were closer to the Chinese Room than the main staircase. And also, Morton thought to himself, less observed by other people than the ones leading to the Great Hall.

Shortly after this interrogation Tracy began delivering tea-trays to the rooms. She took Dee Dee's first and repeated the action of giving a tray to her. Next she took trays to Adrienne's room and to Welch, calling out, "Your tea's outside," as she put the tray down on the little table in the alcove outside Welch's door. Finally she served those nearest to the east wing. Jim and Jemma heard her and re-played their own actions of Saturday morning, coming out to the passage.

"No other footsteps going past," Jim commented.

"And no woman in a night-dress," Jemma added, looking along towards Welch's door. The re-enactment time was seven-ten.

Then, to their astonishment, they did see movement at the far end. It was Hamish and he was coming in their direction, right past Morton, who was standing at the head of the stairs. The Savages both hesitated. Jemma picked up her tray and dodged into her room. But Jim was deliberately slower, so that Hamish had to walk past him.

"On my way to the kitchen to find some coffee," Hamish ex-plained. "I never drink tea." Then he continued towards the back stairs.

Jim went into his daughter's room and they both roared with laughter.

"No way did he go past yesterday," Jemma said.

"The poor devil has to pretend he was with his wife."

"Do we point that out to the inspector?"

"Why should we?" A distant streak of wickedness, or perhaps only wilfulness, took possession of Jim. The re-enactment was fill-ing him with the excitement of the chase. "All it actually tells us is that Hamish was either with Loredana or in the kitchen at the time Welch died."

The noise of someone coming along the corridor made them both fall silent. After the footsteps Jemma opened her door and saw the maid, this time not carrying any tray. Tracy must have come up the back stairs and was now going along towards the State Room. She stopped by the main staircase, close to Morton, and looked im-patiently at her watch, just as she had done before.

"Did Mr. McMountdown come down to the kitchen yester-day?" Morton asked her softly.

"Sure he did." Tracy echoed Dee Dee's Americanisms yet again. "He wanted coffee. I was just taking tea up to Mr. Welch."

"You started at the east wing of the house?"

"Yes. After I brought the tray to Lady Gilroy I took tea to the actress first, then to Mrs. Chancemain, then to the father and daughter, then to that Mr. Welch. Then the others." The tone in which Tracy referred to Welch was caustic enough to alert any detective.

"You didn't like him?"

"He . . . he tried what her ladyship calls 'goosing' me. That's why I wouldn't take a tray into his room. Forget it. No way. Her ladyship said if he tried it again I could sue him."

"So when you'd delivered all the trays, what did you do?"

It seemed to Morton that Tracy had been in an exceptionally good position to poison Welch. She could have slipped whatever substance it was into his teapot and no one would have been any the wiser, and she'd washed all the cups within an hour. But what possible motive could she have?

"I was hanging around up here and that girl, the nice one who's a reporter, she come out into the passage. Just like she done now. Well, I felt stupid just standing here. So I went downstairs, had a quick cuppa tea and then came up again at seven-thirty."

Morton checked his watch. So far the timing was roughly what they had all claimed. She would have gone down again at about seven-seventeen. It was now nearly at the half hour.

"So at seven-thirty you started screaming?"

"That's right." Tracy gathered herself together, walked along the passage and knocked on the State Bedroom door. When there was no answer she entered and emerged again seconds later, screaming lustily.

"She's dead! Help!"

Jim emerged from his room, so did Jemma, and they hurried down the passage, deliberately taking no notice of Morton standing there. Dulcie appeared from the other side of the State Room and after a minute or so Loredana came along, closely followed by Priscilla.

"Oh my God!" Priscilla yelled, not one to forget a part she had already rehearsed, and making a run for the State Room door. "Mrs. Sketchley's been murdered!"

Morton winced. All his instincts and training were revolted by this play-acting, when there had been a genuine corpse in a next-door room. But had Welch been dead then? He did not know precisely when the victim had died and he was not at all sure that the constable inside Welch's room would hear anything worthwhile.

Next Adrienne appeared, not as bleary-eyed as she actually had been, but conscientiously wearing the same night-dress trimmed with lace. She was not much use at acting. She stood outside her late husband's room as if confused.

"So there I was, Inspector," she said, feeling incredibly foolish in her night-gown and resentful at being forced into this rigmarole. "I came out after all the fuss was over and George wasn't awake."

"How did you know?" Morton demanded.

"Well, he hadn't taken in his tea, had he?"

They both looked at the undisturbed tea-tray deposited by Tracy. The constable had not known whether to take it in or not. And this, Morton realized with a sense of futility, was where the re-enactment failed. It was a hundred to one that Welch had been poisoned via his early-morning tea, that most British of institutions, a ritual that had once ruled the world from Australia to the Indies, and found its dying expression in country houses like this. But whoever had poisoned it was hardly likely to come forward now. At least, not unless he or she had exceptional cool.

"Did you go into his room?" Morton asked.

"There was no sense disturbing him, was there?" Adrienne said. "Not with his temper. All I'd have got was an earful."

"So you did not go in?" He was convinced that she must have done.

What wife would not? No matter what any columnist wrote, women were the dominant sex. And likely to remain so, he thought a trifle bitterly. His own wife was an example. He should never have married a policewoman, who knew far too much about what his job entailed. On the other hand, she did understand the tensions. He was lucky there. He was not at all certain that George Welch had been similarly fortunate.

This train of thought was interrupted by Hamish's coming up the main staircase. He too was word-perfect. "What's the matter?" he asked.

Dulcie was waiting for him, but Jim noticed that she answered differently.

"So you found some coffee," she said, as if she had known he had been in the kitchen.

"Can't stand tea, darling. As you know."

She could not resist giving him a filthy look, as if she would like to have rammed the cup down his throat, but made no comment. It was humiliating enough to have this bogus scene played out.

Now Dee Dee emerged from the State Room, resplendent in her scarlet housecoat, announced that breakfast would be at nine and was about to depart when Morton stopped her.

"If you don't mind, Lady Gilroy, I'd like to ask what you did over the next hour or so."

Dee Dee answered with a display of graciousness, as befitted a "grande dame" of English society. "I showered, glanced through the morning paper, then my husband and I had breakfast together."

"Not with the others?"

"Certainly not." The disdain in Dee Dee's voice was perceptible. "We joined them for the main meals, never for breakfast. Lunch is bad enough."

Morton thought about his usual snatched breakfasts of cereal and coffee, before hastening back to the office for whatever emergency had erupted. There always was an emergency. This stately home constituted another world. He recalled a society woman who had poisoned her husband, telling the jury, "For better or worse, but never for lunch," as though that explained everything. She had been sent down for twenty years. Rightly. She had been a killer. Women, Morton believed, were much more sophisticated killers than men.

While Morton was talking to Dee Dee, Jim moved across to the area by Welch's door. For some architectural reason the doorway was in a small recess, like a tiny lobby. A small table had been placed there for the tea-tray, but there was no tray. Presumably the detective inside the room had retrieved it after Tracy knocked on the door.

At this moment, Jim recalled, with certainty, that at the equivalent time on Saturday the tray had been there on the low table, and he felt equally sure that it had not been used. Furthermore, it had been there when he and Jemma had gone down to breakfast later. Tracy had said his cup had been used, so at some point Welch must have taken it in. But he emphatically was not the kind of man who would have helped servants by taking it out again. It hardly needed the sixth sense that had made Jim a successful loss adjuster to tell him that this smelt all wrong.

"And what did I do?" Loredana was now being interviewed by Morton a few yards away. "After the 'murder' I went back to my room. I couldn't understand why it had to be so dreadfully early. Oh yes, when I went down to breakfast I took my tea-tray with me. The staff really are rather overworked here."

Overhearing these remarks, Jim reflected that Loredana was hardly the caring kind either, at least not in her other actions. But she had indisputedly taken her tray down, since Tracy had mentioned it. This thought was interrupted by the arrival of Adrienne, apologizing.

"As I didn't go along for the screaming," she explained, I thought you wouldn't want me now. But then I thought, well, probably he does."

"Did you stay in your room until breakfast time?" Morton asked. "You didn't go along to see your husband?"

"Well, yes," she admitted, "I did at about ten to eight. But he hadn't had his tea, I mean, the tray was still outside his room. So I didn't disturb him. He could be very tetchy, George could. And then"—her voice began to tremble—"when I did go to wake him up later, he was . . ."

Morton reached out to steady her as she collapsed into tears, and guided her to one of the high-backed chairs that were ranged at intervals along the passage.

Then he opened Welch's door, went in and asked the constable what he had heard. The answer was, "Just about everything, I should say, sir."

So the re-enactment was concluded, except that Morton gathered everyone together and asked, with apparent naïvety, if there was anything they had failed to mention.

There was a general shaking of heads and Jim noticed that Morton had his eye on Hamish, who had so obviously lied about his movements. But the inspector said nothing. Nor did Hamish or Dulcie.

"And when did you all leave your rooms again?"

One by one they explained when they had gone down to breakfast. These movements were all after the estimated time span of Welch's death, between seven-fifteen and eight. Accordingly Morton told them they could go, and with considerable relief they all trooped off to their inferior rooms in the servants' wing.

"Damn," Jim said as they passed through the green baize door, "I've left something behind." He doubled back briefly to his former room, not unnoticed by Morton, before rejoining Jemma.

"So," Jemma asked him, when he caught up with her again, "who was cheating?"

"More a question of who wasn't! I'd say just about everyone, except Lady Gilroy. How McMountdown can think no one knows he went along the passage to Loredana at about midnight beats me. I suppose it's only loss of face that prevented his wife from ratting on him."

"It doesn't make sense that Adrienne went to see her husband and then didn't go in either, does it?" Jemma observed. "And she burst into tears at a very convenient moment."

"And what about your mystery woman?"

"She didn't do her thing, for sure."

"Even I cheated, I'm afraid." Jim sighed. "Can't really trust myself. While you were in your room I took the chance of having a quick word with Priscilla."

"You sneaky old thing!"

"I hoped she might have left one of Friday's clues in her original room. But she hadn't." He grinned, rather like a naughty boy. "She was quite surprised. And I don't know if Morton saw me either."

"He would have said so."

"He still might. He was playing that re-enactment very astutely, not challenging what anyone pretended to have done. But I'm going to tackle that man McMountdown."

When they had dressed and gone down to the library again Jim did exactly that, much to Jemma's embarrassment, asking Hamish very quietly why he had changed his movements.

Hamish looked at him in surprise and anger. "That is nothing to do with George's death," he said under his breath. "And none of your bloody business."

"You'll tell Morton privately?"

"He can find out for himself if he wants to. And I'll thank you to keep your nose out of my affairs."

12

THE REACTION to Jim Savage's brief quarrel with Hamish came unexpectedly quickly. When they had all gathered in the library for drinks before dinner, Loredana came up to him, drew him aside and asked to talk to him in private. Privacy was not so easily obtainable, due to the police being around and the restrictions on the rooms the guests could use. As with Dulcie, Jim suggested they take a stroll in the park. Their departure did not go unnoticed.

"Your father seems to be playing the confessor again," Dee Dee remarked to Jemma. "What's he up to now?"

"Search me," Jemma said candidly. "She was quite patronizing to me last night."

"She's too attractive for her own good," Dee Dee said sagely, after they had gone.

"D'you think she could have murdered Welch?"

"What on earth for? From what she says, she never met the man before." Dee Dee reached to take a gin and tonic from the silver salver Dodgson was taking round. "But then why should any of us have?" She caught sight of Adrienne entering the room and corrected her statement. "Well, most of us. Nobody liked him, but to suggest that my husband might have killed him in order to get out of the contract is crazy. Buck hadn't signed it. He'd agreed to it, but he hadn't signed."

"Is that what Morton thinks?" Jemma asked.

Dee Dee laughed savagely. "He'd have Buck in the cooler right now, if he had any proof. But of course he hasn't, because he didn't do it." She was becoming quite defensive of her husband, now that things were turning serious. "My husband is a bit of an idiot sometimes, but he's not vindictive."

"Unlike Welch?"

"Welch was a bastard. He was paying people in the village to complain about the Lion Park, to try and get it closed down by the authorities."

"That's hardly evidence against Lord Gilroy."

"And there's the morphine," Dee Dee said gloomily. "Somebody's been at the morphine in the medicine cupboard. Morton obviously thinks we laced Welch's morning tea, or the flask of coffee he had, or the whisky."

Jemma made further commiserating noises, wondering how her father was getting on. She could see through the high windows that it was a lovely evening for a stroll, though she wasn't sure that Loredana would be the perfect companion.

Outside, it was indeed beautiful. The early-evening sun glittered on the lake, which was stirred by a light breeze, and gilded a little stone pavilion that the first Lord Gilroy had built for picnics.

"Shall we go down there?" Jim suggested.

Loredana glanced doubtfully at her feet. She had on the lightest, most supple Italian evening shoes. "I only wear Bruno Magli," she always told her friends. But would these elegant creations get her through the grass to the lake?

"I'm not really dressed for it," she said.

She was indeed in a silk evening dress, and Jim felt immediately remorseful. He was too accustomed to Jemma racing around everywhere in the clumsy boots that she thought fashionable. Loredana was altogether more delicate.

"Let's find a bench," he suggested. "If it's not too cold."

"Oh, I'm warm enough," she assured him. "Anyway, it won't take very long."

They found a garden bench and settled down.

"So how can I help you?" Jim asked.

Loredana turned impulsively towards him and fixed her hazel eyes on his. "You know about Hamish and me, don't you?"

"I'd guessed."

"We are terribly in love. I've never been in love like this before. It's the real thing. You have to believe me."

Jim nodded. "You're going to leave your husband?" he asked sympathetically.

"As soon as I can. And Hamish is leaving Dulcie, but she's being very difficult. Otherwise we'd be together already and we'd never have come on this dreadful weekend." She shuddered. "I can't believe it's happening. How did we ever get involved?"

"I thought Hamish had business connections with Mr. Welch."

"Not that mattered." Loredana was dismissive. "No, we were here to make up the numbers. George didn't want any other outsiders if possible." She realized she had made a faintly insulting remark. "I'm so sorry, because I know you're outsiders. But you see what I mean."

"Don't worry. I'm not offended." Jim doubted if this was all she wanted to say and prompted her. "So actually Hamish spent last night with you?"

"How did you know?" She sounded genuinely surprised. "Dulcie was fast asleep and he came along to my room."

"Around midnight?"

Loredana paled. "Yes."

"Jemma heard footsteps in the passage. She's a very light sleeper."

"We were together the whole night. When the maid came round with the tea, he went down to the kitchen to get some coffee. And that's where he was when the screaming started." She switched on all her charm. "I admit it was terribly stupid of us. He should have left much earlier and gone back before Dulcie woke up."

"We did hear somebody. It wasn't him?"

"Definitely not. Perhaps it was Priscilla." Loredana smiled. "She is a bit unpredictable."

"You're probably right. Jemma caught sight of a woman in a night-dress."

"Hardly Hamish! He has that awful dressing-gown. That is one thing that will have to go when we're together. That and his striped pyjamas." She laughed prettily. "What nonsense I'm talking. The thing is, we don't want Dulcie humiliated."

"So this afternoon he had to pretend that he'd been with her?"

Loredana nodded. "You see, it would be so hurtful for her if everyone knew. We have to protect her until the weekend's over."

"Yes, I can see that." Jim said non-committally, surprised at this solicitude for the woman she was supplanting. "So you'd rather I said nothing to the inspector?"

"If you could." She gazed at him imploringly.

"But he would keep it to himself," Jim assured her, thinking that Morton must have wondered why Hamish had gone straight along the corridor to the back stairs in his quest for coffee, rather than down the main staircase. Hamish did not seem a back-stairs type of man. Presumably one of the staff had seen him come down the back stairs on Saturday morning, so he had to go that way.

"Can one trust the police?" Loredana asked. "It would be too awful if he mentioned it, and then everyone would be staring at Dulcie and us."

"All right," Jim agreed. "I won't say anything." Then it occurred to him to add what should have been obvious. "Of course, being to-gether does give you both an alibi."

"An alibi?" For a few seconds Loredana was puzzled. "You mean for the murder. Oh, but how silly. Why on earth should either of us want to hurt Welch? I'd never set eyes on him before."

"So that doesn't worry you?"

"Not one bit. The important thing is that Hamish and I were terribly stupid and we must keep it secret."

"Well, I promise to do my best."

"Thank you so much." Loredana leaned across and kissed him quickly on the cheek. "I knew you'd understand."

Back at the house, in his interview-room, Inspector Morton, was already on to the same subject. He was having everyone unobtru-sively watched, and Timmins had seen Jim and Loredana go out.

"Probably sweet-talking Savage into keeping quiet about her lover," Morton remarked cynically, "as though everyone doesn't know. And why did Savage nip off down the passage while we were doing the re-enactment? I must have words with that man." He shifted to a more immediate question. "Whose fingerprints were on the morphine bottle?"

"Mainly the butler's. The others are quite old and overlaid by his." Timmins paused. "You do know, sir, that morphine is very fast-acting."

"The pathologist told me. And it tastes bitter, so it would have made whisky taste odd. If Welch was given morphine he must have only taken it around seven and in a liquid that disguised the taste."

"Strong tea?"

"That's probably how Welch liked his. Used to work on building sites, didn't he?" Morton tapped away on the table with his Biro, as he always did when perplexed. "For the sake of argument, if the opiate—and we still don't know what it was—was in Welch's morning tea, who put it there? Don't tell me! Just about everyone could have done. The butler or the maid before it was taken up. Lady Gilroy when the tray was outside Welch's door. Welch's wife, because it's hard to believe she went to his door and didn't go in. If McMountdown did as he pretended this afternoon, he could have done. But they'd have had to do it before the screaming began, because afterwards there were too many people around."

"Assuming they had the poison," Timmins observed.

"And the motive." Morton began clearing his papers from the table, preparatory to locking them up. "Let's get back to the Carpenters' Arms. I could use a beer."

The pleasure of being hosted at dinner by the Gilroys had lost its appeal for this weekend's guests. The brochure had promised that Sunday evening would see the climax of the murder-mystery weekend, when clues were unravelled. George Welch would have been dramatically denounced as the killer of Mrs. Sketchley. Then there would have been a final champagne toast, a speech by Lord Gilroy, and everyone would have gone to bed happy. On Monday morning they would all have left Wittenham Park, ready to sing its praises to anyone in search of an amusing and unusual weekend.

"Unusual it has been," Dee Dee remarked to Buck as they prepared to join their guests again, "amusing absolutely not. I wish to God that inspector could get on and arrest someone. For my money it's Welch's wife. She admits she stands to clean up a million or so."

But after the avocado mousse decorated with prawns had been served, and they were waiting for the main course of roast turkey, it was Priscilla who became the target. Furthermore, the way that this came about seemed curious to Jim.

The seating arrangements were the same as before, with Dee and Gilroy at either end, while Hamish faced Priscilla across the centre. Quite unexpectedly, Hamish turned the subject on to who saw Welch last.

"That ridiculous re-enactment missed the point," he said. "What matters is who saw George last and who had the opportunity to give him poison." He eyed Priscilla. "You told us yourself that you drugged his cocoa."

"Which then put me out for the count," Dulcie cut in. She was still aggrieved at this having facilitated her husband's infidelity.

"And that he tried to rape you," Hamish continued relentlessly. "What else went on?"

A discreet cough interrupted them. Dodgson and Tracy were in the doorway, waiting to hand round plates as Gilroy carved the turkey.

"I think the whole thing's disgusting," Adrienne complained. "Talking about the dead like that when they can't answer back." She dabbed at her eyes, though she had become noticeably more composed since this morning. Then, as Dodgson placed a helping of turkey in front of her, she looked sideways at him and made an accusation. "And what were you doing, may I ask, letting his cocoa be drugged? Cocoa! George would never have drunk that stuff anyway. What he wanted was whisky, and you know it!"

Dodgson drew himself to his full five feet nine inches and stepped back a pace, making sure that the entire table could hear him.

"That is correct, madam," he said in his screechy voice. "And not once, but twice, since you ask."

"What do you mean, twice?" Adrienne demanded, but sounding unnerved. "There was only one decanter in his room."

"A second was sent up not long before midnight." He glanced apologetically at Dee Dee. "His lordship's instructions were to give the guests whatever they wanted."

"That was carrying it a bit far, Dodgson," Gilroy said, standing back from the sideboard, the carving knife and fork still in his hands. "Too damn far, frankly."

"Are you accusing my husband of being a drunkard?" Adrienne shrilled.

"I'm accusing my butler of being a fool," Gilroy snapped with a terseness that he seldom displayed. The whole scenario was getting on his nerves.

That's torn it, Jim thought. Now Dodgson will spill the beans about Priscilla's having taken up the second decanter. He was right.

"If that is your lordship's opinion," Dodgson said with all the dignity he could manage, while Tracy stood by the door trying not to titter, "your lordship may like to know that the second decanter was requested for him by Mrs. Worthington."

There was a traditionally deathly hush, of just the kind Dee Dee had planned when the murderer was revealed.

"And what were you doing taking my George whisky, may I ask? In the middle of the night?"

There was no convincing answer to this question, which Priscilla knew. However, she made an attempt.

"When I took him the cocoa he asked for more whisky."

"As if you were the maid?"

Priscilla looked imploringly down the table at Jim. "He understands."

Jim decided to do his best and confirmed that the "murder" had required Welch to give "poisoned" cocoa to Mrs. Sketchley, which Priscilla had taken up. Then he had demanded more whisky.

"I think Mrs. Worthington faced a dilemma," Jim said, measuring his words. "She was employed to make the murder plot work. She had not anticipated Mr. Welch's request. What else could she do?"

"Keep herself to herself," Adrienne said bitterly.

"None the less," Dulcie said in her clear voice, "this means that Priscilla was the last person to see George last night, not me."

She had been careful to say "last night" rather than "alive."

While this was going on, the butler had been standing immobile, so Gilroy asked him to continue and, when he returned to the sideboard, muttered, "Sorry, Dodgson. This business is getting on all our nerves."

"I don't believe a word of it," Adrienne restarted the dispute. She had long been suspicious of Dulcie's late-night meetings with her husband, but this was worse. "And how long did you stay in my husband's room, Mrs. Worthington? Half the night, I suppose?"

"No!" The cry was wrung out of Priscilla. "He wanted to talk, but I didn't. I was hardly there ten minutes."

"Talk? At that time of night?" Adrienne could conjure up a good line in scorn and at last she had a target for her resentment at George's infidelities.

This was too much for Priscilla. Genuine tears filled her eyes, her mascara began to run, and she found herself shaking uncontrollably. She was fifty years old and out of work, but she was of good family, and here she was being treated like a slut by a thoroughly common woman. She got up from her chair.

"I can't . . ." she began, then sobbed, "I won't be treated like this. All I was trying to do was help."

As she walked unsteadily towards the door, Jim sprang to his feet, took her arm, and guided her back to the library.

"Dodgson," Dee Dee said with total calm, "you'd better put Mr. Savage's meal in the oven to keep warm. I don't expect Mrs. Worthington will be wanting hers." She turned to Hamish. "Now why on earth did you start all that going? Let's please talk about something else. The weather. Anything."

She was right, Jemma thought. Why had Hamish provoked this conversation? He must have known where it might lead, except that he could not have known that the butler would let the cat out of the bag about the whisky. She was tempted to follow her father out, but decided against it. He would deal with Priscilla better by himself.

In the library Jim guided the actress to a sofa, where she collapsed. He put one arm round her shoulders, trying to comfort her, as she sobbed unrestrainedly. She felt terribly thin under the gauzy top of her dress and it struck him that she probably didn't eat much at home, probably had next to no money. For all her usual bravado, she was rather a pathetic creature, and as her shoulders heaved he felt increasingly sorry for her.

After a few minutes she began to calm down a little, repeating to herself, "How could that woman say such a thing!" in a dazed way. "He was a horrible man."

"What really happened?" Jim asked, remembering how previously Priscilla had joked about the encounter and said she had only just escaped being raped. But it was quite possible that Welch had said more than she appreciated. What had been his state of mind? As Jim probed, a more complicated picture emerged.

WELCH had been dressed when she entered and sitting in one of the bedroom armchairs, a near-empty glass of whisky on a table beside him, together with an empty decanter. He did not get up.

"That took a bloody long time," he said belligerently. "What kept you?"

"The butler wasn't very pleased." Priscilla was nervous. It looked as though Welch was at least half drunk. "I had to talk him into it."

"Ten quid not enough, eh?"

"Money isn't everything."

"Try that on the wife!" Welch hoisted himself more upright. "Why not have a quick one now you're here, eh?" He pushed his own tumbler across the table towards her. "Haven't got another glass."

"I really won't. I've been drinking gin. I'd be ill."

"Well, sit down, girl. Don't just stand there. And give me that bottle."

She approached closer, put the second decanter on the chest of drawers, then sat down cautiously on the other bedroom chair, well away from him. If it hadn't been for the money she would have left, but she lacked the nerve to demand it outright.

"Money ain't everything, you said?" He took a swig from his glass, finishing it. "I'll tell you one thing: my wife wouldn't give a damn if I died. She'd be in clover."

Priscilla murmured something placatory.

"Doesn't understand me. Has to have separate beds. What kind of a marriage is that, for Christ's sake?"

It was so obvious where this was leading that she headed him off by asking how he was enjoying the weekend.

"Bloody waste of time." He picked up a formal-looking document from the table. "Look at this bloody contract! That bugger McMountdown was going to talk Gilroy into signing. What's Gilroy done? Changed the f——ing conditions and wants me to sign first."

Priscilla had no idea what this was about, so she simply nodded.

"And Dulcie says I ought to sign! Me! She's my lawyer, but whose side is she on? Says it's as far as he'll go." Welch leaned forward to emphasize the point. "If I don't get the right bit of land it's not worth so much. Stands to reason. But she'd like to get her husband off the hook."

Again this meant nothing, and Priscilla did not know how she was going to extract the twenty pounds from him either. She'd promised the butler half.

"I really ought to be going," she said. "How about the twenty quid?"

"Twenty smackers for that? You gotta be joking. Here, better take this with you." Welch got to his feet and picked up the empty decanter. "Don't want the wife finding two bottles in here."

Priscilla accepted the decanter and then said, as firmly as she dared, "I have to give the money to the butler."

"Give us a kiss first then." Welch lurched towards her, collided with the table and the tumbler slid off. It fell on the carpet, rolled against the table leg and cracked. Welch swore and seemed momentarily to sober up. "Oh Christ, there goes his lordship's fancy glass." He looked round. "Where's the bloody waste-bin?"

"Why don't you throw it out of the window?" Priscilla suggested, seeing an escape route.

"Now there's a thought." Welch wobbled across to the window, pulled back the curtains and swung one of the windows open. As he did so, Priscilla reached the door and made her escape.

"AND THAT was all that happened?" Jim asked.

"I swear it was." Priscilla had recovered a little in telling the story. "He was just a dirty old man."

"Would you like to go back into dinner?"

She hesitated, then shook her head. She was still trembling. "I don't think I could face them."

"But you must have something to eat." There was hardly anything of her and he firmly believed in women's eating enough, which some of them never did.

"I couldn't swallow a thing. I'll just go to bed."

"Let me take you up." He escorted her back through the Great Hall to the servants' staircase and up to her room.

"Bless you," she said, in quite an affectionate way, when they reached her door. "You're the only one who understands." She gave him a quick kiss on the cheek, making him think that he was being kissed rather more than usual today. And if he "understood," it was basically because he had said nothing, simply listened. Then he returned to dinner.

"Is she all right?" Dee Dee asked. She had obligations as a hostess, whatever her guests might feel. "Dodgson will bring back your plate in a moment."

"She will be in the morning." This assurance earned a scowl from Adrienne, and silence from Hamish.

"We were talking about cricket," Dee Dee said as brightly as she could.

"Hampshire are doing fantastically this season," Gilroy backed her up.

This determined attempt to keep off the subject of murder continued until the meal was finished, though Jim wished the discussion had been less forced. He was a fan of the game himself.

At last, over coffee in the library, he was able to talk to Jemma.

"Why were they ganging up on Priscilla?" he asked.

"I couldn't work that out, Daddy." Jemma was as perplexed as he was. "She hadn't really done anything, had she?"

"Not so far as I can tell. But she'll find it hard to live down being the last person to see Welch alive. If she was."

"You mean someone else wants to emphasize that?"

"It's not impossible. But she solved two small mysteries for me. I now know where the missing whisky glass and the decanter are. And they have nothing to do with the crime."

He had hardly said this before the loud clanging of a bell interrupted all their conversations.

Gilroy leaped up. "The fire alarm," he said "Probably a false alarm, but we'd better all get out on the lawn."

He began shepherding everybody out of the library as a policeman ran in and asked where the fire extinguishers were kept. "There's a fire upstairs," he shouted. "Someone call nine-nine-nine."

Gilroy sprinted to pick up a large red canister from near the hall door, the policeman took another, and the men all pounded up the great staircase.

The smell of smoke was coming from the servants' wing. As they reached the landing, the automatic sprinklers came on, squirting water down on their heads.

"Try our rooms," Jim shouted, seized by a premonition. Gilroy led the way down the corridor and through the green baize door separating the house from the servants' wing. They were met by a distraught Priscilla running down the passage from her room.

"I didn't mean to," she gasped.

They raced past her and found smoke pouring out of her open bedroom door.

"Can't wait for the fire brigade," Gilroy said. "We must put it out." Without tying a wet cloth over his mouth he dashed inside, saw the curtains were on fire and turned the extinguisher foam onto them.

The curtains could not have been alight more than a minute or two. He doused them successfully, stamped out a small fire on the carpet and saw, to his astonishment, that the cause had been a piece of clothing set alight on a tin-tray on the floor.

Twenty minutes later the fire brigade arrived, its appliances churning up the gravel of the drive, and the entire household was assembled in the hall, while the chief fire officer made an inspection.

Priscilla stood clinging to Jim's arm, weeping and saying repeatedly, "I didn't mean to do it. I swear I didn't."

For the first time since the weekend began, Dee Dee hugged her husband, praising his bravery. And for the first time George Welch was forgotten.

"What on earth are we going to do with Mrs. Worthington?" Gilroy asked.

13

"Do you want her charged with arson, sir?" Morton was asking Gilroy.

It was Monday morning and the two men had just concluded a visit to the smoke-grimed bedroom where Gilroy's unquestioned courage had prevented a blaze. Luck had played a part too. The curtains were made of an old, thin cotton print material and were unlined. Although they had burnt, they had not flared with the intensity that more modern materials would have and Gilroy had doused them before either the carpet or the window could catch fire. The ceiling was partially blackened. Powdered ash covered the furniture. And on the floor were the scorched remains of Priscilla's lace-trimmed night-gown on an equally scorched tin-tray which she had borrowed from the kitchen.

"I wanted to get rid of it," she had explained to Morton, her voice only just under control. "But the curtains caught fire." Then she had added, as if it were a complete explanation, "You see, the room hasn't got a fireplace."

"Either she's crazy or she was drunk," Gilroy said. In spite of his own decisiveness at the time, he was still dazed by the realization that the entire house could have been burnt down. This was one hell of a weekend. "Of course, she was extremely upset after Mrs. Welch was so foul at dinner."

"I'd like to know about that," said Morton.

"Ask Savage. He's the chap. Comforted the wretched woman afterwards." Gilroy pondered for a minute. Mrs. Worthington had been employed to help dramatize the original weekend, but not to this extent. Trust an actress to carry things too far. "What's the point in prosecuting her," he asked, "if she's as loopy as they come?"

"Not a lot, sir," Morton said sympathetically. Although Gilroy remained a prime suspect, this episode had slightly redeemed his character. The army must have taught him something, even if heredity had not. "Why do you think she did it?"

"Search me, Inspector. Why didn't she give the night-gown to the maid, or just throw it away?" Suddenly he remembered a remark of hers, a throw-away line about having been called a pyromaniac. "She was accused of trying to burn down a theatre once. She told us it was all libel. If you want to know how her mind works, you'd better ask Savage. Last night she kept saying he was the only person who understood her."

After Gilroy had gone, Morton went through the most recent reports that his interviewing teams had sent in. Whereas Mrs. Worthington was known locally as being eccentric and theatrical, Savage emerged as unshakeably respectable. His daughter was thought a bit wild, but so what? None of the three had any known connection with Welch. Nor, for that matter, did Loredana Chancemain, even though her affair with Hamish was the talk of her village. This didn't rule them out. You could never rule anyone out until you had the truth. Even so, Morton came to a decision that he did not entirely relish. He was going to ask Savage's advice. But he would start with a tough question.

"I'd like to ask you something, Mr. Savage," he began his interview, "and I'd appreciate a straight answer. Why did you go off down the passage after the re-enactment yesterday?"

"I wanted to test a theory."

"What exactly?"

"That what you find depends on what you imagine you are looking for, not what is actually there."

"Fairly obvious, I'd have said." Morton bridled at being told his business.

"To take a case in point, have you found the missing whisky decanter?"

"In fact, we haven't."

"That was what I went down the passage to look for. Unfortunately, Mrs. Worthington was still in her former room, so I failed, and came straight back." Jim didn't mind if he irritated Morton mildly, and in any case he had pursued another objective at the same time. "As you will recall."

"The decanter can't be in that room. It's been searched twice."

"Shall we go and see?"

Somewhat reluctantly Morton allowed himself to be led up the narrow servants' stairs, through the green baize door into the main part of the house and to the small bedroom that Dee Dee had originally allocated the actress. It did not have an en suite bathroom, but it did have a wash-basin. And, as was customary in country houses, there was a carafe of water with a tumbler placed upside-down over its neck. His more affluent friends would have provided their guests with a bottle of mineral water, possibly bottled on their own estates. But economy in small things was the order of the day at Wittenham. Priscilla Worthington was allocated plain drinking water.

"So?" Morton asked, looking around.

"So here is your decanter," Jim said, pointing to the carafe and removing the tumbler. "Not the best cut-glass and missing its stopper. But I'm sure the butler will identify it." He sniffed the neck. "Mrs. Worthington didn't wash it out very thoroughly."

Morton took a tissue from his pocket, picked up the decanter carefully, smelt the faint odour of whisky and was obliged to agree.

"How did you know?" he demanded.

"It was not in Welch's room. She was the last person to see him. She could not have carried it with her when your men moved her to another room. So it had to be here. Quite cunning of her, though."

"She's a very foxy lady, that one," Morton remarked. "Why should she burn her night-dress?"

Jim shrugged his shoulders. He had a theory about that which was too undeveloped to expound. "You'll have to ask her that yourself. But I can tell you where Welch's whisky glass ought to be."

Ten minutes later a detective was recovering a broken whisky tumbler from the shrubbery beneath the window of Welch's bedroom.

"I'll be surprised if it tells them anything," Jim remarked to Jemma, as they watched from a distance. "Any more than the decanter will. Morton admitted the poison was fast-acting. In fact, I got the impression he knows what it was, though he isn't going to let on. Either way, it was a bright idea of Priscilla's to suggest throwing the glass out of the window, so that she could get away. Just the gesture to appeal to Welch. Mud in the eye of the aristocracy, all that sort thing."

"If she's as switched on as that, why on earth did she burn her night-dress on the floor?"

He made a slightly despairing gesture with his hands. "That's what Morton wanted to know. I'm no shrink. I can only guess at what went on in her mind. She's emotional. As an actress she responds quickly. She was very upset last night."

"I don't blame her."

"I think she probably started drinking in her room. She hadn't eaten anything. The alcohol went straight to her head. She needed to protest against being insulted."

"Why burn her own night-dress?" Jemma made a face. "Especially when night-dresses are the only clue I've got to the mystery woman!"

"She might feel it was associated with the whole disastrous night. After all, this was a disaster for her. She was being paid to perform. Welch's death changed all that. Now she's stuck here, not being paid, and being villified into the bargain."

"Could she have killed Welch?"

"I've no doubt she'd like to kill his widow."

"Where is Priscilla now?" Jemma felt quite sorry for her and intended to help her.

"Avoiding everybody, I expect." He knew she'd had breakfast taken to her on a tray. "They gave her another room. The Gilroys would like to have locked her in a padded cell, and called in the men in white coats." He had overheard Dee Dee on the subject.

"I'll go and look for her," Jemma said. "What are you up to?"

"Might go for a stroll."

It was another glorious day. How sad that this drama was being played out against a background of perfect English weather, when everyone should have been enjoying themselves. Not, of course, that they would be doing so on a Monday. Most people would be working. For the first time since he had arrived here Jim remembered that when he did get home himself, he would be going to a life without a job, and felt a sudden pang in his gut. It was all very well being an amateur detective, pointing out clues to the professionals, but the inspector had a job and every prospect of promotion. He himself had neither. Then he pulled himself together and set off towards the Lion Park. He had a feeling that something might be going on there.

He was right. Lord Gilroy was outside the headquarters building, in earnest discussion with Sergeant Timmins and one of the wardens. When he approached them Timmins immediately stopped talking and Gilroy called out, in a strained way, "Want to have a drive round the park? One of the boys will take you."

Jim hesitated. There was nothing much else to do. On the other hand, he wanted to talk to Gilroy about an aspect of the re-enactment that the police seemed to have neglected. Somewhere there must have been a plan for the fictional murder and instructions to the characters on what they were to do. He had been given his own, which had been vague. Others could have been more specific.

"Would you be able to give me a lift back?" he asked. It had taken him quite a time to walk there.

Gilroy looked at Timmins, who muttered something and frowned. "In about half an hour," he replied. "Gary will give you a quick safari."

The warden who was with them went to fetch Gary, while Timmins remained studiously silent, and very soon Jim was in the front of a Land Rover and headed for the gate in the electric fence.

The media stories about the death of Ted Matthews had generated far more visitors than usual. Yesterday having been a fine summer Sunday, the ghoulish had arrived in unprecedented numbers. Even today there was a line of cars waiting to get in, which Gary jumped.

"It's an ill wind what blows nobody no good," he commented as they passed through the gate. "Poor old Ted. He'd have been glad to see the takings go up, but not at the price he paid."

They progressed very slowly behind other cars along the winding tarmac, until they stopped near a pride of lions. The day was warming up and the lions were already somnolent. Their only activity consisted of a lioness's cuffing a cub which was being, in her view, hyperactive.

"Where did the . . . er . . . tragedy take place?" Jim asked. It was almost impossible not to refer to Ted.

"Further on. We was keeping an eye on this lot, while Ted followed Caesar. He darted him just over there."

"Does anyone know what went wrong?"

Gary remained convinced that Ted was not the sort to make mistakes. He said so, adding, "We found the dart yesterday. Needed a metal detector and all."

"You learn much from that?"

"It fell out quite a way from where Caesar finished up." There was doubt in Gary's voice. "Should have worked, though, I'd have thought. Wasn't much liquid left inside."

The cars ahead of them moved on and he shifted into gear again and continued their trundling pace, just two more spectators in a sanitized version of Africa in the English countryside. Except, Jim reminded himself, that it was in no way sanitized. Bringing a lion to Oxfordshire did not transform its natural character. Not far from here the grass had been wet with blood.

"Is there to be an inquest?" Jim asked.

"This arternoon." Gary gave the word his own accent. "I've to be there."

Ninety to one, the verdict would be "accidental death," Jim knew. However you viewed Ted's killing, it had been an accident. Appalling. Tragic. Deserving all the adjectives the media used. But still an accident.

They continued their brief safari, though with Jim's mind focused elsewhere. Why should Priscilla burn her night-dress? Had she returned to Welch's room in the morning? Maybe Jemma would find out. It would have been nice to think that he was in telepathic communication with his daughter and could will her to ask certain questions. In reality, even if he had, he would have got back a very curt reply telling him to stop interfering. Father/daughter relationships were like that. Close, but easily frazzled.

Telepathy or no telepathy, up at the house Jemma was working her way towards the same obvious question. However, she began by trying to persuade Priscilla to put on some clothes and rejoin everyone else. They were sitting in a tiny bedroom, the discarded breakfast tray on the floor, and Priscilla herself still in her dressing-gown. In spite of its being summer she sat huddled on the bed as if it were mid-winter.

"I can't face them," she kept repeating. "I wish they'd let me go home. Oh, my head." She clearly had a monster hangover.

"But you didn't mean to set the house on fire, did you? You ran to get help."

"Of course I didn't," Priscilla tried to convince herself. "That night-dress brought me nothing but bad luck." She was close to tears and Jemma gave her a quick hug. "Your father's the only one who understands."

"He is a bit special." Jemma was more proud of her father than she would have let him know. "He'll tell them. Then it'll be all right. Come down for lunch."

"I might." She shook her head vexedly. "I should never have gone to George's room in the first place. I should have known better."

"Why did you?" The use of Welch's first name put Jemma on the alert.

"It was in my script. I was Mrs. Sketchley's companion and in league with her brother to kill her. Don't you remember?"

Subsequent events had driven the Gilroy's original story-line out of Jemma's head. The Friday-evening briefing seemed light-years ago.

As if anxious to justify herself, Priscilla slid off the bed and opened the suitcase into which her clothes had been crammed after the fire. It was a cheap imitation-leather suitcase and its top sagged as she opened it. She rummaged unsuccessfully for a minute and then turned to her make-up case. This was tall enough to take an assortment of bottles and jars, and when Priscilla lifted out the top tray Jemma saw that lotions were not its only occupants. There was the recognizable top of a flat-sided half-litre liquor bottle. However, Priscilla hastily put back the tray, having found what she wanted. It was a computer-printed slip of paper, like the clues they had all been handed on Friday evening. She gave it to Jemma.

"At 9:30 P.M. you take her poisoned cocoa up to Mrs. Sketchley. But you do not go direct. You take it to her brother's room next door. He will deliver it."

Jemma read this twice, struggling with her memory. Hadn't Priscilla quarrelled with Welch over taking it up? And, of course, Priscilla herself had doped it for real.

"Why did you ask Welch to take it up?" she asked. "When that wasn't in the script."

"That man was such a pain, darling." Priscilla sounded relieved at talking about him. "So I put a few sleeping tablets in as well. I was supposed to go to his room again in the morning."

"For what?" Jemma felt a thrill of discovery. Maybe Priscilla was her mystery woman after all.

"I was to go through his room and the bathroom to Mrs. Sketchley's room, make sure she was dead, and bring the cocoa cup down. So no one was seen going to her room from the passage. Darling, don't tell Lady Gilroy, but it was the most crummy plot. A five-year-old would have seen through it."

"Did you do that on Saturday morning, then?"

"I thought of it, because the old fart still owed me twenty pounds." Priscilla was becoming quite chirpy now. "But I'd never have got it off him. He was far too mean."

Suddenly the light dawned, and Jemma asked the question that no one had asked so far.

"Did you know Welch before?"

Priscilla stared at her. "How did you guess? You promise not to tell?" Luckily for Jemma, she did not wait to be given the promise. "Five years ago. I was in a comedy at the Birmingham Playhouse.

One evening this man came round to the stage door with a huge bunch of roses and asked if he could take me out to dinner."

"And that was Welch?"

"That was George. I hadn't got a boy-friend at the time and I didn't fancy going out for fish and chips with the others, so I accepted. He took me to the best place in Birmingham. Then he propositioned me."

"I can imagine."

"I bet you can't, darling!" Priscilla was enjoying telling her story and had quite cheered up. "Of course he asked me back to his hotel. Which I refused. Then he offered me a thousand pounds to burn the theatre down."

"You're joking!"

"I never did understand all the complications. But he wanted to redevelop the site and he knew the theatre owner was underinsured. Darling, I couldn't believe it. A thousand may not sound like much, but it was to me."

"So what happened?"

"Well, if it had burned down we'd all have been out of work, wouldn't we? It was a repertory company and we had contracts for the season. So I refused. And then he took me to dinner again and offered me two thousand. I thought, well, if I started a tiny fire in my dressing-room, the kind that would set the alarms off at once, perhaps I could get the cash and do no harm to anyone."

It was not difficult to guess the outcome. "The fire got put out and he refused to pay?"

"In the end I rang him at home and his wife answered. Well, darling, you know what she's like. She wouldn't let me speak to him. What I never expected was to meet them here."

"What an incredible coincidence."

Priscilla laughed nervously. "Someone used to say that you're allowed one coincidence in every plot. We were as surprised as could be to see each other. And I didn't let him forget about the two thousand either. Not that I stood a chance. All he was after was what he didn't get in Birmingham. Mean bastard. And his wife guessed."

"He didn't ask you to burn this place down?" Jemma tried to make a joke of it and failed.

"Oh God." Priscilla veered back into depression. "How can I ever face them again?"

"Look." Jemma mixed decisiveness with coaxing. "You get dressed and I'll go and talk to Lady Gilroy. Don't worry. We'll sort it out."

She went downstairs in search of her hostess, having put Mrs. Worthington back on her list of suspects. The woman might be crazy, but she often seemed to have been crazy with a purpose.

She located Dee Dee in a small room on the ground floor of the servants' wing, which she had converted into a temporary study.

"This is one good thing about having a huge house," Dee Dee said, "there's always a spare corner somewhere. So you've been talking to that mad actress? Why did we ever hire her?"

This was not a question Jemma could answer, but she did assure Lady Gilroy that she was sure it wouldn't happen again.

"How do you know? Why not?"

"I just don't think it will. She's terribly ashamed of herself. But she can't stay in her room all day."

"You mean I have to welcome her back into society?" Dee Dee groaned.

"If you want her to behave."

Dee Dee looked intently at Jemma. How come this twenty-something-year-old was telling her to do things? "You know about criminal behaviour?" she asked.

"A little," Jemma said, then realized that even this claim was extravagant. "I write about crimes all the time. I have a feeling that if you encourage her to come down, she won't do anything again."

"She had better not, I tell you. Well, I'll see what I can do," Dee Dee conceded.

"She talked a lot about her role in the 'murder' plot. Is there a copy of the whole thing? I mean a master plan for the weekend?"

"Of course there is. Or there was. I had it all worked out."

"Have you got a copy?"

"Somewhere. It's not been the most important thing on my mind." Dee Dee shifted through a pile of the papers that the police had allowed her to bring through. She found a red folder and extracted a print-out. "Here you are. No secrets worth having any more. But I'd still like to have it back."

Jemma thanked her and carried off this trophy to her own room. There she sat down and read the whole document. As Priscilla had commented, it was a crummy plot. But one thing was crystal-clear. All the actions and clues assigned to the characters related to the Friday evening. With the exception of the maid's screaming session, and Priscilla's going to Welch's room, no one had movements allocated to them after the discovery of the murder.

While Jemma pondered this, her father was on the way back to the house with a dejected Lord Gilroy.

"Bad business with Ted," Gilroy muttered. "Now they think it's negligence. But it was his own, poor fellow."

"Must be 'accidental death,' " Jim prompted.

"Absolutely." Gilroy lapsed into silence, but after a minute he glanced quickly at Jim and said, "They think I murdered Welch."

"Why?" This was no surprise, but Jim did his best to mask it.

"It's obvious. That sergeant looks at me as if I was something the cat brought in and Morton never stops asking questions about the contract."

There, Jim thought, Morton had it dead right. The contract had to be at the heart of the case. "Did you have a quarrel with Welch?" he asked.

"Who could fail to? The man's an out-and-out—well, you know what I mean. Remember when you were in the hall after dinner on Friday evening?"

"We heard a bit of an argument. We also overheard one before dinner. Was that the row that the clue referred to?"

"Before dinner?" It took Gilroy a moment to recall the original "murder" plot and his attention lapsed, so that he nearly ran the Land Rover off the road. He swerved back onto the tarmac, swore, then regained his concentration. "Good God, no. The fictional row was with my wife during dinner. Wasn't so damn fictional, either."

"Welch certainly thought he was being insulted then." Jim remembered the developer's angry reactions.

"My wife couldn't resist putting the knife in a little. I paid for it later. Phew." Gilroy shook his head. "Welch wanted to develop land by the lake. There was no way we were going to sell him that. He made one hell of a fuss. So did his bitch of a wife."

"Do you have to sell?"

"Lloyds." The single word expressed a volume of misery. Gilroy had enough thick reports on Lloyd's requirements to fill a bookshelf.

"Is it really so bad?"

"If you believe that fellow McMountdown, it is." Gilroy's expression became puzzled, as his brain shifted with difficulty into overdrive. "Come to think of it, there hasn't been a letter from Lloyds today."

"So that was all a false alarm?"

"Could be," Gilroy said gloomily. "Doesn't alter the fact that I'm still up to my neck in it. I do need to sell land, but I'm damned if I'll ruin the estate. That's what I told them. Welch blew up. 'It's sods like you what's ruining the country. Here's a decent bloke like me trying to give people the homes they need and you're pouncing on about the view.' Bloody man."

They had reached the house and Gilroy stopped alongside one of the police cars in the drive, giving it a baleful look, as if it were a trespasser he would like to see clamped. But he did not get out immediately. This conversation had set him thinking.

"You know," he said, "with hindsight I think Welch was desperate to buy and that's why he lost his temper when I wouldn't sign for what he wanted after dinner."

"How did it end?" Jim asked.

"Oh, his wife walked out and then the lawyer woman calmed him down a little. She and I tried to sort out a compromise."

"Hardly a reason for murdering him," Jim suggested.

"Exactly what I keep telling the police. Between you and me, I think his wife told them I'd threatened him. Well, I did, as a matter of fact. Told him I wasn't going to be insulted in my own house and he could leave in the morning."

"But he refused?"

"Didn't have the chance, did he? He would have refused. There'd have been a long palaver about having paid his money for the weekend. I wish to God that inspector would get on with it and arrest someone." Gilroy heaved himself out of the Land Rover.

"Thanks for the lift," Jim said. They walked to the house together, then Gilroy excused himself and Jim went through to the library, hoping to find his daughter and asking himself how much Gilroy had been concealing in his account of the quarrel. What was needed next was to talk to Dulcie. It was Dulcie whom they had overheard say, in a most challenging voice, "Go ahead then!" Since Gilroy had not been in the room at that point, she must have been talking to Welch himself. What had she been challenging him to do? And would she, being as circumspect as lawyers were, be willing to reveal it?

The group were gathered for "elevenses" in the library and still absorbed by the subject of Priscilla's fire-raising escapade. This was hardly surprising, given their enforced idleness and a collapse of their small-talk conversation. By now no one had anything to say to anyone else. They were all obsessed with how to get away from Wittenham. Consequently a misdeed that could be unequivocally pinned on a particular person was welcomed.

"She ought to be locked up," Jim heard Adrienne say, before he was collared by Jemma and told that Lady Gilroy was waiting to speak to him. He grabbed a cup of coffee and they retreated to a relatively private corner of the room.

"Mr. Savage," Dee Dee began, "you were the last person to see Mrs. Worthington before she set her room on fire. Was she drunk?"

"Not when she went upstairs. She was upset about things and she's quite a highly strung person. Mrs. Welch had been very rude to her."

"Well, it's very difficult to know what to do. We can't ask her to leave." Dee gave an exasperated sigh. "But what if she tries some other crazy stunt?"

"I'm certain she won't. She's made her statement, her protest."

"And nearly burnt the house down. I'd call it arson."

At this moment a complete hush descended on the gathering. Jim looked round. Priscilla was coming in from the Great Hall, fully dressed in a skirt and blouse, but moving with caution, as if someone were about to leap on her. She looked at the main group, hesitated, saw Jim and came his way.

"How dare she show her bloody face!" Adrienne said loudly and challengingly. "She ought to be ashamed."

Priscilla stopped dead, looked imploringly at Jim, then turned towards Adrienne and said in a very quiet, understated voice, "And who killed George Welch?"

14

"ARE YOU accusing me of killing my own husband?" Adrienne glowered at Priscilla, as everyone else fell silent. She was not tall or impressive, but she hadn't lived with George Welch for twenty years without learning how to give as good as she got, and she was convinced Priscilla had been one of George's many girls in the past. "You filthy bitch. How dare you!"

The others, who had been grouped around the long table at the side of the library with the coffee on it, instinctively distanced themselves from the confrontation, leaving an open space for the two women to fight it out. Hamish tugged Dulcie back protectively a few feet towards the fireplace. Loredana followed. Jim and Jemma had already taken their coffee to one of the groups of chairs in a corner. Only Dee Dee remained by the table. Now Jim stood up, prepared to intervene if Lady Gilroy did not. He mentally kicked himself for being a fool. Adrienne was the most obvious suspect for Welch's murder. Why had he not anticipated that Priscilla would retaliate by suggesting it?

Trembling, Priscilla stood firm. "Why did you go for me?" she asked. "I can't have been the last person to see him. Someone else must have done." She would have liked to explain the whole tangled background of why she had set her her night-dress on fire, but she couldn't find the words, and anyway, no one would have believed her. "Didn't you see him in the morning? You must have done!"

"No, I did not." Adrienne refused to be put on the defensive.

"I've told everyone. George didn't like to be disturbed." She looked round for support, as though appealing to a jury. "It's the truth."

"I don't doubt that for a second," Hamish offered, moving very slightly away from Dulcie. "Your husband could be a very difficult man."

Loredana glanced at her lover in surprise, accidentally caught Dulcie's eye, and looked away again. What was going on now? Why was he suddenly Adrienne's defender?

"Thank you," Adrienne said warmly. "It's nice to know who one's friends are. Not that I've many here." She sniffed loudly. "This is the most unfriendly place I've ever been in. The way you're behaving, you'd think I never loved my husband at all."

Hamish turned to Priscilla. "You owe Mrs. Welch an apology, you know," he said in his rather languid tone.

"I do?" she shrilled. "How about her?"

Realizing that Priscilla was about to break down again, Jim Savage intervened, walking towards the two women, who were facing each other like boxers in a ring.

"There's no point in accusations," he said firmly. "Everyone's overwrought at the moment. Why don't we all sit down again?" He took Priscilla's arm and led her to Jemma, where she immediately burst into tears on the sofa.

"Thank God for someone with common sense," Dulcie said quietly. "This is becoming a madhouse."

"That's one hundred percent right," Dee Dee agreed, putting down her coffee. "I'm going to find my husband. This can't go on."

After she had left, Dulcie pointedly turned turned her back on Loredana and told Hamish, who was now consoling Adrienne, that she would see him at lunch-time. Then she crossed the room to join the Savages.

"Jim," she said forthrightly, "you seem to be the unofficial lightning-conductor in this place. Where do we all go from here, apart from a lunatic asylum?"

"We might try intellectual processes, instead of emotion," Jim suggested, getting to his feet again.

This was the opportunity he had hoped for. The contract must have been directly connected with Welch's death, though he could not for the life of him reason out how. It did not seem a sufficient cause for murder. Jemma had agreed with him. Drug dealers got themselves gunned down over contracts. Mobsters were killed for territory. But Welch, though a rough diamond, did not appear to have been in that category, and much less had anyone else here. Possibly Dulcie would help illuminate the problem. Not, as Jim kept reminding himself, that it was really his business. It was Inspector Morton's. At the same time he was increasingly caught up with it.

"Where do we go to talk?" Dulcie asked.

"Outside, where we can't be overheard. It's becoming a tradition," Jim remarked wryly. "Thank God it's not raining."

The policeman at the front door nodded them through and this time Jim did lead the way to the little stone pavilion by the lake. It had no doors, simply a columned frontage, giving onto a three-sided stuccoed room, with niches for statues.

"This was where George wanted his housing estate," Dulcie remarked, after they had sat down on a bench inside. "Right by the lake. Boating, fishing. He had it all worked out. But Gilroy wouldn't sell."

"Do you blame him?"

"Not at all. He'd have been a fool to. He was only prepared to let go five hundred acres on the other side of the estate. But George thought he could pile on the pressure."

"Was that what the row on Friday evening was about?"

"Partly." The directness of the question reminded Dulcie that they were supposed to be discussing what they could do next. "But what we have to decide is when to leave."

"You're the lawyer."

"And you seem to be our channel of communication with Morton."

"Believe me, it's a one-way street. He's delighted to have information. He doesn't give much away." Jim nudged the conversation back to where he wanted it. "Incidentally, Jemma and I overheard your quarrel. We were passing through the hall."

Dulcie frowned in aggravation. "I never thought eavesdropping would be your style."

Jim flushed. "The 'murder' scenario told us all to listen out for a row. 'Two characters are in fierce argument,' it read, if I remember right. 'Who are they and why are they in dispute?' Of course we were listening."

"I'm so sorry." Now it was Dulcie's turn to be embarrassed. "I'd completely forgotten. We were only here for the sake of the contract." It struck her that if they had been merely passing through, they would not have heard much and she might as well tackle this head-on. "So what did you hear?"

"You said, 'Go ahead then!' That was all we heard. Gilroy materialized and naturally we got out of the way."

"Hardly an incriminating sentence," Dulcie suggested. She knew exactly when she'd said that, a moment before Gilroy had returned from fetching some documents. And it had been a crucial moment, too. One she did not wish to discuss.

Jim read most of these thoughts in her face. "Morton knows," he said, "because he confiscated my notes. Why don't you tell me?"

"So that you can tell him?"

"No." Jim shook his head vigorously. "So that I can fit another little piece into my jigsaw and just possibly speed this business up." He made an appeal. "Unless you killed Welch yourself, what harm can it do now?"

This was the sort of plea Dulcie herself was in the habit of making to clients. Come clean, it can only help your case. Be frank and I can clear your name.

"I assume you were talking to Welch about the contract," Jim said.

Dulcie shifted on the bench to face him more directly, though not in the coquettish way that Loredana and Priscilla had done. Jim knew there would be no rewarding kiss on the cheek, no cry of "You are a darling." Dulcie had a good brain and no need to rely on being flirtatious, even if she sometimes took advantage of her sex.

"Are you going to solve this murder?" she asked. "Because if you're not, then I shall not betray confidences."

"I think I may, if Morton doesn't get there first. We are travelling by different routes. He's the professional. He has all the technical resources. I have better access to the suspects."

"Of which I'm one?"

"As am I." Jim smiled. "We're all in the same boat."

"Let me tell you what happened, then. But don't forget that this is my version. You might hear others."

THERE HAD been four of them in Gilroy's study: Gilroy himself, Dulcie, Welch and his wife. Adrienne had insisted on being present, despite Dulcie's subdued protests.

"I'm a director of his company. He's brought me along. I don't want him making commitments I don't know about." What she had left unsaid was her resentment at Dulcie's influence over her husband. She suspected they were having an affair. Why had Dulcie sat in the front of the Roller with him on the way here, while she was consigned to the back with that gormless Hamish? "You lawyers," she had limited herself to commenting, "are only interested in your fees."

Dulcie had been forced to swallow that insult and get the meeting going. It had not started well. Gilroy had categorically refused to sell any land by the lake.

"The other bloody farmland's no use to me," Welch had protested, knowing that he must come away from this weekend with a development site in order to raise more loans. "How do I get planning permission?"

"What about the golf-course site?" Dulcie suggested a compromise. "Could we see those plans?"

This was when Gilroy had left the room to fetch them and Adrienne had turned on Dulcie.

"I thought your husband was supposed to work on him. Make him so scared of Lloyds losses that he'd sign?"

"Didn't you hear Hamish at dinner? He was doing all he could."

"I told you," Welch said aggressively. "I told you on the way 'ere. If I don't get this land, I'll sue that useless man of yours for fraud. He got me into the Lloyds mess. He can bloody help me now."

"Gilroy will agree to sell some land," Dulcie insisted, keeping her temper.

"Not the part I want."

"If my George gets second best, my girl," Adrienne cut in, "we'll sue you, and that's a promise. And you'll get no fees."

"Wait a minute, love." Welch backed off, suddenly worried at having gone too far with the lawyer he depended on. "She's doing what she can."

"For who, I'd like to know?" Adrienne dismissed George's plea and turned on Dulcie again. "I tell you, we'll sue your hubby till he don't know if he's on his ass or his elbow."

Adrienne had taken it too far. "Go ahead then!" Dulcie said in her steeliest voice, and would have said more if she had not been interrupted by Gilroy's return.

"I DIDN'T like my husband being threatened," Dulcie said.

"But you still tried to negotiate?" Jim asked.

"Of course. It was what I was here for. I persuaded Gilroy to give away quite a lot that evening. Possibly George hoped for more. We'll never know."

"Either way, your husband was saved a court case."

"True," Dulcie conceded. "But it was one he wouldn't have deserved and George might never have brought, because George knew he was on risky Lloyds syndicates." She gave Jim a half-sad, half-quizzical look, as if to ask what else could anyone expect. "It's not unfair to say that Adrienne likes money. George got a genuine buzz out of what he did. He was almost creative. That was the likeable side of his character, though no one here saw it. Adrienne was always more interested in the bank balance."

"And Hamish?"

"I wouldn't have wanted him to be sued, but I wouldn't have minded his getting a shock. This weekend has really been the end." She sighed. "I don't know what he sees in Loredana. I'm not sure I even want to. Come on, you don't need to hear all that. Let's go back."

When they were nearing the house Dulcie asked him if their discussion had solved anything.

"It gave me some ideas. Especially about who took the contract and left it in my room."

"Who?"

"Ah. That would be telling."

"You old devil! And after all I've told you!" Dulcie pretended outrage, yet actually she was relieved to have revealed, if not every-thing, at least more than she had confided to the police. There was something about Savage's unassuming approach that generated con-fidence. "And when are you going to get us out of here?"

"I ought to leave that to you, if the Gilroys fail, and I'm sure they're trying. Thank God it'll soon be lunch-time."

JIM'S GUESS was accurate. In Dee Dee's temporary office she and Buck were discussing how best to tackle Morton, and indulging in some understandable marital recriminations.

"Darling," Dee Dee was saying in a voice that now seemed per-manently strained, "only four days ago I was asking you if this weekend would make money and you promised it would."

"Not exactly promised," Gilroy protested, recalling last Thursday vividly because it had been at that memorable tea-time that the guest list had arrived with Welch's name on it. He should have known that the proverbial bad luck of the Gilroys was about to reach new heights, or plumb new depths, whichever it was that bad luck did.

"You said, 'The weekend must show a profit.' I can hear you now. And it's a disaster. I've just had to phone through another huge order to the supermarket. We have to get rid of these people, quite apart from the strain. They're all at each other's throats. Any minute now there'll be another murder."

"Do we tell Morton that?"

"Oh my God!" Dee Dee clenched her fists in exasperation. "No, we do not. If necessary, we'll get that lawyer woman to talk to him on behalf of all of us."

"You don't suppose she did it, do you? Killed Welch, I mean?"

"What does it matter?" Buck's inability to see the wood for the trees was maddening. "The point is she knows all about powers of arrest and what the police can do. Morton said himself that he couldn't keep anyone here against their will. We've co-operated long enough."

"I doubt if he'd listen to me. He thinks we're the murderers."

"How totally stupid." Dee looked at her husband with alarm. Buck had disliked Welch intensely. He had unburdened himself about it at length on Friday night, and he had felt himself cornered. He hadn't signed the contract, but he knew he was going to have to. "You didn't put morphine in his tea or anything like that, did you?"

"Dodgson or Tracy might have done. Someone's been at the stuff."

"They've been worried that we might sell the whole place and they'd have to go. Dodgson told me as much yesterday. He's been even gloomier than usual since this happened." Dee considered the possibility. "The poor guy would never get another job."

"Except at an undertaker's."

"No." Dee Dee shook her head, her American upbringing asserting itself. "He's too gloomy. And that voice! Funeral parlours need re-assuring people. Dodgson looks as if he's just escaped from a grave himself. Why do we keep him on?"

"Because he worked for my father and he has nowhere to go." Gilroy had heard this argument before and always provided the same answer. "Noblesse oblige and all that. Anyway, if we did sell up I'd give him a pension."

"Have you ever told him that?"

"Not exactly," Gilroy hedged. "I mean, he must know we'd do the decent thing."

Dee Dee gazed at her husband with a mix of affection and despair, the despair predominating. There he sat, wearing his habitual Guards tie and boating jacket, along with a hangdog expression that would make even a pawnbroker wonder if he was trying to hock stolen goods, and he expected the servants to trust him with their futures at a time of crisis.

"You're crazy," she said. "I also think Dodgson could have done it. He'd have overheard conversations, he had the morphine, and he could have laced anything that tasted strong enough. Coffee, tea, whisky. Welch had them all. Tracy would have helped too. She already had it in for Welch in a small way. Not to mention that madwoman Mrs. Worthington. I bet they were all in it."

"I suppose they could have been," Gilroy said, then went on with remarkable lack of tact, "of course, you were in the room next to Welch. You could have—"

"Buck," Dee Dee snapped, "snap out of it. Nothing would have pleased me more than to see that odious man off the premises, but not as a corpse. Go and tell Morton that we've had enough."

"Anything you say, darling," Gilroy obeyed, "but you do realize we're both suspects?"

"Get out of here before I scream!"

Down in the library Jemma had been reading a magazine and covertly watching Hamish and Loredana. They had evidently taken advantage of Dulcie's absence to get together. But it didn't appear that their conversation was going smoothly. Loredana was making emotional gestures and Hamish was defending himself.

"Why are you making such a fuss about that woman?" Jemma heard Loredana say. "She can more than look after herself."

Hamish's reply was inaudible.

"Well, maybe, but she's recovered amazingly quickly," Loredana said and Jemma realized they must be talking about Adrienne.

Then Dulcie came striding in, faltered momentarily when she saw the two together, but continued and told Hamish that she needed to talk to him. She took no notice whatever of Loredana. Shortly after they had gone, Loredana came across and sat down next to Jemma.

"What do you really make of Priscilla?" she asked in a gossipy sort of way, as though it were Priscilla she had been discussing with Hamish.

"She's quite highly strung." Jemma felt sorry for the actress. "I'd say this has all been too much for her."

"Is it true that she was trying to burn her night-dress? It's incredible."

For reasons that she could never have explained, because her reaction was instinctive, not rational, Jemma took the subject further.

"It's an odd thing about the night-dress," she said. "On the real morning of the murder I saw a woman in a night-dress going into Welch's room at about ten after seven."

"Who was it?" Loredana sounded intrigued.

"That's what I don't know. I only caught a glimpse of her back."

"Who could it have been? What kind of night-dress was it?"

"The hem was trimmed with white lace. That's all I saw."

"And no one was wearing the same at the re-enactment?"

"On the contrary, everyone was except for me and you. Adrienne was, Priscilla was, Lady Gilroy was. I don't know if you were, because you had a long silk dressing-gown over yours."

"Well, of course I noticed all the lace," Loredana said a little huffily. "I meant was anyone wearing exactly the same?"

"It might have been Priscilla's."

"Which she tried to burn! How riveting!"

"You didn't see her, did you?" Jemma asked. "You must have taken your tray down to the kitchen about that time."

For a second Loredana was startled. "I quite forgot about that. No, I didn't see anyone. Did you see me?"

"No," Jemma confessed. "But I only peeked down the passage on my way to the bathroom."

INSPECTOR Morton was perplexed and, which was unusual for him, irritated. He had been on the phone to the pathologist again and very little had been definitely confirmed, except that the poison was a powerful opiate. Traces of a substance the forensic lab had not yet identified had been found in Welch's blood, but not his urine. That meant it had been administered shortly before his death. Tea had been found in his stomach. But so had alcohol in his blood. If he had driven a car, he would have been well over the limit.

"We can say for certain that it was in something Welch drank," the pathologist had said.

"And how long before we know what it was?"

"Chromographic tests could take the rest of the week, I'm afraid. It's like consulting a dictionary. You have to identify a substance before you can look up the reference."

Technical explanations had followed, which Morton was obliged to accept. He knew that it could take three days to complete a full blood-alcohol test, and that was when the lab technicians knew what they were searching for. And with this they did not, beyond that Welch's lungs and liver had been congested and he had died of respiratory failure, indicating an opiate.

So Morton was sitting there, tapping the desk with a pencil and reviewing his list of suspects, when Timmins announced that Lord Gilroy would like to see him.

"Give me five minutes," he ordered and quickly went through the file on the owner of Wittenham Park. It was already voluminous.

Gilroy's character was variously described as weak, friendly and untrustworthy. He had been under a lot of pressure from Welch. Down at the Lion Park Timmins had found a memo from Ted Matthews suggesting that Welch had instigated a series of local complaints about the lions. Investigations in the village had shown this to be true. There had been rows on the Friday evening between Welch and Gilroy. Although Mrs. McMountdown had been circumspect, it was clear that there had been bad blood between both Lord and Lady Gilroy and Welch. No one at the Friday evening dinner had doubted that Lady Gilroy had been deliberately insulting to the developer.

And yet, Morton asked himself, since Gilroy had not signed the contract, why should he resort to murder? It did not add up.

"What can I do for you, sir?" he demanded when Gilroy was shown in, and immediately widened the subject by adding, "I understand there's been a quarrel between two of the ladies."

"There certainly has." In a sense this was what Gilroy had come to talk about. "The strain's becoming too much, Inspector. The women are at each other's throats."

"Over what?"

"Mrs. Worthington is accusing Mrs. Welch of murder. Well, I suppose it's possible. She's by far the most likely person to have gone to Welch's room before breakfast that day."

Morton gave an encouraging grunt, an unspoken assent to the idea. The least convincing aspect of his interview with Adrienne Welch had been her insistence that she had not wanted to disturb her husband, even though the maid had been screaming her head off outside his door only minutes earlier.

"Of course," Gilroy began to backtrack, "I wasn't in that part of the house, so I can't tell. But the point is the two women are at each other's throats now and the others are taking sides. Surely you could let them all leave today? Haven't you got enough statements?"

"As I've told you, sir, I have no power to keep anyone here. But I hope they will continue to collaborate." This was Morton's sole ace. Anyone who insisted on leaving would automatically throw suspicion on themselves.

"You can't make an arrest?" Gilroy asked hopefully. That would solve the problem. Then all the others could be on their way and he and Dee Dee could start getting things back to normal.

"Not without a smoking gun, as you might say."

"Can we at least have more use of the house?"

Morton considered this. All the main rooms had been exhaustively searched. After two full days they had yielded nothing more significant than coins down the sides of armchairs and discarded clues for the "murder." The broken whisky glass had tested negative for poisonous substances. So had all the cups and saucers and teapots from the kitchen. He was convinced that the evidence he needed would be derived from personal relationships, not objects.

"I'll agree to that," he conceded, "and I'll make an announcement later about when they can leave."

"Thank you, Inspector." Gilroy was mightily relieved and hastened back to tell Dee Dee. He felt he ought to have thrown his weight around and insisted on his rights. But there was a solid, rocklike quality about Morton which made that impossible.

After he had gone, Morton called in Timmins again.

"They're starting to crack up," he said with satisfaction. "Keep your fingers crossed for this evening."

15

THE SINGLE, agonized scream coming from the servants' wing was enough to set everyone within earshot racing towards the back stairs. Morton got there first, closely followed by Jim Savage. What they found was totally unexpected.

Lying at the foot of the stairs in a contorted heap was Loredana, her arms outstretched to save herself, one leg buckled beneath her body at an unpleasant-looking angle. And bending over her, futilely trying to lift her from the step above, was Hamish, while Dodgson made unavailing efforts to free her legs.

"Leave me alone," she moaned. "Oh, my leg!"

Morton leaped into action, brusquely telling Dodgson and Hamish to get out of the way and lifting Loredana gently by the shoulders, so that Jim could ease her legs away from the bottom step, where her feet had become wedged against the wall. Together they carried her through to the Great Hall and laid her down on a sofa.

A policeman went to fetch a blanket, while Morton arranged cushions beneath her head, Gilroy telephoned the doctor and Hamish stood helplessly by. Gradually Loredana calmed down, her breathing became less agitated and she started tentatively feeling her limbs with her fingertips. Occasionally she gave a tiny exclamation of pain.

"What happened?" Morton asked, when she was more composed.

"I slipped. It was so stupid. Oh God," she said, continuing to explore her injuries, "I have hurt my leg."

"Better stay still until the doctor comes." Morton turned to Hamish. "You were with her?"

"I was behind her on the stairs."

"You couldn't save her?"

"Of course I tried. I was just too far away." Hamish's expression showed acute embarrassment. "The truth is we'd had a slight argument."

"I just wanted to get away from him," Loredana said weakly from the sofa. "Then I slipped up on that beastly carpet."

Shortly after this the doctor arrived and began his examination of Loredana, giving Jim a chance to escape and take a look at the stairs himself.

The servants' staircase turned through a right angle half-way down and its steps were covered with a narrow strip of worn, brown-patterned cord carpet. The wood showing on either side of the carpet was painted a dull brown. It was all another reminder of Gilroy's parsimony where the staff were concerned. In fact, the carpet was so threadbare and scuffed that Jim had difficulty making out where Loredana had slipped or, more likely, tripped. But a long scratch on the paintwork near the bottom had presumably been made by one of her heels.

When he returned, Doctor Thompson was delivering his verdict.

"A lucky escape," he was telling Loredana, "you'll have some beautiful bruises, no doubt, but nothing's broken. If I were you, I'd spend the day resting."

He began putting his gear away in his black bag, then asked for a word with Morton before leaving again.

Having been re-assured that she was not badly injured, Loredana cheered up a little, but refused to go to her room to rest.

"I'm quite happy here," she insisted, then thought of something and called out to Jemma. "I left the book I'm reading upstairs. Could you be an angel and fetch it for me? It's a Barbara Taylor Bradford."

Jemma dutifully went to the small room Loredana had been allotted, not far from the head of the servants' staircase. The room was immaculately tidy. Jemma herself normally left clothes, towels, boxes of tissues, make-up and magazines strewn everywhere. She was impressed, yet slightly chilled. Loredana must be a pain to live with. She saw the novel at once, lying on the counterpane of the bed. Then she became curious and began examining Loredana's other possessions.

They reflected a very orderly person and also one who was obsessed with her own appearance. An array of what Jim called "lotions and potions" stood on the small dressing-table. A set of hair curlers had its electric flex neatly coiled. Loredana's cream silk dressing gown hung from a peg on the back of the door. So did two night-gowns, one much more diaphanous than the other.

Jemma could not resist running her hands over their expensive fabrics and, in a moment of bitchiness, guessed at the demure one being for when husband Trevor was around, and the sexier number, with its low-cut neck and lace trim, for receiving lovers. Lace again! If Loredana had been wearing the lacy one on Saturday, that could add her to the list of mysterious women. Then she realized that the hem of neither would have been visible under the silk dressing-gown, which during the re-enactment had practically swept the floor.

She'd already been in the room several minutes and Loredana would be getting suspicious. She picked up the novel, noticing it had a slip of paper as a bookmark. Still curious, she saw the bookmark was a clipping from a magazine and almost laughed out loud as she read it. So that was where the horoscope had gone!

As she was on the way down again she bumped into Tracy, almost literally bumped, because the maid was coming up the stairs and was so fat that they had to squeeze past each other.

"Oh, miss," Tracy said, seizing the moment, "your dad says you're a crime reporter. Is that for real?"

"Pretty much."

"Can I talk to you about it? That's what I'd like to do. Be a reporter."

"No problem." Jemma had few illusions about how little she could help Tracy, but equally she had time on her hands. "When would you like?"

"After I've done the lunch. I have the afternoon off and I was going to the village."

"Why don't we go together."

"If that Mr. Morton'll let us."

"I'll ask him."

In fact, Morton was busy and she had to ask Timmins. To her surprise, he had no objection. Still with time on her hands, Jemma returned to the library, only to freeze in the doorway as she realized that a serious altercation was going on there between Loredana and Hamish.

Loredana was reclining on a sofa near the fireplace, with her back to the door, but there was nothing relaxed about her voice, while Hamish was perched on an upright chair alongside the sofa, apparently defending himself.

"Why are you making such a fuss over Adrienne? Because she's suddenly become rich and unattached, I suppose? The way you've been all over her is disgusting." Loredana spoke sibilantly, almost hissing out the words, in a tone Jemma had never heard her use to Hamish before, though it was reminiscent of the way she had addressed her unfortunate husband on Saturday. "I suppose I don't matter to you any more?"

"Darling, you're imagining things. I was being nice to Adrienne because I can no more believe she's a killer than that we are."

"I told you upstairs, you and I have nothing to do with all this. Why get yourself involved?" She glared up at him.

"I was simply trying to be nice to her."

"Well, you're a fool. Anyway, if anyone did have a motive to kill George Welch, it was Adrienne."

Jemma coughed discreetly, feeling she had heard enough of this, and Hamish jumped up as fast as if a wasp had stung his backside.

"We had no idea you were there," he said in an accusing voice.

"The last thing we wanted," Loredana added, unexpectedly backing him up, "was to be overheard. But since you obviously listened to everything, you might as well know that I think Mrs. Welch is as guilty as hell. He does not agree. We almost came to blows over it upstairs, before I tripped on that wretched carpet." She made a show of reaching forwards to massage her ankle and Jemma noticed that dark bruises were coming up on her arm. Hamish tried to assist and she pushed him away. "Hamish, please."

"I'm so sorry." Jemma decided to retreat until they'd sorted out this argument. Interpersonal relationships were evidently not Hamish's big thing, though it was hard to feel sorry for him. She had decided that he thoroughly deserved Loredana, tantrums and all. She left the room quickly and went to find her father.

"Hmm," he grunted, "odd that they should be quarrelling when the pressure's off. I wonder if Adrienne really is the reason. Perhaps we'll discover more at lunch."

However, lunch was an uneventful and strained occasion, with Loredana hobbling to the table on a borrowed stick and nobody except Jim talking to Priscilla at all. Furthermore the generosity of earlier menus had been diminished. This one consisted only of cold meat and salad, followed by cheese and fruit. It was quickly over and soon after Jemma borrowed her father's car and the two girls set off.

For Tracy this was a huge treat. She normally bicycled, huffing and puffing her considerable girth along the three miles. So she was both cheerful and gossipy. The village itself was a typical English tourist trap, where most of the few shops sold Cotswold postcards and souvenirs, antiques or pottery, but little of practical use. However, there was an Olde English Tea Shoppe, with a bow-window displaying all kinds of cakes and cookies. Here they ended up, with Jemma buying tea and scones for them both. As she devoured the scones and cream and jam as if she hadn't eaten for a week, Tracy became more confidential.

"You could write a thriller about what's been going on," she confessed. "Could we write one together? Just fancy having my name on a book! That would put old Dodgson's nose out of joint, in real time too."

"I bet he's a pain to work with."

"Worse than ever this weekend." Tracy leaned conspiratorially across the table. "Missed his Sunday fix."

The idea of the doddery old butler taking a fix of anything was so unlikely that Jemma almost laughed. "What of?" she asked.

"That medicine-cupboard stuff. Morphine, its called. I reckon Lady Gilroy forgot it was there. He's been taking a tiny drop in his tea on Sundays to jazz himself up. But now the cops have confiscated the bottle."

"He didn't put some in Welch's tea, did he?"

The remark was meant as a joke, but Tracy took it at face value.

"He could have done," she said, an edge of excitement in her voice. "He easy could. You see, usually I make the early-morning tea, but seeing how many guests there were, he made the tea in each of the pots and I took them up."

"Did he have anything against Welch?"

"Not half. His Lordship thinks we never hear anything. But we knew all about what Welch was after. And Mr. Dodgson asked him straight out if we'd lose our jobs. 'Don't you worry, old chap,' he said, 'it probably won't come to that.' What a nerve. Didn't worry me, but it did old Dodders."

"But . . ." Jemma was about to point out that the land development didn't mean the whole place would be sold, when she remembered Lady Gilroy's saying that a housing estate by the lake would be unbearable. No doubt that had been overheard. "I suppose he'd have nowhere to go?"

"Too right," Tracy said indistinctly, her mouth full of pastry.

After this the conversation lapsed until they got onto the subject of the back stairs.

"They're real dangerous," Tracy remarked. "I've always said so. No wonder that lady came a-cropper." She giggled. "Screamed a lot better than I did."

"You must have heard her fall."

"The first thing we heard was her yelling. Otherwise I'd have been there before anyone else. You know something? I wouldn't be surprised if her boy-friend didn't push her."

"Seriously?" This was a startling idea, though not one that Jemma could believe.

"I heard them quarrelling earlier on. D'you know," Tracy went on, "some people behave as if you aren't there. She's one of them. All matey with Lady G, and all airs and graces with us. You know she brought down her tea-tray Saturday morning?"

"At what time?"

"A good twenty minutes before any one else. She said she wanted to save you trouble."

"Not on your nelly! She was after getting her breakfast right.

Must have her grapefruit all cut up the way she wanted. Lightly boiled egg. 'Only three and a quarter minutes, please. Not a second more.' No crusts on the toast. You name it. Choosy bitch she is." That hardly made her a criminal, Jemma thought, and turned the conversation to crime writing. Whether Tracy was more enthralled by her second lot of scones or by the literary advice was uncertain, but it evoked one more piece of gossip.

"You'll never guess what I found in one of the library wastebaskets this morning."

"What was it?"

"A tiny glass bottle with a funny top, almost like it was out of a doll's house. No label or anything. I'll show you when we get back, if you like." Tracy giggled. "Could have been drugs, I thought. D'you reckon any of them are junkies?"

Jemma considered this fairly lightly. Then it struck her that quite possibly Priscilla might be on drugs. She was scatter-brained enough to dump the evidence in a waste-basket.

"I'd like to see it," she said. "Maybe we ought to be getting back."

Tracy reluctantly finished the last of her tea and they set off, arriving back at Wittenham just behind a police car.

"Something's going on," Jemma remarked. "Let's go and see."

But Tracy felt she couldn't. "Her ladyship'll go bananas if I come in the front door. We have to go round the back. Thanks a million for the outing, and ta for now." She left the car and hurried round to the servants' entrance, while Jemma went to the main one.

Something was indeed going on. A policeman insisted on checking her identity at the door. Inside the Great Hall the guests were grouped to one side, listening to an altercation between Dulcie and Morton, while Adrienne stood sobbing hysterically beside Sergeant Timmins, who was in his uniform.

"Have you a warrant for her arrest?" Dulcie demanded, squaring up to Morton like a very small pugilist confronting a Goliath, her head up and eyes fixed on his from beneath her neatly cut mop of blonde hair.

"Is she your client?" Morton asked firmly but equably. He was at his best in this kind of tense situation.

"She is now." Dulcie turned to Adrienne. "You would like me to represent you?" Adrienne nodded, unable to speak and having to be supported physically by Timmins.

"Then I am asking again. Have you a warrant for her arrest?"

"I am arresting Mrs. Welch on suspicion of having murdered her husband, George Ernest Welch," Morton said. "Under the Police and Criminal Evidence Act I can hold a suspect for questioning for up to twenty-four hours."

He turned to Adrienne and delivered a wordy caution that had been much modified by British law's having removed a suspect's right to stay silent. "You do not have to say anything unless you wish to do so, but it may harm your defence if you do not mention, when questioned, something that you later use in your defence. Anything you do say may be used in evidence."

"Don't say a word," Dulcie snapped and then faced Morton again. "She has the right of access to her solicitor before being interviewed. Are you going to grant her that access here, or at the police station?"

Morton considered this. There were rigid procedures to follow. Mrs. Welch would have to be handed over to an officer at a "designated" police station, be fed, kept warm, not be interviewed unduly late in the evening, allowed eight hours' sleep, et cetera, et cetera. Mrs. Welch would be within her rights in refusing to say anything until she had spoken to a solicitor, while he could not start interviewing her until they reached the police station.

It was unusual for a solicitor to be present at an arrest. However, few things about the Wittenham Park murder seemed to be normal. In fact, Morton reckoned that if he ever came to write his memoirs, Wittenham Park would merit a chapter of its own. So he gave way and allowed the two women to be taken to Gilroy's study, for Dulcie to counsel her new client. The quicker this was done, the sooner he could start his interviewing and discover how much Mrs. Welch really knew about the state of her husband's finances.

Amid the hubbub of excited conversation that broke out among the guests, Jim took Jemma aside.

"Either he's deliberately breaking up the log-jam by making that arrest, or he's got evidence that neither of us have dreamt of."

"How do you mean?"

"He may hope Adrienne will collapse and confess. More likely he hopes this will make all the rest of us feel we're off the hook. Then who knows what might not surface."

The truth of this observation was reinforced within seconds, when Hamish accosted Morton and said he presumed that everyone was now free to leave.

"If you don't mind, sir"—Morton was at his most diplomatic— "I would prefer you to wait until after breakfast tomorrow."

"But that's absurd," Loredana said, hobbling across on her stick. "Who wants another night in this dreadful place?"

"Thank you, dear," said Dee Dee caustically, having overheard her. "I will pass your compliments to the staff."

"I'm so sorry." Loredana backed off apologetically. "I didn't mean it personally. It's just that now he's made his arrest it seems so pointless keeping us."

"I don't like to disappoint you," Jim cut in, not unhappy at putting Loredana in her place. "But holding someone for questioning is not the same as charging them with murder."

"Oh. Isn't it?" Loredana sounded disappointed.

A few minutes later Dulcie emerged with Adrienne, who was calmer, if still extremely shaky.

"She'll need to pack some clothes," Dulcie told Morton. "I assume you'll send someone upstairs with her?"

Morton agreed, then turned to his unwanted audience. "I shall shortly be taking Mrs. Welch to Oxford. I shall not need to talk to anyone of you again this evening."

Dee Dee glanced at the tiny jewelled wrist-watch Gilroy had given her as a wedding present, saw that it was still only five-thirty, and decided the hell with it. "I need a drink," she announced. "Anyone else who would like one can come to the library." She turned to the butler, who had also been watching. "Please come out of your daze, Dodgson, and do your stuff. And tonight we shall eat properly in the dining-room."

This clear statement did more than anything to make everyone appreciate that, at least as far as the Gilroys were concerned, life was returning to normal. Nor did Morton dispute it. Shortly afterwards he and another officer took Adrienne away, Dulcie promising that she would visit her in the morning.

"Those people make me angry," Dulcie commented as Morton disappeared. But she would not explain why.

Meanwhile Jemma slipped along to the kitchen and returned unobtrusively with Tracy's tiny bottle wrapped in a tissue in her bag. When she showed it to Jim, he was puzzled.

"Looks familiar," he remarked. "But I can't think why." He examined it, carefully holding it with the tissue. The bottle was barely an inch and a half long and had a rubber-sealed clip-on metal cap. He eased the blue-coloured cap off and sniffed. There was no smell and the bottle appeared empty. "It'll come to me eventually. Let's keep this safe." He went through to the hall, took one of the crested envelopes from the rack on the writing-table and popped it in. I shall call this Exhibit A for the time being."

"How original can you get," Jemma cracked. "You're not still playing detective, are you, Daddy?"

"I most certainly am. And if you're not being my accomplice, why did you bother with this?"

"You don't think Adrienne's guilty then?"

"I'm one hundred percent certain she lied to us and probably to Morton about the contract. I'm equally sure she's no murderess. Let's follow Lady Gilroy's advice and find a drink, shall we? We could have a strenuous evening ahead."

16

 "DEE DEE, darling," Buck said, as they were changing for dinner. "D'you realize we're going to be rid of this ghastly bunch tomorrow? Why don't we have some champagne?"

"Why not!" For the first time in three days she looked at her blundering husband with affection. The "Agatha Christie" weekend looked set to retreat into the annals of a family history which future generations would marvel at, if more in despair than admiration. The threatened Lloyds demand had not arrived and a phone call had established that it had never been issued. Buck was now convinced that Hamish McMountdown had tried to con him and was wondering why. The only answer was that he had been in cahoots with Welch.

One thing the Coldstream Guards had taught Buck Gilroy was how to open a bottle of fizz without the ostentatious fuss of a racing driver spraying stage champagne all over a crowd. He twisted the cork out with only the mildest "pop" and deftly poured two glasses.

"To us." He toasted his wife.

"To us." Dee Dee kissed him. "And to Mrs. Welch for getting rid of that loathsome man. She deserves a medal, not jail."

Naturally they consumed the bottle before going down to host the final evening, and Buck became increasingly of a mind to confront McMountdown. With less of the Widow Clicquot's vintage restorative inside him, he would have shied off the idea like a bolting horse. But now he began to feel alcoholically indignant.

"You know, Mr. Savage," he said, as he and Dee Dee encountered Jim and Jemma on the stairs, "I think there was a conspiracy against me this weekend. What do you think?"

"I'm quite sure there was." Jim looked at him in amazement. "Didn't you know they were ganging up on you?"

"Only just came to me. You mean, you knew?"

"I deduced it. You remember I was asking about the row my daughter and I overheard before dinner on Friday? That was Mrs. McMountdown telling her husband in no uncertain terms that if he did not collaborate with Welch in fooling you, then Welch would sue him for something. I can only guess what it was, but the threat was real enough to make him spin you that tale about Lloyds losses during dinner."

"Which was a bloody lie," Gilroy said with unusual animation.

"A necessary one for Welch. Everything this weekend centered on your signing the contract."

"Including Welch's murder?"

"Everything except the murder. That might have been thought about before, but it was prompted by an opportunity."

"But his wife was involved with the contract."

"That doesn't mean she did the deed."

"I suppose not." Gilroy absorbed this idea slowly. His brain cells had been working overtime since Adrienne's arrest and the champagne did not improve their efficiency.

"She wasn't deeply involved with the deal, anyway," Jemma chimed in. "I mean, I'm sure she pretended to be, but I could see she wasn't."

"Exactly," Jim agreed. "Even though she nicked the document later on."

"She what?" Gilroy exclaimed, amazed.

"Took possession of the contract. Can't say 'stole' because she was a director of the company."

"Why?" Now Gilroy was indignant. "We were looking everywhere for the damn thing!"

"To see what it let her in for." Jim persisted. "I'm virtually certain that she took the contract from Welch's room when she found him dead. Either she did go in when she says she was afraid to disturb him, or she put it in her bag before calling for help later. Since it turned out to be unsigned, there was no commitment to alarm her, and eventually she got rid of it by dumping it on my bed."

"I'm still going to have it out with that bastard McMountdown," Gilroy said vehemently, reverting to his earlier thoughts about having been conned.

"Buck, darling," Dee Dee cut in, "I don't think that is such a great idea."

"Oh." Having wriggled back into his wife's good books, Gilroy didn't want to annoy her. "Let's forget it then."

They left the Savages and continued down the stairs and through to the library, ready to greet their guests as they came down.

Meanwhile Jim and Jemma lingered in the Great Hall, over in a corner where they could watch the others descend.

"He's pretty slow," Jim remarked. "It's taken him a long time to cotton on to Welch's tactics."

"Adrienne can't have been part of those. Do you think she's innocent, Daddy?"

"Yes. Do you?"

Jemma told him why and he listened with care to her conclusions.

"We ought to tell Morton this," he said.

"Except that he's not here to be told. Why don't we bring it out into the open?"

"It's impossible to prove."

"But it's not impossible to hassle people into admissions. That's what attorneys do all the time in court."

"My love, I'm not an attorney and we're not in court."

"Well, I don't agree," Jemma insisted. "I think Lord Gilroy's drunk just enough to challenge Hamish and we should take it from there."

"Let's play it by ear then, shall we?"

So they went on through to the library, where Priscilla was making a nervous entrance.

"Oh, Lady Gilroy," she gushed, "I am so glad this is the last night."

"So are we," Dee Dee said icily. "There's a taxi coming for you at ten tomorrow to take you to the station. Now please behave yourself this evening."

"Scout's honour," Priscilla promised, which privately meant that, since she was not a boy, she would do no such thing. She had existed in a half-world between the theatre and life for too many years.

One by one the others filed down and joined in somewhat stilted conversations, with Loredana leaning on a stick and showing a livid bruise on her left arm, whilst still contriving to shimmer in the Versace dress that had caught Welch's eye so successfully on the first evening. But despite Dee Dee's efforts the conversation inevitably coalesced around the arrest of Adrienne.

"Is it true she stood to walk away with a million from the insurance?" Loredana asked.

"Whether it is or it isn't," Dulcie retaliated, "in my belief, she's not guilty."

"You would say that, wouldn't you, being her lawyer?"

Dulcie gave her a look that ought to have stripped the Versace off her back, but the damage was done. Buck Gilroy took up the subject again.

"If she is innocent," he asked, "who did kill Welch?" He turned to Jim. "You must have a few ideas."

"He certainly does," Jemma chimed in, "don't you, Daddy?"

"Could we at least wait until after dinner?" Dee Dee asked. She was counting the hours to her final release from this torment and knew she could always excuse herself once they had eaten. "If we're going to be foul about anyone, let's at least be foul on full stomachs."

But restraint was a lost cause. The subject re-erupted after the main course, when Dodgson was carrying round a summer pudding, with Priscilla arguing provocatively that any one of them could have murdered Welch.

"Even the butler could have poisoned his early-morning tea. Couldn't you, darling?"

"I beg your pardon, madam." Dodgson paused in the act of serving her. "But I did no such thing."

"You could have done, though," Jemma commented. "You had

access to the morphine bottle and you could have dropped some into Welch's teapot while Tracy was taking the other trays upstairs."

"This is absurd, my lord," Dodgson appealed to Gilroy. "I must protest."

"But you did have access to the morphine," Savage said gently, wishing to stir up the subject with absurdities first. "And it is a fact that the teapots and cups were all washed up immediately after their use."

For a moment they all thought the butler was going to drop the salver. His face turned quite purple and he began to stutter unintelligible phrases. Dulcie, who was closest to him, stood up quickly and rescued the pudding, taking it to the sideboard.

"Thank you," Dee Dee said gratefully, "that was very sensible. Dodgson, you may go. I should like a word with you afterwards."

"I didn't do it, milady!" Dodgson managed to transform his mumbling into shrill speech. "I know I could have done, but I swear I didn't."

"Should bloody well hope not," Gilroy muttered. "Can't have one's butler going around murdering people."

"Thank you, sir," Dodgson said and fled.

"You'd better all help yourselves to pudding," Dee Dee suggested and turned maliciously to Priscilla. "Perhaps we should investigate your part in it next?"

"I suppose George was always fooling around with other women?" Loredana said pointedly.

"Or trying to, the old goat." Priscilla fended her off with feeling. "But I wouldn't have murdered him for that."

"Adrienne might have done," Loredana suggested. "She struck me as being a very jealous person."

"She certainly noticed him looking you up and down the first evening," Jemma said. "And she was very suspicious of Priscilla."

"Well, darlings." Priscilla decided to put a brave face on her past. "Since Jim here knows, you might as well all know. I first met him five years ago, and he was only interested in money and sex. In that order."

"Any fool could see that," Loredana observed.

"But neither was exchanged between them," Jim put paid to

Loredana's bitchiness, something he'd been wanting to do all weekend.

"Thank you, darling," Priscilla said. "It's nice to know someone understands."

"Priscilla's problem with the police," Jim went on "has been that she was the last person to see Welch alive. At least, she might have been."

"Who else could have done?" Dulcie asked.

"A lady in a lace-edged night-dress," Jemma said, "whom I saw go into Welch's room at about seven-ten. But I only saw her back and legs, because she was leaning forward to open the door."

"In my plot it was supposed to be Mrs. Worthington," Dee Dee remarked to Jim. "I'd completely forgotten about that until your daughter reminded me."

"No such thing happened in the re-enactment," Hamish insisted.

"Very little that was accurate did," Jim countered him, "As you know yourself. And I don't imagine Morton was deceived by your supposed movements either."

"I don't know what you mean." Hamish flushed. "I did what I actually did. Went downstairs for coffee."

"Who d'you imagine you're fooling?" Dulcie asked wearily.

"Talking of deception," Gilroy interrupted, "you told me a pack of lies, McMountdown. There was no Lloyds call for money today."

"I'd been assured there would be," Hamish protested. "I resent that remark and I demand an apology."

"What was your cut going to be?"

"He wasn't getting a cut," Dulcie said. "He was saving his own skin."

"Surely," Loredana said, worried by this attack on Hamish in spite of their quarrel, and switching the subject to the night-dress, "the mysterious woman must have been Adrienne?"

At last Jim became totally serious. "Before we carry this joke any further," he said, "we ought all to recognize that if Adrienne is innocent, then Welch's killer must be one of us."

A hush fell over the room.

"That's quite a challenging statement," Dulcie observed. "True, furthermore."

"Adrienne is a most unlikely killer. Unless, of course, she had set up her insurance scheme with the intention of killing her husband this weekend, but I think not. Would she have bought new clothes for the occasion? Hardly. I'm sure she intended simply to have an enjoyable time, in spite of her husband's business purposes."

"But something got in the way," Hamish observed.

"The business got in the way," Jim said curtly, "because there were only two things Welch was serious about, and as Priscilla just told us, they were money and sex."

"Which brings us back to night-dresses," Priscilla said, with a totally false laugh.

"Come to think of it, everyone had lace night-dresses," Loredana suggested, widening the field of suspects.

"Except for me," Jemma said. "And if you had one, it was underneath your dressing-gown."

"So you're ruling out the men?" Dulcie asked Jim.

"Since Lord Gilroy was asleep around that time and we've exonerated the butler, and Hamish was down in the kitchen, that only leaves myself." Jim paused. "Oddly enough, Welch had threatened me the night before."

"Why?" Dulcie asked sharply.

"He knew my profession and I knew he'd been suspected of insurance fraud. He told me to keep my nose out of his business here."

"George made enemies unnecessarily. He was very stupid over that."

"Which led to his death, d'you think?"

"Possibly." Dulcie became guarded and again a hush fell on the room.

"Well," said Priscilla, making Dee Dee wince at yet another intervention, "as it wasn't me who went to his room at seven-ten, who was it?"

"How do we know it wasn't you?" Loredana asked.

"Because Priscilla's night-dress had a blue ribbon through its lace and the woman's didn't," Jemma said. "In fact, your spare one looks more like it than anyone's."

"How do you know I have a second one? How can you possibly know?"

"I saw it in your room when I went for your book," Jemma said simply.

"You sneaky little bitch!" Loredana exploded, then knew she had over-reacted and said with enforced calm, "I always wear a gown over my night-dress." Everyone was watching her. "Anyway, why should I have gone to George's room, for heaven's sake?"

"I think," Jim said, all eyes now on him, "that you went because your horoscope told you that Saturday was a day for decisions."

Loredana gave a little cry. "It's true. It did. But it was nothing to do with George. It was deciding to run away with Hamish."

"Since Hamish's wife was throwing him out because of his affair with you, was that such a difficult decision?"

"That is true," Dulcie confirmed in a very level voice. "I was, and I still am."

"And Welch swore to sue him for fraud if the contract wasn't signed. It had not been signed. Dulcie told Hamish that late on Friday night, before she fell asleep. Lord Gilroy was being difficult over the terms."

"Damn right I was," Gilroy cut in.

"Trevor had seen through you at last and was going to boot you out," Jim continued to address Loredana remorselessly in the same very quiet voice that he had used professionally with fraudsters. "You were foul to him once too often. You wanted Hamish. You wanted him desperately, but not penniless. Not when you adore Versace dresses and Bruno Magli shoes. You'd realized weeks ago that Welch would have to be dealt with. This weekend brought it to a crunch." He turned to Hamish. "Or possibly you cooked up the scheme to kill him. You're a cold-enough and hard-enough person."

"It's not true." Loredana had gone extremely pale. "How dare you accuse me!"

"You know what I believe you did? It was neat, simple and ingenious. You put poison in your own teapot, then took your tray down the passage, perhaps with your dressing-gown over your arm, and knocked on Welch's door. That was when my daughter caught a glimpse of your back. You took in your tray, told him you'd brought his tea and spun him some story about why you were there. Perhaps you asked if he'd got the contract signed. Probably he said no, then made a grab for you, but you evaded him, because your night-dress had certainly not been not torn."

"It had not," Jemma affirmed, earning a furious look from Loredana, but no comment.

"Doing that was taking a risk, but with luck everyone else would be in their rooms. Your luck held. You escaped and returned to your room, with the dressing-gown on. Within minutes Welch was dead. When the screaming started you came back, wearing your other night-gown. Now came the riskiest part. You had to retrieve your own tray before anyone discovered that he had one inside his room and the other was still outside. You went down for breakfast earlier than anyone else and on the way down you passed Welch's room, darted in and took your own tray down to the kitchen to ensure the pot and cup were washed up. But you did one last thing before going down. You poured out some tea into what had been Welch's proper cup and left it there outside his room, so that the maid would assume that he had drunk his tea and finished with it. That was intelligent." Jim turned to Hamish and said sardonically, "I assume you thought of that?"

"I've never heard such a cock-and-bull story in my life," Hamish protested.

"But how do you know what did or didn't happen," Jim said equably, "when first you were with your wife and after that in the kitchen, fetching coffee?"

"You know perfectly well I was with Loredana." Hamish turned to his wife. "Sorry, Dulcie," he said, as if everyone did not know this already, and sounding every bit as sincere as a traffic cop apologizing for fining a driver.

"And what else did the horoscope say?" Dulcie asked frigidly. "Kill George now before he sues?"

"What with?" Hamish asked, while Loredana began to cry softly. "It's a marvelous theory, it's worthy of Agatha Christie, but it's nonsense. Where did the poison come from?"

"From the Lion Park." Jim took the tiny bottle out of its envelope and held it up in its tissue. "When Loredana stole some of the tranquillizer she poured the small amount she took into this. There were several of these bottles in the laboratory."

"I've never seen it before," Loredana sobbed. "How can you be so cruel! It's all lies."

"Probably poor Ted Matthews told you it was lethal to a man. So fast that it's a favourite for vets committing suicide. That sparked the idea that it could be used on Welch. You had no idea exactly how, you acted on instinct."

"How can you say these things!" Loredana screamed.

"I'm not listening to any more of these slanders." Hamish got up. "The police have made an arrest. We had nothing to do with George's death." He took Loredana by the arm. "Come on, darling. We're leaving."

But, to Dee Dee's surprise as much as everyone else's, Gilroy was faster. He reached the dining-room door well ahead of them and barred their way.

"Do you have any proof at all?" he asked Jim.

"There'll be fingerprints on the bottle. With luck hers will show through below the maid's." He looked at Loredana with something close to pity. "Throwing the bottle into the library waste-basket was about as stupid a way of trying to throw suspicion on someone else as I can think of." He saw from Hamish's furious expression that he thought so too.

Loredana began to protest and then to weep. "You're inventing it all. I hate you."

"Well," Dee Dee said decisively. "I think we should call the police. It's not as though there aren't enough of them around."

17

"WE'D NEVER get a conviction on the fingerprints alone," Morton was saying to Timmins, "and that pair are rock-solid in their denials. The woman Loredana claims she was given the stuff legitimately by the keeper to put down her cat, which is why her fingerprints are on the bottle, and the maid stole it from her."

"The maid could have done," Timmins commented "She had the opportunity. The problem is motive. Why kill a man simply because he goosed you? Mrs. Welch had much more reason."

"It doesn't begin to add up." Morton sifted through his voluminous papers on the case. "It's a hell of a pity all these tests take so long."

It was late Tuesday morning and much had happened. The poison that killed Welch had been positively identified as veterinary tranquillizer. The pathologist confirmed that it was very likely to have been administered in tea. Welch would have died almost instantaneously and there was little possibility that the poison had been administered earlier, since it was present in his blood, but not in his urine.

Nearly all Jim Savage's suppositions had been shown as correct. Traces of the drug had been found in the tiny laboratory bottle. Loredana and Hamish were now "helping police with their inquiries," in the understated British phrase. Adrienne had been released. Priscilla had been warned against ever starting a fire again and been put on a train home. Dulcie had also gone home to discuss what to do next about their respective spouses with Trevor. Jim had wondered, idly, if those two would end up getting together. Now that Trevor had recovered his nerve, he could be a different man. But that was irrelevant speculation. The reality was that everyone except the Savages had left Wittenham Park.

"You reckon that Mr. Savage is right, sir?" Timmins asked.

"One hundred percent, damn him. I'm going to talk to him again."

It was stupid to be resentful, and Morton knew it was, but he could not help himself. However, he would do his best to conceal his feelings.

"Could we go over the way you saw events once again?" Morton asked Jim, when coffee had been brought to the library, which he had chosen deliberately because he wanted the Savages to feel relaxed. He was confident that they could not have been connected with the crime, save as observers.

"The key was the way people kept acting out of character," Jim explained. "Lord and Lady Gilroy never did that. They were consistent from the moment the weekend began. They loathed Welch and they hated having to sell their land. They made no secret of it. The rows we heard before and after dinner on the Friday night were all about pressurizing them."

"Unpleasant, but not criminal," Morton observed.

"You'd be the best judge of that," Jim said tactfully. "It was when Gilroy refused to sign that things went wrong."

"In what sequence?"

"Dulcie McMountdown tried to engineer a compromise. Her final act was to take the amended contract to Welch at around eleven P.M., urging that this was the best she could achieve. He told her it wasn't good enough. She left him, incidentally taking the drugged cocoa—a complete red herring so far as any investigation was concerned. Everything Priscilla Worthington did confused the issue. She'd been asked to make the weekend dramatic and found herself unable to stop.

"She's one from the cuckoo's nest," Jemma said.

"Anyway," Jim continued, "Dulcie had already told Hamish that she'd had enough and was going to divorce him. Before she fell asleep she warned him that Welch was still going to sue him for fraud over Lloyds."

"Could Welch have done that?" Morton was no expert on the convolutions of the insurance market.

"Managing agents have been sued. Fraud, incompetence and malpractice are the words."

"And then?"

"As we know, once his wife was asleep, Hamish sneaked out along the passage to Loredana's room."

"We heard him go past, didn't we, Daddy?" Jemma confirmed.

"We heard someone go past our doors. Presumably him. When he told Loredana that Dulcie was definitely throwing him out and Welch would be suing him, they evolved their plan."

"None of which can be proven?" Morton asked.

"It's informed supposition. But what transpired supports it. Take Loredana's behaviour. Why, when her affair with Hamish was so secret, did she insist on telling me how she had found true love at last? Because they were each other's alibis, that was the reason. What is less explicable is that accident on the back stairs yesterday."

"I think they genuinely had quarrelled," Jemma said.

"Perhaps they were getting the wind up after the inspector's questioning," Jim said. "Or else Hamish was trying to back out of the affair now that his own problems were solved and that Trevor had woken up to what was going on."

"They were certainly nervous," Morton agreed. One of the few complete conversations that his bugging device in the library had picked up was that one, but nothing had been said that could incriminate either Hamish or Loredana. Not that he intended Savage to know this.

"I suspect it all lies in Loredana's character," Jim suggested. "She's a creature of instinct, of impetuous action. Jemma, remember how she insisted on having the 'gazelle-like' role at the start, and all the fuss about knowing Africa? She likes dramas. She might well have persuaded Hamish before they arrived that Welch had to be killed. Look at it from her point of view. She was bored stiff with her husband, who didn't earn enough to indulge her and was often away and she'd taken up with Hamish."

"Who wanted an easy lay, but not a divorce," Jemma said.

"Exactly. Hamish didn't intend to burn his boats with Dulcie. He was having a very satisfactory love affair on the side. Divorce is expensive, and anyway, he probably had no thought of actually marrying Loredana. She's not the most intelligent woman in the world, whereas Dulcie is extremely switched on."

"That would figure, Daddy," Jemma said. "He's a calculating so-and-so."

"But this weekend changed everything. He was being divorced, and he was being sued. It had become a now-or-never situation. If she could possibly do so, Loredana had to bounce him into total commitment. She'd acquired the poison, almost by chance. The next stimulant was the horoscope. Last night she didn't even try to deny the influence that had on her. That made her decide to act."

"Horoscope?" Morton queried.

"She had taken her stars for the month out of a magazine," Jemma explained, "the usual spiel. The astrologer said Saturday was a day for decisive action for future happiness."

"You might just break her down over that," Jim suggested. "It's a very weak point in her psychology."

"So you think the horoscope decided her to kill Welch?" Morton asked.

"I think she'd thought about how to deal with him a lot. The poison practically fell into her lap. The horoscope convinced her that she had to act at once after she heard that Gilroy hadn't signed the contract. The horoscope said Saturday and she sees everything in immediate terms. I believe she then talked Hamish into their using the poison. And once he was party to a murder she'd got him where she wanted him. Or thought she had."

"You don't think he planned it?" Morton suggested.

"He could have done. He's one of those Dr. Crippen characters," Jemma said. "Totally cold, totally calculating."

"Either way," Jim said, "she then went through the routine we've already discussed and poisoned Welch very successfully. Hamish certainly took no risk himself. But she overdid it with the maid when she eventually took the tray down. Having said she wanted to help the staff, she couldn't resist explaining exactly how she wanted her breakfast done. Result? The maid remembers that she came down at least twenty minutes before anyone else. She had to if she was going to be unobserved going into Welch's room again. But pretending to be helpful to the staff was entirely out of character. Just as it would have been out of character for Welch to put his dirty tea-things out in the passage, where we all saw them and were fooled into assuming it was the tray he had actually used."

"Her only problem was that I saw her go into his room the first time," Jemma said, "although I didn't recognize her night-dress until I saw it later."

"It was both premeditated and an opportunist murder," Jim said. "And she took a lot of trouble to cast suspicion on Adrienne."

"I couldn't go on holding Mrs. Welch," Morton admitted. "Her fingerprints were on the contract, but so were several others."

"Adrienne was a worried woman," Jim said. "She'd been worried about what her husband was letting himself in for the night before, because she knew what financial trouble he was in. When she first found him dead she saw the contract on his bedside table and must have snatched it with the idea of destroying it if necessary."

Morton nodded. This was precisely what Adrienne had claimed she did.

"And, as I told you, when I hinted in front of her that I knew where it was, it appeared on my bed."

"Thank you, Mr. Savage," Morton said, convinced that these explanations held water. "It's all very plausible." He gave Savage a friendly smile for the first time ever. "Now tell me how do I get Mrs. Chancemain into court?"

Jemma looked at the inspector. "I thought the police often started with a lesser charge and worked up from there to a confession."

"You've been reading too many crime magazines, miss."

"Writing them, actually."

"Well." Morton considered this. "Could it be proven that the tranquillizer bottle was stolen? She claims it was given her and Ted Matthews isn't alive to dispute that."

"Wait a minute," Jim said, showing excitement for the first time himself. "You might have a witness. Gary, the assistant keeper, the boy who insisted that Ted never made mistakes. He'd know if a bottle had been officially missing."

Half an hour later Gary was with them, in his ranger's khaki uniform, and explaining that Ted had complained about a missing bottle. Shown the vial, he recognized it at once.

"I remember now. Ted was very particular about equipment. He'd had two empty ones of these by the lab sink and he asked me if I'd taken one. Well, I hadn't. Nor had no one else. Then, after Ted got killed, we forgot all about it." He looked hard and long at Morton. "You mean that dart was interfered with, like?"

"Some of the tranquillizer was transferred to this bottle and the other must have been topped up with water."

"Well, I can swear on oath it was stolen, if that's what you need." Gary looked both horrified and bewildered. "Bastards," he muttered.

"Don't worry," Morton assured him, "we'll get them."

THE TRIAL several months later at Oxford Crown Court was far from being an open-and-shut case. Loredana was charged with murder and Hamish with being her accomplice. But they had hired good lawyers and the most Loredana would ever admit was that the horoscope had made her decide that she and Hamish must elope.

When the trial ended, after eleven days, the jury was divided, unable to agree. Both the accused walked free, though to boos and catcalls from the crowd outside.

Morton felt strongly that the prosecution should have opted for a lesser charge, though Savage knew that once they had realized the weakness of the case, neither Loredana nor Hamish would have given way.

In the meantime Jim Savage had found a job as secretary of a country club, which kept him occupied but was hardly exciting. He and Jemma were both called as witnesses by the prosecution and when the trial was over he felt curiously empty, as though an era of his life had ended.

The Gilroys were more than thankful that it was all over, although the publicity had doubled the gate money at the Lion Park.

"Agatha Christie would not have approved," Dee Dee told her

husband as they drove back to Wittenham "And that is absolutely the first and the last of our murder weekends."

However, Buck was ready for her. "Definitely," he agreed, "but I've had a brilliant idea, darling. Why don't we go into hosting ghost weekends instead?"